"A guy walked out of the water and into the woods, then disappeared."

"Tessa also said the boat has been out there, no lights and no movement, for more than a day," Hansen explained.

Tessa switched her gaze from the glare she had locked on Ben since they walked in, back to Hansen. "So, you were listening to me."

He ignored that because the truth was he spent far too much time paying attention to her. She was impulsive and sexy, adorably cute and could talk on any subject *forever.* So, naturally, he wanted her. He couldn't think straight some days because he wanted her so badly. But he wasn't on the island to date . . . no matter how tempting she was.

Also by HelenKay Dimon

THE PROTECTOR
THE PRETENDER
THE NEGOTIATOR (novella)
THE ENFORCER
THE FIXER
UNDER THE WIRE
FACING FIRE
FALLING HARD
PLAYING DIRTY
RUNNING HOT (novella)

SECRET

A NOVEL

HELENKAY DIMON

AVONBOOKS

An Imprint of HarperCollins*Publishers*

This is a work of fiction. Names, characters, places, and incidents are products of the author's imagination or are used fictitiously and are not to be construed as real. Any resemblance to actual events, locales, organizations, or persons, living or dead, is entirely coincidental.

First Avon Books mass market printing: July 2019

Print Edition ISBN: 978-0-06-289278-2
Digital Edition ISBN: 978-0-06-289276-8

Cover design by Amy Halperin
Cover photograph © Shirley Green (man); © Andrey Yurlov/Shutterstock (wave); © Belle Cloma Santos/EyeEm/Getty (beach)

FIRST EDITION

19 20 21 22 23 QGM 10 9 8 7 6 5 4 3 2 1

This one is for all my fellow romantic suspense authors out there. People think writing suspense is easy. It's not. They wrongly believe that because you make it look effortless. The reader part of me thanks you for that.

HER OTHER SECRET

CHAPTER 1

People didn't wash up on Whitaker Island's pebbled shores by accident. No one just stumbled around and found the small strip of land tucked into the northwest corner of Washington state. It was a destination. A person had to want to land there. By ferry or private plane, it took effort.

Trees shadowed over half the twenty square miles, and the scent of lavender from the nearby fields drifted over the land. The island once housed a prison and continued to be the perfect place to disappear. A sanctuary for people on the wrong side of the law who needed a restart, for battered wives mysteriously gone missing, or for anyone searching for a new life.

Tessa Jenkins ended up there because she had nowhere else to go. The island offered hope and quiet. A new start . . . and, unexpectedly, him. Nothing prepared her for Hansen Rye. A six-foot-three hottie with black hair and thick dark glasses that only highlighted his hotness. Part Asian—Korean, she thought but hadn't asked—and all kinds of fine.

He'd proved many times that he could build or fix almost anything, and as the island's most sought-after handyman, he was often called on for the oddest of chores. Today, she was the one who did the calling.

His sneakers crunched against the tiny gray pebbles lining the island's oddly named Throwaway Beach. "Why are we here again?"

That voice. Deep and husky and somewhat annoyed. Hansen wasn't much of a people person and seemed to wear that as a badge of honor. He gave off the impression he only tolerated other humans, preferring to live in semi-isolation and only pop out when he needed to earn some money to pay for food.

He had a few friends, but he listened more than talked. He tended to watch people, assessing, almost waiting for them to make a wrong move. Not that he was mean. But his mood often hovered around grumpy.

Almost every woman on the island—age four through ninety-four—seemed to harbor a secret crush on him. There was no end to the list of "chores" women and men, everyone actually, created that required his expert handling. If he noticed the attempts to charm and seduce him, he hid it well. Even with her, unfortunately. Not that she went on the attack or stripped down or anything, though she had been tempted more than once. But she did flirt.

A woman could flirt . . . and it would be nice if the guy noticed.

He snapped his fingers in front of her face. "Hey, Tessa."

Okay, that was a little much. "Don't do that."

"What?"

He actually looked confused by her comment. She was just about to tell him what she thought about his thoroughly unnecessary dude gesture when she glanced up into those dark brown eyes and her brain blinked off. Just for a second, but there it went. "Huh?"

He exhaled. "You said you wanted to show me something."

The actual chore. Right.

"The boat." She ignored the sharp smell of fish and salt highlighted with each incoming wave and nodded in the direction of the yacht that hadn't moved for more than twenty-four hours.

Hansen just shot her a blank stare.

She tried again. "In the water." When he doubled down on the staring, she pointed at the vessel bobbing not that far off the shoreline. "Right there."

She didn't know much about boats, but she estimated this one to be more than fifty feet long. Sleek and white with slashes of black highlighting the sides. It rose up three stories from the deep blue water—the open upper deck, the main one with the windows and back area where swimmers could jump into the water, and then the obvious cabin below. She guessed it had a bedroom but there was no sign of life on the thing.

After following the direction of her finger, he exhaled again. Put a lot of oompf behind it this time. "Yeah, I know what a boat is."

She ignored the sarcasm, though that was getting

tough since it seemed to be his go-to tone this morning. "Why is it there?"

"Where else should a boat be?"

Sarcasm *and* snottiness. That was a powerfully unattractive combo. He was lucky he looked like that, all fit and chiseled with a healthy glow that didn't fit the usually cloudy skies blowing over Whitaker, and had those handyman skills, or no one would talk to him. "You're annoying."

He shot her one of his usual what's-wrong-with-you scowls. "Me?"

"I think something happened to it. The boat, I mean. It could be disabled. The people might need help."

"Is it possible you're jumping to conclusions?"

Yes, of course. Not that she'd admit that out loud.

"No." She recalled the mental list she put together last night when she vowed to call him if the boat still hadn't moved this morning. The one she'd memorized in case a situation just like this happened. "It's too close to shore. It hasn't moved. I haven't seen any sign of life. Not one person. And there were no lights on it last night."

"Wait a second." He held up a hand, as if she didn't know what *wait* meant. "You're saying you've been stalking the boat since last night?"

"Is that the point?"

He actually snorted. "Maybe it should be."

The dismissive noise grated across her nerves. The guy really could use a How Not to Piss Off Your Neighbors course. "We have a harbor. There's more than one marina on Whitaker. There's the Yacht Club, which is right on the water. A boat could pull in there."

"The boat is in the water right now." He stopped as if he were trying to make some big point before starting again. "That's basically how boats work. You get in them and then go out on the water."

He grew less attractive by the second. "Are you trying to be difficult?"

His serious expression suggested he teetered on the verge of delivering the same lecture he might give an unreasonable four-year-old. "Look—"

"No." She was not in the mood for him to launch into some sort of condescending male speech. Honestly, it would be far too disappointing. She'd had a thing—not serious and not really worth discussing—for Hansen since she met him, which happened approximately thirty-eight minutes after she moved to Whitaker. If it turned out he really was all-ass-all-the-time instead of just a little testy as she decided sometime during the last six weeks of knowing him, well, that was more than her very active fantasy life, which centered solely on him, could handle.

"Okay." He nodded, all strains of frustrated male gone as if he'd found a well of calm somewhere in that pretty head and was dipping into it. "Let's start over."

Better. It was good to know that maybe she hadn't wasted all of that fantasy time on him.

"Last night I was—" A blur to her right grabbed her attention. It started with a wave as the water lapped against the shoreline. Then the ripple grew into a full-grown man. He wore a business suit and walked right out of the water, head down with his dark hair hanging over his face. His movements were somewhat slowed by what had to be a hundred pounds of wet wool. He walked across the pebbled beach about thirty feet behind Hansen.

But the big news about the drenched dude's dramatic movie entrance was how he walked away from them without saying a word, as if all of this was perfectly normal.

Hansen cleared his throat. "You know you stopped talking in the middle of a sentence, right?"

"The man . . ." Good lord, how did she even describe it? Instead, she reached for Hansen's arm and tugged and shifted until she had him turning around, facing the man who was now walking toward the line of trees that grew right up to the edge of the rocky beach. "Do you see him?"

Hansen frowned. "Huh."

She stepped in front of him. "That's the sum total of your response?"

"It's weird. I'll give you that."

"Why are you standing here? Go get him!"

The man disappeared into the wall of trees. Didn't stop. Didn't turn his head or look at them. Didn't acknowledge them in any way.

Once he was gone, Hansen looked down at her again. "Why?"

"Why?" She shook him because *come on.* "He could be hurt."

Hansen had the nerve to shrug. "He looks fine."

"Or maybe he's a criminal."

"Then why would I run after him?"

She didn't bother to launch into the list of reasons, the most obvious being that his best friend happened to be what counted as law enforcement on the island. "He's getting away."

"Where is he going to go? We're surrounded by water."

"You're actually serious right now?" When he didn't say anything, she tried very hard to ignore the disappointment flowing through her at Hansen not being all heroic and ready to do battle.

Her fantasy man would have chased the stranger down.

Just as she started to move, Hansen caught her arm. "Whoa there."

She didn't even spare him a glance. "Someone has to go."

"Seriously?" His fingers grazed her cheek as he turned her head to face him again. "No way."

Instead of answering, she rolled her eyes at him.

That drew an exaggerated male sigh out of him. "Fine. Stay here."

"I'm not agreeing to that."

Before she could get her bearings or assess how she felt about him hovering so close and resting his hand on her forearm and that sexy soft touch, he was gone. The Hansen she knew usually took his time and moved slowly. It's part of what made him such a joy to watch.

He could chug a water bottle like no one she'd ever seen, throat guzzling, firm chin up. It was quite the sight. But this version of Hansen, the athletic, racing-into-danger type? Also very good.

Small rocks kicked up behind him as he shot across the beach, dodging stray pieces of driftwood. He moved into the crowd of trees and out of sight before her mind restarted. That didn't stop her from trying to follow. She just reached the edge of the treeline when he popped back out again, not even breathing heavily, and how sexy was that? But he was also alone, and that part she didn't get.

"Well?" she asked.

"I lost him."

"Not possible."

"Actually, it is. The trees are densely packed. Very little light gets in and there's lots of ground cover. Once he went off the path he could hide anywhere."

"He was weighed down by a soaking wet business suit and probably doesn't know the island, and he beat you?" She couldn't fight off the wince.

"Beat me?"

That stunned voice wasn't good. Apparently she'd hit on some sort of soft spot on his ego. "Wrong word?"

He gave a stiff nod. "Yeah."

Since his voice sounded gruff now and he had that whole furrowed brow thing going on, she let his failure go. "Let's find Ben."

"What for?"

Good. Grief. "He's the police guy on the island. Admittedly, he sucks at it, but still."

Hansen coughed. It clearly sounded fake, as if he were trying to bite back a laugh. "You think he sucks at his job?"

This was a touchy subject for her and a dangerous one to wade into, what with the two men being friends and all. "Yes."

For the first time all morning, Hansen smiled and it lit up his face. "Did you tell him that?"

"Yesterday." She tried to beat back the warmth that spread through her at his happiness. She needed to concentrate on his refusal to see the seriousness of this situation first. "But even I can admit he needs to know if there's some sort of merman on the island."

Hansen's smile fell. "What did you just say?"

She could only assume he'd never read a book. "Male mermaid."

"Nope." He shook his head. "That's not a thing."

"Which part?"

"All. Of. It."

She had no idea why he was so touchy about this topic. It's not as if she believed the wet guy really was a merman or that they really existed, but they were a thing in fiction. "*Merman* is a real word."

"I will go with you to see Ben if you promise never to say *merman* again." He sneered as he said the word.

"You're more than a little weird, Hansen."

"Right back at ya."

CHAPTER 2

The front two legs of Ben Clifford's chair smacked against the hardwood floor as he sat forward in his desk chair. "You saw what?"

A phone rang in the outer office of the small building hooked to the end of the library. Ben didn't make a move to answer it. He was too busy shooting them a wide-eyed, what-the-hell-are-you-talking-about stare. Hansen thought the expression might be the funniest thing he'd seen in weeks. His usually calm, always diplomatic, hard-to-ruffle best friend looked frozen to the spot behind his big desk.

Ben was thirty-four and had seen some scary shit as an MP in the army. He'd been in combat and right now looked like he'd rather be back there than trapped in his ten-by-ten office with the peeling green paint on the walls, facing down Tessa.

Hansen wasn't sure how he got tangled up in this mess of a story, but he suspected this sort of thing wasn't all that out of the ordinary for the woman standing beside him. He couldn't help but sneak a peek at her. He did that a lot lately. Looked, listened, imagined her legs wrapped around his waist. All things that could not happen because his stay on Whitaker was temporary and no woman should get dragged into his mess of a life.

Still, it was hard to ignore her. Those big blue eyes and the wavy brown hair that fell just below her shoulders. He'd seen her racing around the island in shorts. Those long, lean legs always zapped his concentration. Everything about her did. Energy bounced off her. She'd been on Whitaker for six weeks and everyone knew her, liked her, and loved to talk with her.

That shit wasn't normal.

"Ben needs a better description of the guy." Tessa practically beamed up at Hansen. "I know we made that stupid deal, but can I tell him my theory?"

"No." The way her eyes sparkled with amusement almost derailed Hansen's plans to get in and out of this situation and this office quickly. She wanted to say *merman* and he wanted to survive the next ten minutes, so no.

It took another twenty seconds for Ben to speak. Even then his mouth dropped open and closed twice before he said anything. "Maybe he was out boating and—"

Tessa sighed loud enough for people a hundred miles away in Seattle to hear. "I told you he wouldn't get it."

Ben leaned forward, balancing his elbows on the edge of his desk. "Get what?"

This part . . . Yeah, Hansen had to admit he enjoyed it. Just a little.

Whitaker was a private island, which meant a governing board ran everything. The mysterious owner of the land never spoke up, preferring to let the board handle the details instead. The board also hired Ben and tried to micromanage his every move. Never mind the fact people loved Ben—except Tessa, apparently—and his presence kept the crime rate to almost zero. The hoops he had to jump through to keep the board from calling a no-confidence vote about some new gripe every two seconds would have made most people lose their cool.

Hansen could only imagine Ben trying to explain this case to the board. He planned to give Ben crap about that right after he figured out what was happening between Ben and Tessa. He didn't get involved in anyone's life but he had to know. "Apparently she questions your abilities."

Ben shot Tessa a quick look. "She's made that quite clear."

Just as Hansen was about to ask for more details, Tessa started talking. "The unknown guy was in a suit as if he jumped off a boat in full work attire, including a tie, then washed up on the beach and kept walking. He had to see us, or at least hear us, so why walk away? Why hide from Hansen in the woods?"

Ben made a humming sound. "I agree. It's strange."

That was about as ruffled as Ben got but Tessa didn't seem to appreciate it. "Gee, you think?"

Rather than let them wrestle this out, Hansen stepped in. The sooner Tessa told the rest of her tale, the sooner he could get Ben alone and ask what the hell happened to set Tessa off. She was nice to everyone . . . except Ben right now.

"Tessa also said the boat has been out there, no lights and no movement, for more than a day," Hansen explained.

Tessa switched her gaze from the glare she had locked on Ben since they walked in, back to Hansen. "You *were* listening."

He ignored that because the truth was he spent far too much time paying attention to her. She was impulsive and sexy, adorably cute and could talk on any subject *forever.* So, naturally, he wanted her. He couldn't think straight some days because he wanted her so badly. But he wasn't on the island to date. He still hadn't recovered from the last time he gave a shit about anyone and was in no position to get involved . . . no matter how tempting she was.

"The guy didn't swim to shore. I didn't hear any splashing. I didn't see his face and wouldn't even have noticed he was behind me except for Tessa's warning," he said, trying to keep his mind on the problem in front of them.

She turned back to Ben again. "Some people believe me."

Maybe her need to solve problems was rubbing off on him because Hansen couldn't wait any longer. "I give up. What is going on with you two?"

"Doug Tottenridge." That's all Ben said.

Tessa agreed with a sharp nod.

Hansen still didn't get it. "Ruthie's son? About fourteen or so?"

"And handsy." Tessa wiggled her fingers in front of her as she talked.

All the amusement ran out of Hansen. His mood switched from charmed to pissed in two seconds. "Wait. Did he touch you?"

"We were in the market parking lot. He palmed my butt and I smacked him. This happened in front of his friends. He got embarrassed, I guess, because he started yelling at me." Tessa's gaze switched from Hansen to Ben and back again as she talked. "I walked away and when I came back out from shopping, my car had been keyed."

"I couldn't prove it was him and—"

Tessa didn't let Ben finish. "We both know you didn't want to throw the son of Ruthie—the town matriarch, the head of the Whitaker board, and your boss—into prison."

Ben frowned. "Prison? He's a teenager."

"Last I checked a kid won't do hard time for acting like a jackass, but he should pay for the damage and get some sort of warning about destruction of property and the concept of assault. It's not okay for him to touch people without permission." Hansen also thought it would be perfectly fine if he had a talk with the kid. Kind of a scared-straight sort of thing.

"That's what I said." She stared at Hansen as she gestured in Ben's general direction. "He, your dear friend here, refused to do anything about the situation."

Ben sighed, sounding as if he'd had enough, and stood up. "That's not true."

"And I bet you think the fact some dude is walking around the island in a soaking wet suit isn't a big deal either."

Ben closed his eyes. It looked like he might mentally be counting to ten. "I'll look into it."

"Forget it," she said. "I'll do it myself."

"Tessa, don't—" But it was too late for Ben to make his point. She'd taken off, shutting the door behind her with enough force to make the glass rattle. "Right. You're on it."

"She's not your biggest fan." Hansen knew that wasn't actually true. He'd been out with Ben more than once and ended up spending a few hours with him and Tessa, listening to bad music in the sandwich shop turned after-hours-lounge at night. They'd laughed and talked about some of the more interesting inhabitants of Whitaker. Ben and Tessa seemed so comfortable that Hansen had felt more than a subtle kick of jealousy.

One night, two weeks ago, he broke down and asked Ben about his feelings for Tessa, and Ben just laughed. He insisted he saw Tessa—who admitted to being twenty-six, but who knew the truth about anyone's real age or past on Whitaker—as a sister. Hansen decided right then and there something was wrong with Ben's female radar.

"The Tottenridge kid is an entitled jackass," Ben said as he sat back down.

"You talked to him about Tessa?"

"Of course."

"Want me to rough him up to, you know, drive home the point?" Hansen didn't really mean that, but he was pretty sure he could find the right words to scare the crap out of the kid.

Ben's eyebrow lifted. "Let me guess. You're volunteering because Tessa has a *thing* for you and you happen to *thing* her back but are too much of a loser to tell her?"

"Okay, no." Actually, yes, but that wasn't the point. "Because the kid shouldn't touch a woman without her okay."

"Agreed. And I did threaten him but made it sound like I was willing to do him a favor. I'm making him volunteer in the office. Did a man-to-man deal with him, but made it clear this was his only warning." Ben shrugged. "We'll see if it works."

Sounded like problem solved, or mostly, so Hansen didn't see the issue. "You could tell Tessa that."

"I will as soon as he starts the volunteer hours. She'll want to dictate when and how many hours he should do before I can even get him in here." Ben leaned back in his chair. "My leverage against him is limited without evidence. His mother will go all protective mama bear if she finds out this really is about the allegations and not for school credit. Tessa doesn't need the pressure Ruthie will apply. Frankly, neither do I."

That sounded more like the Ben he knew. "I guess you do know how to do your job. That's a relief."

"Thanks." Ben sighed. "So, let's get back to this random guy walking out of the water. What the hell is that about?"

"No idea. But, damn, he disappeared before I could get a good look at him."

"Were you really trying to grab him?"

This part didn't make him look very good. Hansen knew that but explained anyway. "It seemed ridiculous at first, like a prank or something. I figured I'd follow, he'd hear me and then turn around and give me a reasonable explanation that I could take back to Tessa."

Ben's eyes narrowed. "Like what?"

"No idea, but it didn't happen that way. He hit the trees and must have started ducking and hiding because I didn't see or hear him. I gave up and ran back to Tessa because I didn't think she should be alone, just in case the guy doubled back."

"Makes sense."

Hansen didn't think any of it did, but okay. "I tried not to make a big deal of it because we both know if I did, Tessa would take that as a sign to launch into a private investigation, or worse, a personal crusade, and potentially put herself in danger."

Ben nodded. "And then there's the part where you love her."

"I'm ignoring you every time you say that."

"Fair enough. This could be innocent, but this could also go really wrong."

Hansen more or less assumed that could happen at any time, so he might not be the right guy to ask.

"There's no rational explanation that I can come up with. I don't have any idea where he went."

"I'll start searching the island and asking around." Ben folded his arms behind his head. "Now, back to you and Tessa."

Interesting how he tried to slip that in. Hansen still wasn't biting. "Not a topic that's up for discussion. Ever."

"Fine, live in denial."

"The weather is lovely in denial, thank you."

"We both still have a problem." Ben slowly lowered his arms again. "Tessa's on the trail and will not let this go, despite the fact I'm investigating."

Hansen's mind spun with the possibilities. Tessa tracking the stranger through the woods. Tessa swimming out to the boat and climbing on. Tessa getting herself entangled in something without having all the facts.

Tessa being threatened or hurt.

His stomach sank. One of the sexiest things about her, besides that face and those killer legs . . . and every other part of her . . . was this sense of curiosity that wound around her. She didn't come off jaded or reclusive, like a lot of people on the island.

That meant one thing . . . "You're saying I need to go find her."

Ben shrugged. "You can, or I will, but I need to search for our mystery man as well. It's a busy morning on Whitaker."

"In other words, I get to talk to Tessa because she hates you right now."

"I disappointed her." Ben's eyebrow lifted. "Maybe you should take that as a lesson."

Hansen wasn't in the mood for cryptic conversation. The whole morning had been a mystery so far. "Which is?"

"Stay on her good side."

He doubted his ability to do that. Not with his history. He couldn't fight off the nagging sensation that he was about to ruin everything.

CHAPTER 3

Morning slipped into afternoon and Tessa, after conducting a quick check of the area for Water Man, wandered over to her favorite spot, Berman's Lodge. There was a long, convoluted, and highly romanticized history of the Berman family helping to build up the island. For as long as anyone could remember, the Bermans had been around . . . until now.

The last of the Bermans, a great-however-many-grandson, preferred city life and never moved back after college, forfeiting his unwanted birthright. His parents sold the lodge to Sylvia Sussex, the person most likely to tick off the town matriarch, Ruthie Tottenridge.

Rumors aside, the Bermans and Ruthie were engaged in a long-running feud. The Bermans were winning because along with owning the lodge, the place with the best food on the island, they made sure Sylvia "inherited" the Berman family seat on the Whitaker board. She voted on every motion and her opinion carried a lot of weight, which Ruthie hated. So, the feud waged on.

Tessa sat on a barstool and balanced her elbows against the bar. It took ten minutes, but she'd retold the story about the boat and the man, leaving out the merman joke because people scattered around the room in those big wooden booths listened in. Most of them looked as if they possessed *no* sense of humor.

"Wearing a suit?" Sylvia frowned as she reached for the phone. "We need to call Ben. This stranger could be dangerous. At the very least, Ben needs to check on him and ask some questions."

As Tessa predicted, Sylvia got it. The whole scene had been more than just weird, or whatever word Hansen used.

"Already done," Tessa said as she watched Sylvia do ten different things, including making mimosas, at the same time.

"Good. And you should . . ." Sylvia's voice trailed off as she glanced toward the doorway that led to the lodge's wood-paneled open center hall.

Tessa didn't have to ask. The hush that fell over the room clued her in. This happened whenever Hansen Rye showed up somewhere in town. Conversation shifted to hushed tones. People looked at him and played this game where they'd pretend not to notice he was out, walking around with other humans, while remaining riveted to his every move.

Fact was, he showed up and all activity stopped. Not just for her, but for everyone. He radiated that kind of power. He commanded a room even though he acted like he'd rather be anywhere else.

Without saying a word or nodding a hello to anyone, he stalked across the room toward the bar, those long legs carrying him in a quick but deliberate pace. He shot Sylvia a quick smile, but it faded by the time he glanced at Tessa. "I've been looking for you."

She doubted that was true. "I'm talking with Sylvia right now."

"I can see that but—"

Before he could finish the sentence, Sylvia grabbed a glass from under the bar, filled it with water, the only thing anyone had seen him drink, which was another source of gossip about him, and put it in front of him. Cool as could be. "How are you, Hansen?"

Sylvia never flinched. She did not ruffle easily. All anyone knew was that she'd shown up on Whitaker less than a decade ago, after a rough divorce. She was part of the island's need-a-restart crowd. In her late forties, she looked much younger with her runner's build and straight blond hair. She could be found almost around the clock working at the lodge and rarely entered into the gossip game of who's-sleeping-with-who that the locals liked to play.

Hansen downed the water and set the empty glass on the bar. "Exhausted."

It was as if he knew how sexy he looked with his head thrown back as he downed a drink. Even when furious with him, Tessa could admit the whole clueless-to-the-world-around-him thing worked for her.

"Have you been running around town?" Sylvia asked.

"After her." Hansen nodded in Tessa's general direction.

She didn't appreciate being the object of his wordless gesture or him acting like he was in charge of babysitting her. The man really needed to get over himself. "What do you want?"

Sylvia laughed. "Tessa. Wow."

"He deserves the tone. Trust me." He brought out the worst in her. She'd been nothing but friendly and welcoming, and all he did was grumble back at her.

Hansen nodded. "I probably do, but I still need to talk with you, Tessa."

"Right now?"

"That depends." His eyebrow lifted as he stared at her. "Is your immediate plan to go out looking for the stranger?"

She toyed with the idea of not answering. It wasn't her style to be rude, but he hadn't done anything to support her in Ben's office. Not really. Now he loomed over her, looking ready to pounce.

After a few seconds of quiet—the kind that echoed around the room as the other diners seemed to hold their collective breaths waiting for an answer—Sylvia jumped in. "Tessa stopped in to get coffee before heading out to find this mysterious island visitor."

"Traitor." Tessa didn't even try to whisper the comment.

Hansen nodded. "Then, yes. We need to talk now."

Tessa didn't even notice Sylvia had left until the

door behind the bar swung open and she walked back in with a to-go coffee cup in hand.

"Here you go." Sylvia handed the cup to Tessa, then looked at Hansen. "You?"

"I'm fine. Thanks."

Sylvia nodded, then scurried around the end of the bar and went to check on other customers. She employed waitstaff but she welcomed everyone personally. She also tended to pick up a good deal of gossip, even though every single person on Whitaker insisted this was the kind of place where people minded their own business.

Sure it was.

"Such good manners . . ." Tessa took a sip of the piping-hot coffee. "To other people."

Hansen had the good sense not to sigh at her. He didn't deny his crappy behavior either. "I know you're ticked off at me."

"At you, Ben, and men in general."

He sat down and leaned in close until only a few inches separated them. This veered away from his usual looming. This felt more intimate. Friendly even.

"All men?" he asked.

On those two simple words, her breath caught in her throat. She pretended she couldn't smell his woodsy shampoo and didn't swallow three times before she kicked the words out. "Is this really why you needed to talk with me?"

"You can't run around the island by yourself right now." His voice was softer and carried a note of concern.

She didn't know if this was some sort of ploy, but for

a few seconds his hard outer shell seemed to crumble. All of the noise from creaking dining-room chairs and clanking silverware faded away. It was so tempting to get sucked in, but self-preservation surged through her. Hansen was a practical guy and a smart one. If he thought being unusually nice would get his way, he'd try it.

She went for another angle—common sense. "Why?"

His expression went blank. "What?"

"You didn't think the man walking out of the water was a big deal. What was the word you used . . . *odd*?" She rolled her coffee cup between her palms, letting the warmth seep into her skin on the overcast day. "Ben doesn't seem concerned. He hasn't made any sort of announcement or asked around yet."

Hansen slowly stood up straight again. Wariness thrummed off him.

Smart man.

"Your point is?" he asked.

"If this mysterious stranger is not dangerous, and if him showing up on the beach isn't a big thing we should worry about, then why is it unsafe for me to walk around the island?" He glanced away from her and she knew she had him. "Under your reasoning, I'd be as safe on Whitaker today as I was yesterday."

"I'm not sure now is the time for verbal games."

"Uh-huh." She refrained from shouting *touché*. "But you will admit I have a point, right?"

He hesitated for a few seconds before responding. "Reluctantly."

"Was that so hard?"

He winced. "A little. Yes."

"I'm starting to think you have a problem with women." Tessa spotted eighty-year-old Louise Stone sipping tea and another couple openly staring at them from their table ten feet away. Tessa shot them a half wave hello.

"People."

Her head snapped back until she faced Hansen again. "What did you just say?"

"People. I'm generally not a fan."

As if that were news. "On behalf of people everywhere, thank you."

"Not you." He shrugged. Even took a step back. Generally looked uncomfortable in his skin, which never happened. "You, I like."

She almost spit out a mouthful of coffee. "Since when?"

"Let's say you're growing on me." He sighed and crossed his arms. Then uncrossed them again.

For once he made her look smooth. No one would believe her if she told them how Hansen fidgeted and mumbled while talking to her. Then it hit her . . . but it couldn't be. Not from him, right? "You're not very good at flirting, are you?"

His gaze shot back to hers. "Is that what you think we're doing?"

Good grief, he was. Sure, he was bumbling his way through it and looked as uncomfortable as a human could look without actually peeling off their own skin, but still she saw that weird spark in his eye and heard the note of amusement, genuine and kind of sweet, in his voice.

Some of her frustration about the day and the man and Hansen's failure to even pretend to be excited about it all faded away. "You're older but not wiser."

"I'm thirty-five."

He barely looked thirty, but the bigger point was that little tidbit was the first personal information he'd ever shared with her. She wasn't sure if she should feel honored or call an ambulance. "A lot older then."

He snorted, healthy ego and self-assurance seemingly back on course. "Nine years is not a lot."

But she refused to let this go. They'd made progress . . . sort of. At least she intended to see it that way. "And you just happen to know how old I am?"

"I know a lot about you."

Amazing how the guy could kill the mood with a few simple words. Her history—her life—was one big disaster. The thought of him figuring out her secrets shook her more than she wanted to admit. "That isn't very comforting."

"Back to the point of my tracking you down." He stared at her fingers where they wrapped around the coffee cup. "Let Ben handle this."

"I thought there was no *this*."

He looked ready to launch into a lecture sure to annoy her when something even more annoying slinked into her peripheral vision. Ellis and Arianna Wells. On an island where people tolerated a lot of nonsense from their odd and secretive neighbors, these two pushed the boundaries.

They lived on a boat in the marina. He taught high school history and everyone agreed he sucked at it. She helped out at the marina office. And they had this nasty habit of—

"We just came from the Yacht Club," Arianna said as her opening volley.

There it was. *The Yacht Club.* A phrase the two of them managed to work into every conversation. Then there were the clothes. Arianna always wore long, flowing dresses, no matter the weather. Ellis looked one step away from putting on a navy blazer and captain's hat. Never mind the fact the club they loved so much consisted of half the residents of Whitaker and *all* the ones who owned a boat. These two acted like membership to the club, which pretty much anyone could get, made them super special.

"Of course you did," Hansen mumbled under his breath as he stood up.

"Did you hear about the stranger walking around the island?" Ellis asked. "No one is claiming to know him."

Before Tessa's mind could unscramble long enough to respond, Arianna jumped in again. "We heard he had some sort of accident."

As usual, the Whitaker gossip circle ran at bullet-train speed. Equally unsurprising, the information had gone sideways. That's what happened when people tried to cultivate a mysterious air.

Unless someone knew more than she did about the boat—and Tessa really doubted that since she'd been watching it nearly nonstop since it appeared—the story had blossomed into a full-fledged fairy tale. "Accident?"

Ellis nodded. "The boat is destroyed."

"Since when?" Hansen's voice didn't even rise.

A pretty impressive talent as far as Tessa was concerned.

"That's what Cliff said," Arianna said as she looked from Tessa to Hansen and back again.

Hansen made a noise that sounded like *guh*. "Cliff, as in the older guy who sits on his front porch all day and grumbles at anyone who walks by?"

Now that he mentioned it, Tessa noticed the resemblance. "Are you guys related?"

He didn't even spare her a glance. "Not funny."

Arianna blustered forward as if Hansen hadn't said a word. "Cliff has a view of the boat from his house."

This time Hansen snorted. The sound drew more than a few looks from the customers at nearby tables. "No, he doesn't."

Since the conversation felt as if it were galloping out of control, Tessa tried to reel it back in. She put her cup down and stood next to Hansen. "The boat is off Throwaway Beach, which is on the other side of the ridge and not within Cliff's view."

"That's not what we heard." Arianna ran a hand over her short spiky hair.

Ellis nodded. "Someone said there was blood all over the beach."

Hansen glared at both of them. "What is happening right now?"

"I think it's a messed-up game of Telephone or Whisper Down the Lane or whatever it's called." That was the only explanation Tessa could come up with on such short notice.

Now Hansen glared at her. "What?"

As far as she was concerned he could take that look somewhere else. She wasn't the one spreading crappy information across the island.

"We'll leave you two to it." Ellis slid his hand under his wife's elbow and guided her away from the bar and toward a nearby table. "Let us know if you hear anything."

"Right." Hansen nodded. "That sounds like something I'd do."

Tessa waited an extra minute for them to sit down and settle in with the menus Sylvia dropped on their table as she sped by before talking to Hansen again. "You didn't have to be rude to them."

"Agree to disagree."

Since it looked like Hansen planned to continue glaring at the Wellses, Tessa shifted. She grabbed her cup and put her back to the bar. The move forced Hansen to focus on her and not them, which was good because he had a friendship errand to run. "You should let Ben know the news is out. If he doesn't do something about this stranger, Ruthie Tottenridge will threaten to fire him. Again."

"I'd think you'd be on Ruthie's side."

"I don't want Ben fired." She didn't. She really liked Ben and his comforting style. The way he put people at ease. She'd never felt a zing with him despite the fact he had the tall, dark, and handsome thing down, but he was ticking her off right now. His calm affect had backfired on her and her innocent car. "I want him to take me seriously."

"Oh, he does. Trust me."

She glanced at Hansen's lower half, which was no hardship and in the general area of his back pocket, where she assumed he kept his cell phone. "Call him."

His eyes narrowed. "What are you going to do?"

"Go home."

"Straight home?"

He was not a stupid man. Looks, deep hottie voice, and a brain. If he were a tad less grumbly, he'd be perfect . . . and then she'd be in trouble. Harmless flirting? Fine. Letting him get wrapped up in her life? Nope.

"I'm not a child, Hansen." But her voice didn't hold any heat. A part of her appreciated that he cared, even if it was only a little and likely because he didn't want law-enforcement strangers and the media all over the island.

"I am well aware that you are a full-grown woman." His gaze did a little bounce. Not far down, and not in a creepy, he-deserved-a-good-punch way. No, this was more of a smooth glide that heated a trail through her.

Damn him.

She smiled because, despite the fact she didn't want to go any further down the flirting road, he did make her happy. Sometimes. Certainly not always. "You're getting better."

"At what?"

"Flirting." But she was sure he'd screw it up in no time.

CHAPTER 4

Talking Tessa into going home until Ben could do a quick check of the island took every ounce of Hansen's communications skills. He threw in some charm and tried very hard not to think about her comments about flirting. He did not flirt. He stayed aloof for a reason. His past was not something he wanted dug up and passed around. Flirting led to dating, which led to sharing, which led to him running far away.

All of those thoughts and a flash or two of her smile ran through his mind as he stepped off the rotted wood of Cliff's front porch step later that night. Hansen and Ben had been searching the island, keeping in touch via cell, and had not found any stranger, wet or dry, lurking about.

By the time they met back at Ben's office around nine, the sun had gone down and a steady driving rain fell from the dark sky. Sheets of water pounded the ground, transforming every inch of the island into a slick, muddy surface.

Hansen dumped his drenched jacket over the back

of a rickety steel chair Ben kept in the corner for just this purpose. Water ran down the side of his face from his hair. A reminder of his time outside dripped off his shirt and pants until a puddle formed at his feet.

"Find anything?" he asked as he grabbed a bottle of water from the small dorm-size refrigerator Ben kept next to his desk.

"Some missing laundry from the Taylor backyard over on Sunset. Otherwise, nothing." Ben frowned at him. "You're making a mess."

"You afraid I'll ruin the expensive carpet that you don't have?"

Ben lounged in his chair, tapping his fingers against the edge of his desk with not a drop of water in sight. "Do you need a towel?"

"Is there a reason you're still dry?" Hansen shook his head, letting the beads of water scatter over Ben's desk blotter. "Because I'd think the person who volunteered should be more dry than the one who gets paid to do this shit."

Ben pointed at the coatrack. "Raincoat and umbrella."

"You didn't think to offer me one?"

"No." Ben flattened his hand against the desk. "So, what did Cliff say?"

"He insists he heard a noise in his front yard and that his motion sensor light clicked on last night." Hansen shook his head. "He talked about voices and a fight, but who knows what he actually heard. I had to yell his name four times before he opened the door to let me in."

"Despite that, we both know Cliff is telling his version to everyone, getting them riled up. This is no longer about some guy showing up in town. Cliff's created some story about a fight and an accident."

Neither of which Hansen actually believed happened, but it's not as if he could find the mysterious stranger, drag him into Berman's Lodge, and make him tell the truth. "You didn't expect Cliff to keep the Whitaker news of the decade all to himself, did you?"

"By the time I talked to people at the marina, the story had escalated to where you would have thought a serial killer was wandering around the island." Ben's head fell forward. "I really hate gossip."

"Then you're living in the wrong place."

"Haven't you heard? The residents here mind their own business." Ben snorted. "Right."

This was Hansen's least favorite topic, so he switched to another. "The rain is making things messy out there. Checking on the boat and doing a serious door-to-door search will need to wait until tomorrow."

As soon as Hansen finished the comment, he heard the thump of sturdy rainboots behind him. A not-so-subtle throat clearing came next. "Gentlemen."

Ruthie Tottenridge. The only person on Whitaker that Ben went to ridiculous lengths to avoid, and here she was, alternating between dripping and scowling in his doorway.

"Great." Ben coughed over the word but anyone could still make it out.

"Mr. Clifford, I need to see you about the dangerous

stranger you've failed to apprehend." Ruthie walked into the room like she owned it. As the head of the Whitaker board, she kind of did. Not the island, because a private and very mysterious individual, who most thought didn't even live on Whitaker, owned every single inch of land and rented it out to all of them. But Ruthie wielded a great deal of power. She ran the board that made the rules. At least, for now.

She ran for the seat years ago after her father, the previous head, died, and she'd held on to the position ever since. No one else wanted the trouble or the paperwork, and despite her dictatorial tendencies, she kept everything running without trouble. But over time she'd made enemies. While she might have thought the position amounted to a for-life kind of thing, some residents thought it was time to cut back on her power. More than a few pushed Sylvia into thinking about challenging the matriarch who acted like a one-woman judge, jury, and dream-killing machine.

Hansen half hoped he still lived here when the next election came around.

Ben stood up, but he took his time doing it. "As we've discussed, you may call me Ben."

"I'm not sure such informality is the best under the circumstances, hmm?" With that, Ruthie continued past them both and headed for the small conference room to Ben's left.

Hansen watched her move, head held high and rubber boots squeaking against the cheap linoleum floor with each step. When she closed the door behind her,

Hansen looked at Ben again. "Are you supposed to answer her question?"

"No idea."

"You going to be okay meeting with her alone?" If Ben said no, Hansen wasn't quite sure what he'd do. It wasn't as if he knew how to handle Ruthie or wanted to, but he could stand there and stare. He'd gotten pretty good at that sort of thing.

"She needs a vote of the entire board to fire me, so I should be safe tonight." Ben fidgeted with his belt. "I'll also remind her that firing the only law enforcement on the island while a stranger is on the loose is not great optics."

The town's hysteria was starting to rub off on him. "*On the loose?* That's a bit dramatic, don't you think?"

Ben shrugged as he slipped from behind the safety of his desk. "Blame Tessa."

Yeah, about her. "I usually do."

"Going to pay her a visit, are you?" The office phone rang. Ben stared at it and seemed satisfied when it cut off after a few rings. "Looks like the answering service still works."

The answering service consisted of one person—Maddie Rhine. Hansen thought she was the only person on the island more reclusive than he was. He'd met her exactly twice and both times she'd been in the middle of going somewhere else in a rush and couldn't stop to say more than hello. People felt as if they knew her because hers was the voice they heard if they called Ben's office with an emergency or even a question . . . and they called on every subject, most unrelated to law enforcement, which Ben chalked up to general island boredom.

The result was that everyone smiled when they said Maddie's name but no two people gave the same description when talking about what she looked like. Hansen almost envied her ability to move in and around Whitaker and still maintain complete privacy. He'd lost his soon after landing on the island when he agreed to help an older woman named Winnie get her dog, Mr. Higginbotham, out from where he was hiding under her car.

Hansen circled back to the one topic he couldn't avoid. "I want Tessa to know we didn't find anything. Further, that we plan to go out and check the boat after the storm blows out again."

Ben smiled. "Uh-huh."

"Don't do that."

"Right." Ben nodded and kept nodding. "You're a loner and don't spend your days dreaming about her. Got it."

Was he wearing a fucking sign? "Try shutting up."

Some of the amusement left Ben's face as the office phone rang again. "It's going to be a long night. We really do need to find this guy tomorrow and straighten this out before we get a front-row seat to a lot of panic."

"I'm trying to imagine all two hundred and eleven residents panicking at the same time."

"Don't even joke about that." Ben shuddered. "And I'm sure there's a rational explanation for the guy in the water, not that I know what it could be."

"Nothing is going to happen in this weather." Or at Tessa's house. Hansen already decided he'd knock on her door, deliver the status, then go on home and find warm clothing. Simple. "We'll head out again tomorrow."

Ben didn't move. "Enjoy your date."

Hansen refused to take the bait. Instead, he nodded in the general direction of the conference room. "You, too."

WHEN TESSA HEARD the clanking noise outside her living room window for the third time, her heart started to race. It zoomed right up her throat and lodged there. She tried to inhale and calm down her senses, but an endless round of shivers coursed through her.

The summer heat had faded for the night. The satellite television blinked out five minutes before the electricity. Now it was just her and the candlelit darkness and the steady beat of rain against the roof of her artist's cottage. Not hers, actually. She rented it but did not design it. As much as she liked bold colors, that didn't mean she would have picked a flashy new shade of blue for each wall in the bedroom and variations of purple for the family room. The kitchen cabinets were painted and awash in stenciled designs she couldn't identify.

Her place could best be described as eclectic, which was why she grabbed it for such a low rent. She was a big fan of cheap.

Glass doors led out to the small lawn. Towering trees lined up about twenty feet behind her house, giving it a protected, closed-in feel. Floor-to-ceiling windows showed off the gravel area and hill that dipped down to the water out front.

She knew every patch of grass and planted flower out there. Right now she couldn't see any of it because the rain made everything blurry. Sounds muffled.

Clink.

That was a new one. Softer but still not the normal creaks and groans of the wooden structure that she'd grown accustomed to during her last six weeks of living here. She blamed the wind and rain. This wasn't a light summer storm. This blew in and thrashed.

This was the perfect night to stay inside. She huddled under a blanket in the corner of her small L-shaped sectional. Curled her legs under her and pulled the soft material tight against her chest. Sank right down until she rested in a cocoon of cushions. Here she could work through her theories about the man in the water.

Some said she was nosy by nature. She preferred the words *inquisitive* and *caring*. Whenever something felt off to her—like a man walking out of the ocean without seeing people right there who could help him—she tried to fix it. She feared this mysterious guy might have gotten hurt or became disoriented and needed someone, so she couldn't just ignore the situation. She had to jump in.

Bang. Bang.

She jerked at the sound and sat up taller, trying to separate the random noises and come up with a reasonable explanation for each one. The rapid thuds made her think a shutter blew free and danced against the side of the house.

Yeah, a shutter. That was as far as she allowed her mind to wander.

She'd gone to camp as a kid outside of Washington, D.C., and had ridden out summer after summer of thunderstorms. But now a choking sensation swamped her. She never obsessed about the worst thing that could happen but now her imagination threatened to run wild. People might get off on the adrenaline rush. Not her. She liked life quiet and peaceful. Fixed, explained, safe, and without surprises.

She yelped when the doorknob rattled and turned—back and forth, back and forth—as if someone would do anything, break through a wall, if necessary, to shelter inside with her. She lifted her head to call out and ask who was out there, but the sound died in her throat. A second later, tiny rows of goose bumps broke out on her arms. She felt frozen from the inside out and stuck to that spot.

She glanced around, looking for her cell phone, when the banging started again, this time right on the front door. Sounded like someone was pounding with the side of his fist. The door thumped against the frame as if the wind, or a hand, shook it.

The noise grew until it echoed through her. She knew she needed to get up and grab a frying pan or a lamp. Any makeshift weapon would work. Her mind raced with the moves she'd learned in self-defense class. How to deflect. How to scream and run.

Every nerve ending sparked to life. Energy blared through her, ramping up her breathing and shaking through her muscles. The fight-or-flight response kicked hard to the surface. She was a big fan of the flight side but one look into the pitch-black night beyond the glass doors to her backyard and she reassessed. Out there she didn't stand a chance. In here she had things to throw.

She dumped the blanket on the floor and forced her legs to uncurl from beneath her. Her hands shook as she reached for the lamp and yanked the cord from the wall. Her fingers clenched and unclenched around the blown glass base as she lifted it.

The kitchen. She needed to get in there. Hunker down. Grab a knife.

"Tessa?"

The muffled sound refused to make sense in her brain. Her name, the wind . . . someone desperate on the other side of the door. The possibilities blended together.

"Tessa. Open up."

She knew that voice. Loud and frustrated.

Hansen.

All the fear crashing through her morphed into fury in the short time it took her to stomp from the couch to the door. She threw it open, ignoring the pelting rain and shock of dampness. The smell of wet earth mixed with the heat thrumming off him as he stood there, soaked pure to the bone. Hair hanging down and glasses beaded with water.

He was a dead man.

A white-hot rage bubbled up inside her and she aimed every last bit of it at him. She shoved against his chest with her open hand. Smacked him, ignoring that he barely seemed to move or notice.

"What is wrong with you?" Her voice wobbled from the force of her anger. "Why would you do that to me?"

He slicked his wet hair back with one hand and frowned at her. "What are you talking about?"

She'd never found him less attractive. A man who preyed on women, who liked to see them terrified, made her want to punch things . . . mainly him. "You."

"Me?" He wiped his glasses on his wet shirt, smearing and streaking and making an even bigger mess.

"The knocking and turning the doorknob. You scared the crap out of me." Her heartbeat refused to calm down. It thundered in her ears and hit with enough of a punch to make her chest ache.

He froze. "When?"

"Just now. The last five minutes." She seriously considered slamming the door in his face. "What were you thinking?"

"Get inside." His face went blank as he guided her into the house and shut the door to the raging storm behind them. A second later he threw the lock and started moving around the candlelit room.

"What do you think—" Her voice cut off when the flickering light showed his expression. Determined. Angry. Lethal. "Hansen?"

"I would never try to terrify you." He shoved his

flashlight in his jeans' back pocket. "Damn it, Tessa. Give me some credit."

"But then . . ." She had no idea what he was saying. Her brain refused to restart. Terror held her in its killing grip and she couldn't shake it loose. "Okay."

He moved fast, all sleek and quiet. He continued to scan the room as he stood in front of her with his hands resting on her forearms. "I just got here."

"Yeah, I know."

He pulled her in closer until only a breath of air separated their bodies. Those dark eyes didn't blink as he watched her. "I never touched your door. Didn't knock. Nothing. All I did was call your name."

"But someone . . . did you see . . . anything?" When he didn't say anything, she knew. Her knees buckled but he held her up. "Ohmigod. It wasn't you."

"No."

"So then . . ." But she couldn't finish. She knew and dreaded him confirming her suspicions.

"There's someone else out there."

CHAPTER 5

Hansen wanted to hide her somewhere and throw his body in front of her to block out anyone who might hurt her. The instinct rose out of nowhere and he didn't question it. But his brain fought to be logical. Whatever banging she heard had stopped, which meant the person left . . . or they were already in the house.

He unclamped her fingers from the lamp and set it on the floor. "Go sit by the . . ."

He had no idea how to finish the thought. He'd never been inside her place before. Even in the shadows, color assaulted him from every side. Ignoring that, and he barely could, this had to be the least safe house he'd ever seen. Windows everywhere. If someone decided to smash their way in, she'd be showered with glass.

"I'm coming with you. Wherever you go, I'll be right there." She grabbed on to his arm with the strength of an Olympic athlete.

"I need you to—"

"You're big and can fight." Her fingernails dug

through his wet shirt to hit skin. "The plan is to hide behind you and scream my head off."

He couldn't exactly argue with that reasoning. "Smart."

He lifted the flashlight out of his back pocket and aimed it around the room in one last check. The wind wailed outside and rain slammed against the front windows by the door. He couldn't hear anything but her labored breathing as he pivoted around the room, making sure it was clear.

Ready to move on, he angled her behind him, then whispered to her over his shoulder. "Hold on to my shirt and don't let go. You see anything, you yell. Got it?"

"You're going to be amazed at how loud I can scream."

He hoped he didn't find out, but he really liked her attitude. She would go out fighting.

He followed the flashlight beam. Shuffled his feet, keeping his steps short because she'd practically wrapped her body around his. He half carried her, half dragged her through the small structure. The bedroom with blue everywhere appeared clear. No one in the closet or under the bed.

Next, the other small room. The one she clearly used as an office, which he knew from the papers stacked on the bed and the two computers lining the desk. He tried to remember the word for the type of writing she did. She told him once. Clearly it was something that generated a lot of paperwork.

He'd walked away from that life, temporarily anyway. Stopped commuting to an office. No longer attended meetings. Finally reached the point where he didn't hear the office phone ringing in his sleep.

The memories rushed through him. He tried to fight them off, but they flicked through his brain, one after the other. The long hours. All that takeout food and the meals out. He'd once, not that long ago, thrived on the pressure. Thought he had it all until his world imploded.

"I think we're alone in here."

He heard her voice but what she said didn't register until she pinched his arm and said it again. "Uh, right."

He clicked off the flashlight as they walked back into the living room. The safe room . . . the one without a bed or her bra on the floor. Even with the tension slapping him, he'd noticed that in her bedroom. Light pink and lacy. Now he knew.

"I'm not making it up. There was someone out there."

He looked at her, really watched her now. Her pale face and big eyes. The way she shifted her weight from foot to foot. Those tiny PJ shorts that showed off every inch of those sexy legs . . .

This was not the time for that. Reality was, he didn't have *any* time for that, but especially not now. "I know."

"You believe me?" The doubt lingered in her voice and in her eyes.

"Of course." That level of fear? Totally real. Even now she shivered as if she were freezing, and the room was cozy warm. "Are you okay?"

"I don't think so." Her teeth actually clicked together as her jaw bounced up and down.

"Shit." Without thinking it through, he took a step forward. "May I?"

She hesitated before nodding.

Then his arms wound around her. He pulled her tight against his chest and ran his hands up and down her back. This was about keeping her warm and calm. He kept repeating that refrain in his head as he whispered words in her ear that he hoped sounded comforting.

He realized that she was suffering from a nasty bout of shock. The unspent adrenaline rushed through her. He knew because he'd experienced it before and hated the lack of control.

The entire time he held her his gaze roamed the house. Every nook and cranny he could see. Someone had scared the crap out of her and could still be out there. The mysterious stranger who washed up. Had to be. Hansen couldn't imagine a Whitaker resident walking around in this. Fishermen, maybe, but none of them would terrorize Tessa.

No, someone came for her. Either that or her house was the unlucky winner when they tried to break into the first one they saw. That struck him as odd since the houses outside of the main shopping and eating area around Berman's Lodge, like hers, were spread out across the island. Some out alone and tucked deeper into the forest—like his. Some up high on hills to maximize the water views and others down closer to the rocky beaches. Most were surrounded by trees or at least required a drive or a walk through them to get out of the residential setting.

The area around her cottage was green and lush, and it sat in a group of other small houses. She could see her neighbors on either side but they weren't on top of each other. She'd need a mighty loud yell to get someone's attention, which might have been the reason hers was the target.

But the reason someone picked her house over someone else's didn't matter right now. No one scared her and got away with it.

A few minutes later, her body relaxed. Her weight fell heavier against him and her fingers flexed against his waist. For the first time he remembered that he was drenched and likely soaking her and her clothes . . .

Shit.

He pulled back and turned away from her. Acted like his body had caught fire because it fucking had. Her soft skin. The smell of her hair. The way she melted against him. All bad. Very bad.

"Hansen?"

She sounded confused. That made two of them.

"Give me a second to think." He couldn't face her yet. Chalk it up to a mix of need and stupidity, but all he wanted was to put her on that couch and crawl on top of her.

The timing was wrong. His feelings were off. Basically, he hovered right on the edge of messing up six weeks of pretending she was *fine* and nice and all but meant nothing to him.

She popped up in front of him. Leave it to her to refuse to give him five seconds to regain his control. "You're soaking wet."

And half-hard and all stupid. Yeah, that described him pretty well. "It's no big deal."

"You should take those off and—"

He said the first thing that came into his head. "Why isn't your generator working?"

"What?"

Everyone on Whitaker had a generator. When the ferry only ventured by the island two times per week and the weather could whip along the water, residents had to be prepared for outages. Most people invested in whole-house generators that clicked on automatically when the electricity shut off. A few used those plus portable generators for smaller storms. No one went without.

He finally met her gaze. Big fucking mistake. The pinkish color had returned to her cheeks but her PJ top, which was already cropped and formfitting with bunnies all over it, now stuck to her.

He couldn't remember the last time he'd had sex and he knew he wouldn't be able to think of much else.

"Your generator?" Because they needed lights and she could use a jacket.

"I have two portable ones."

Not the answer he wanted to hear. "Which are where?"

"Outside." She winced. "I have them in the carport. Because of the wind they're likely wet."

He counted to ten because yelling at her about not

being prepared after someone tried to scare her spitless struck him as an asshole thing to do. “Okay.”

She stood there in her fluffy white socks, curling her toes into the hardwood floor. “The storm blew in and I was out running around and thinking about the guy in the water.”

He wasn’t at his best right now either, so he got it. “And you didn’t plan ahead.”

“Right. Look, I think it’s safe for you to go, if you need to take off and . . .”

“Yes? If I need to do what?”

“Shower.”

She was trying to kill him. There was no other explanation.

“First, I’m not leaving you alone after someone tried to break in.” He thought that would have been obvious, but he said it anyway.

She nodded. “The merman, most likely.”

“I’m ignoring that reference.” But he did have to swallow a smile because he could hear the amusement in her voice when she said the word. After her scare, he’d worried that her usual spunk might abandon her. Apparently not. “Second, I’m not sure who or what tried to get in, but without electricity and with the rain still coming down, I’m not going to run around out there and try to find out.”

“Good call.”

“Thank you.” That was the first semi-compliment she’d given him since the incident with the man on the beach. He’d been pretty sure his lack of an excited reaction to her big reveal about the boat disappointed her. He shouldn't care, and really, it was good to push her away. Still, the idea of her not talking to him, not calling him, or worse, thinking he was some sort of loser . . . Not okay.

"I'm assuming you don't have anything that would fit me." He looked around, trying to ignore all the purple. "This isn't how I thought you'd decorate."

"I wouldn't. Ever. The house came this way." She shook her head as she stared into the kitchen. "I thought it would grow on me and I'd find it charming."

"And?"

"Turns out I was wrong." She sighed. "I'm pretty sure the room I use for an office has giraffes stenciled on the floor molding."

"Good lord."

"Right? I find something new and confusing every single day."

Yeah, she was better. More relaxed. She'd somehow turned off the fear or tamped it down. Compartmentalized so she could move forward. Impressive skills but they made him wonder why she'd had to develop them in the first place.

"I have an oversize college sweatshirt and we could wrap . . ." She eyed his pants and screwed up her lips as if she were assessing what she saw.

He wasn't sure if he got a good mental review or not. "Wrap what?"

"Wrap a blanket around the rest of you."

Or he could just go home. That would make sense.

Get her to grab a coat and some shoes and take her with him because he refused to leave her alone. But that meant letting someone into his space. There were no good options here.

"I can try to start your generator." He made a move toward the door.

She stepped in front of him. Basically, threw her body right into his path. "Absolutely not."

"I'm already wet."

"And there may or may not be a rogue merman out there."

"Now you're just saying the word to annoy me."

She laughed. "It's cute the way you growl."

An alarm flashed in his head.

"Be careful." He wasn't sure if he was talking to her or himself or both of them.

"It's a joke." She walked over to the ottoman in front of the couch and bent down to grab the lid and open it.

Her pajama shorts rolled up her thigh, flashing him. He doubted she knew it was happening and he certainly should look away. He did . . . for a second. Glanced at the ceiling until her bare skin called to him again. He took in the lean muscles and the—

"Are you gawking?"

She didn't sound angry or interested, unfortunately. More like amused with a touch of *gotcha*. The smile did him in. It lit up her face. The teeth-rattling was gone. She no longer looked ready to bolt or climb on top of him for protection.

The smart, capable, kind of adorable, and hot as hell

version of Tessa returned. And that scared the crap out of him. He had very few defenses against her when she was like this. He'd tried being grumpy. Threw sarcasm at her. Even spent a few days trying to ignore her, until he finally made a lame excuse to go into town and see her at the lodge where she had coffee with Sylvia almost every weekday morning.

"I'm not dead." No, but he was interested even though he didn't want to be.

"I'll take that as a compliment."

She winked at him, then left the room. Headed for her bedroom, the one room that needed to stay totally off-limits to him. Just as he was about to call out to her, she walked back in with a pile of clothes in her arms.

"I have a few oversize plaid shirts, the sweatshirt, a bunch of towels, and some blankets." She nodded toward the opened ottoman.

He was not getting naked in her house. "I'm fine."

"If you get sick, the women of Whitaker will hate me."

"What does that mean?"

She sighed at him. Didn't even pretend she was doing anything other than finding him tedious.

"You can't be that clueless." She dropped the stack on the chair and reached over to lift off his glasses. She cleaned them with a square of cloth. "I use this on my computer screens, so I figured it would work for sexy glasses."

"They're nerd glasses." He chose them for that purpose. They were thick and black and after decades of wearing contacts he used them as a shield of sorts.

She handed them back. "Sexy nerd glasses."

"Tessa, I . . ." He stopped because that was really all he had. Her name and stuttering. He'd lost the ability to think around her and he had no idea what to do about that. It had been years since a woman had him spinning and confused. And the timing was all wrong for it to happen now.

"You saw where the bathroom was. Strip down, get dry, and I'll grab you a glass of wine."

Did she have to say *strip*? "I don't drink."

She gasped. "Right. Sorry."

He knew his beverage choice was a topic of some discussion on Whitaker. No one dared ask, which showed the residents might be gossips but they were smart gossips. But he didn't want her to feel bad or shift back into being guarded. "No need to apologize. It's just a personal preference. No alcohol."

"How about some yummy bottled water?"

"That's more my speed."

He hated to leave her in the living room. Intellectually, he knew she was safe. The house couldn't be more than nine hundred square feet. He could get to her in a few steps and wouldn't think twice about throwing his body in front of hers, if needed. But a voice in his head shouted for him to stay close. Maybe it was the storm or the darkening sky, but the mood on Whitaker felt off ever since the stranger walked up onto the island and disappeared without a word to anyone. He'd feel better once the guy was found.

Hansen repeated that idea as he stood in the bathroom. Again after he washed off and toweled down. He opted for the plaid shirt with the snug fit across his chest and a blanket wrapped around his waist. Every stitch of clothing he'd worn there was draped around the bathroom, over the tub and curtain rod.

He knew tomorrow they'd be stiff and damp, but that wasn't his biggest concern right now. Surviving the night in this house was. He'd be a few feet away from Tessa. He'd hear her, see her. He could now fill in every detail of her room . . . of her legs . . . when he imagined her in bed.

The thoughts ran through his head as he stood in front of the closed door, knowing when he turned the knob and stepped out into the hall things would change. Leaning forward, he balanced his forehead against the wood and inhaled. The scent of her shampoo filled the room.

"Hansen?"

He almost swallowed his tongue at the sound of her soft voice.

She might be on the other side of the door, but he could hear her just fine. "I'm coming out."

He pulled it open and there she was. Her gaze bounced down, wandering over his shoulders to his waist, then dipping lower. By the time she looked him in the eye again, she wore a big smile. "Very nice."

"I'm never going to live this down, am I?"

"I don't see that happening. No."

She lifted her arm and he saw that she held a water bottle. He took it, ignoring the way energy surged through him when their fingers brushed against each other. "Thanks."

"You might be dehydrated."

Right. That was his problem.

"I promise to behave tonight." The words popped up. He had no idea why he said them. He certainly was thinking the opposite.

"Hmm." She tilted her head to the side and her hair drifted over her shoulder.

The strands looked so soft and shiny. He felt a kick of excitement in his gut. "What?"

"I know that's the right answer in theory . . ."

Her sexy voice lured him in. "But?"

"It's a shame."

IT WAS THE longest night of his life. He slept all of fifteen seconds and Tessa was one hundred percent to blame. She mumbled in her sleep. Not loud and not all the time, but enough to draw his attention and have him running into her room from his restless moving on the couch every five seconds.

Every time he'd find her sprawled out on the mattress. One leg sticking out from under the covers or her arms flung above her head. She slept with the same abandon that carried her through life.

He wanted her so badly he could taste it, which meant he needed coffee.

The electricity had kicked on around two in the

morning. He knew because he'd been staring out her back glass doors when the refrigerator whirred to life and the light by the door clicked on.

He somehow managed to drag his wet clothes on, creating friction as they rubbed against his skin. The lack of caffeine and the stiff jeans made him grumpier than the lack of sleep.

This was why he didn't step in and help other people these days. It never ended well.

He got the whole way to the door before he heard her footsteps behind him. Of course she was up by six. He was that unlucky.

"Are you slinking away?" Tessa asked.

"What?" He faced her and immediately regretted it. She still wore the pajama set, which seemed to shrink overnight. She also looked cute and rumpled and half-sleepy.

He was six seconds away from begging to climb into bed with her.

"This is a weird walk of shame," she said after she finished a yawn.

His brain cells refused to wake up and help him out. "What?"

"You're not a morning person, are you?" She shook her head as she stepped farther into the room. "Why are you running out without saying anything?"

"I was going to get us coffee." That was sort of the truth.

"I can make us coffee." She pointed toward the kitchen. "The electricity is on."

He swallowed back a curse. "I know."

"Why do you sound more ornery than usual?"

Rather than admit he hadn't slept, he shifted back into his protective space. "I had things to do today."

"And standing in my living room at"—she narrowed her eyes and squinted at the clock on the kitchen wall—"ten after six is preventing you from doing them?"

"Look—"

"You can leave." She actually wiggled her fingers at him as if she were shooing him away.

"Excuse me?"

"You were nice last night, and I know you hate that. Go ahead and scurry away. I won't be offended." She walked over and reached around him to unlock the door. "Believe it or not, Hansen, I get you."

No games. No complaining. She took his shit and threw it right back at him, not letting him get away with anything.

That was so damn sexy.

"Really, Hansen. It's okay." She opened the door. "You have a grumbly I-hate-people reputation to maintain."

Okay, now the conversation hit him full force and he didn't like the sound of any of it. She'd figured him out and was not impressed with what she'd uncovered. And she seemed a bit too *okay* with letting him leave. She'd called him sexy last night—he remembered because the moment kept replaying in his mind—and now she was kicking him out. He admired the move even though it left him feeling more grumbly than usual.

"You can come with me." His only excuse for saying the words was that his mouth and brain no longer seemed to be connected. "Maybe put on pants first."

She looked down at her legs.

So did he.

Her head shot back up and she smiled at him. "I could wait in the car while you get the coffee. That way I won't need to change."

Which meant he'd be coming back here to drop her off after. Which meant he was screwed. "Uh, sure."

"Then, once I'm fully caffeinated, I'll change and we can go out searching for the merman."

"What did I tell you about that word?" He nodded toward her shoes. "Come on."

"You know," she began as she slid the sneakers on, not bothering to untie them. For the second one she had to stomp her foot against the floor a few times to shove her foot in it because heaven forbid she reach down and unfold the material at the heel. "I think you're nicer than you pretend to be."

If she kept wasting time, she might not think so. "Whatever you say."

The keys jangled as she swiped them off the hook by the door. They stepped outside into overcast skies and a cool breeze.

"Do you need a sweater?" He turned to look at her but realized she hadn't followed him off the porch. "What are you doing now?"

The blood rushed right out of her face. "Hansen."

He followed her gaze to the grass. Just off her porch, faceup and wearing a suit, was a body. Male and not moving.

"Shit." He tossed her his cell phone as he jogged over and squatted down to search for a pulse. "Call Ben and the ambulance."

"Right." She stood over him tapping buttons.

Hansen could hear her voice, but the words no longer registered. Not after he got a good look at the man's face.

She crouched down on the opposite side of the man. "Ben is on . . . What is it?"

Hansen tried to suck in enough air to catch his breath as he lost his balance and dropped to his knees. This couldn't be happening. Not now. Not after all this time.

"Hansen?"

"He's dead." But that wasn't what had Hansen fumbling.

"Are you sure?" She lifted her head and whatever expression she saw on his face gave her the answer. "Oh, God. How did this happen?"

All Hansen knew was that his past had caught up with him in the worst possible way.

CHAPTER 6

Ben and the ambulance showed up within three minutes of the call. Every neighbor, including Sylvia, got there a minute after. In the middle of it all stood Ruthie, or she did until Ben moved her back, on the other side of the rier.

Trampled flower beds, blood, and yellow tape all over Tessa's front yard.

She watched as the volunteer ambulance crew headed by the island's only full-time fire employee, Captain Rogers, guided the gurney with the stack of body bags on top of it out of the ambulance.

Sylvia stepped up beside Tessa, coffee in hand. She offered it to Tessa. "You okay?"

"No." Why lie? There was no way to be okay with a dead man on her lawn.

"I take it that's the mysterious stranger."

Tessa tried to take a sip of the coffee but settled for holding the warm cup in her hands. "Definitely."

They hadn't been on top of each other back at the beach, but she'd recognized the man. The soaking wet dark suit also gave him away. No one on informal Whitaker Island wore a suit. Not even the doctors, one male and one female, or the one lawyer.

Sylvia frowned. "He must have gotten lost in the storm and fell."

That didn't sound right. The knocking and shaking the doorknob. He'd shown up on her porch acting desperate. Tessa had filled in at least those pieces. "He came—"

Hansen stepped in front of them with his usual flat-lipped stare. He nodded at Tessa. "I need to talk with you."

Sylvia frowned at him. "Hello, Hansen."

"Sylvia." He nodded his greeting before glaring at Tessa again. "Well?"

"Since you asked so nicely." She tried to cut him a break because it had been a particularly terrible morning. It had started off okay, except for his attitude and the sneaking around thing, then the whole day slid into a hellscape of death and confusion.

He inhaled before talking again. "Sorry, but this is important."

That was as close to a sincere apology as she'd ever gotten from him, so she took it as a win and let him guide her away from the bulk of the gawkers. Nothing much happened on Whitaker, so this was a big deal. A big, horrible deal.

Residents came out, most she recognized and a few others she didn't. Almost all appeared holding coffee and wearing sweatpants or whatever they had nearby to throw on when the ambulance's wailing siren started. Ellis and Arianna made the trek from the marina. Tessa even thought she saw Cliff peeking at the action from the back of the crowd. That was a miracle because nothing dragged that man off his porch. He paid local kids to run his errands and even insisted the doctor make a yearly housecall for his checkup.

Tessa stopped scanning the crowd long enough to look at Hansen. He needed to be clear about one issue. She'd spent too many years covering for other people, living a lie, and now hiding to protect her privacy. She never should have done it for one man and would absolutely not do it for another. "If you're going to ask me not to tell people that you slept over, forget it. I've been asked by the best to lie and said no. You get the same answer."

For a second he continued to stare at her without saying a word. "What are you talking about?"

Not a discussion she wanted to have now or ever. "Nothing. What is it?"

He reached out as if he was going to touch her arm but stopped. "We need to be careful about what we say."

There it was. The request for her silence. So annoying. "Did you not hear a word I just said? We're telling the truth."

He watched Ben talk to some people, then face off with Ruthie before looking at Tessa again. "About what?"

Maybe this was something else. His usual calm demeanor had vanished. This Hansen hovered right on the edge of control, and she had no idea why. "You seem . . . I don't know. Weirder than usual. What's going on?"

He waved off her concerns. "None of that matters."

She hated that the most. The dismissive thing. She took a long sip of coffee, purposely making him wait before throwing down her ultimatum. "You have ten seconds."

"Until what?"

"I call Ben over here." And she would do it, too. "You want my help? Then be honest with me."

"This is between us only." When she didn't say anything, he stepped in closer. "I'm serious."

Whatever that meant. "I can tell by the way your eyes are bugging out. What is it?"

He slouched a little. At six-three, he towered over her by a good six inches. Bending down put his mouth right by her ear. "I knew him."

"From the beach. Yeah, I recognized him, too." She dropped her voice to a whisper to match his even though she didn't know what the big secret was. "I guess he's been wandering around. I just can't believe he ended up at my place. What are the chances?" The more she talked, the faster her heart raced. She wanted to blame the topic and the chaos unfolding around her, but she feared the closeness was the culprit. "He probably came to the door for help and I ignored him."

And that part. The idea that the poor man could have been out there in the rain, banging around, asking for help, and she hid on her sofa. There was nothing heroic about that move.

Hansen shook his head and his hair brushed against her cheek. She tried to ignore the unintended touch and the shadow of scruff around his mouth and chin. She had a front-row seat to his adorableness and the timing could not be worse.

His hand went to the small of her back. "Tessa, this is a lot to put on you, but I feel like I'm losing it. Maybe if I say it, it will somehow make sense."

The fumbling was so out of character. He had her full attention now. "Hansen, what is it?"

"I'll tell Ben, but I need a few hours to think."

He'd totally lost her now. "About what?"

"I knew the guy *before* I came to Whitaker."

Did he just . . . ? "What now?"

"The dead guy. We have a . . ."

"History?" She filled in the word and internally winced when Hansen nodded in agreement. "How? Who is he?"

"Not important."

She planned to disagree when they weren't standing ten feet from a crowd with the gossipmongers staring at them, watching every breath and every touch. "Why didn't you admit that you knew him back when we were on the beach?"

"I didn't see his face then. Now I have."

The situation was so much easier when she thought of the guy as a merman.

Then it hit her. *Knew him*, as in a relative or co-worker or friend. Any of those meant this moment had to suck for Hansen. It explained his jerky movements and extra helping of surly attitude.

Guilt slammed into her. She skimmed her fingertips over his chin in the barest touch. One she hoped might be soothing. "Hansen, I'm so sorry. Should we let someone know? Contact someone for you? Was the man a friend or—?"

"You don't understand." He reached for her hand and held it. Trapped it against his chest and didn't let go. "I can't tell anyone that I know the stranger, especially not Ben. Not yet. Not until I can piece together a timeline and some facts and make this all make sense. I need you to keep that bit of information just between us."

Her nerve endings started firing. The sweet gesture battled with his harsh whisper. She didn't understand the contrast at all. "I barely understand what's happening."

"I get that, but Ben has a job to do. Me telling him everything about my past and this guy, especially my past with this guy, is going to put him in a rough spot."

She still didn't get what was happening. "Why?"

"Trust me." The pleading was in his voice and his eyes.

"Hansen . . ."

He gave her fingers a gentle squeeze. "I know it's asking a lot, and I probably don't deserve your trust, but I'm begging here."

Begging. By Hansen. If he had used any other word, she might have pummeled him with questions. But that one stopped her. She groaned even as she knew she would give in, at least up to a point. "Okay. For now, but my agreement is very temporary. You need to figure out whatever you need to know very fast."

"I swear I just need a little time."

She didn't know if the touching, so intimate and close, was a trick to get her to shut up. For now, she let him get away with it because that look on his face, all wide-eyed and vulnerable, suggested the morning had touched off some sort of frenzy inside him. "On one condition."

He sighed at her. "Make it quick."

He made it *so* hard to be on his side. "Really? You think that's the smart response here?"

"Sorry. Please just say it."

"Until you come clean with Ben about knowing the man on my lawn, you're stuck with me. You don't leave my side."

His eyes narrowed and the old Hansen, all skeptical and frowning, made an unwanted appearance. "Why?"

Only the sound of crunching pebbles stopped her from answering. Ben stood in front of them, hair disheveled but otherwise steady. "We have a problem."

"You have no idea," she mumbled under her breath.

Ben stopped talking and looked at her. "Meaning?"

Hansen picked that moment to shift his hand to her lower back, as if he wanted to anchor her in place. She got the point.

"What is it, Ben?" Hansen asked.

"He's been stabbed. Not sure how many times but I can see the slashes on his stomach and chest."

Every muscle froze. Tessa didn't think she could have moved if she had to. "Wait, the boat guy has been murdered? He didn't just fall or have a heart attack or something?"

Ben nodded. "Looks like foul play."

And Hansen knew the guy, which meant . . . She hated to think what that meant. "Damn."

"I don't think that language is strong enough." Ben waved to Captain Rogers as he moved people off her lawn and the pebbles and farther away from the house. "I'm guessing he wasn't bleeding on the beach."

"No. I would have mentioned that." That's what started all of this: her seeing that boat and now they had a dead guy. Tessa's mind spun trying to make the connections and fit Hansen into the puzzle in a way that made sense.

"Well, he wasn't here either," Ben said.

Hansen froze. "What?"

"Bleeding. There's not enough blood. Whatever happened likely happened somewhere else."

"And then he was dragged and dumped in my yard?" That struck her as one horrifying fact too many.

"Sorry, but we have more issues to deal with right now. We've got another storm coming, so the ferry can't get in, which means we're on our own for a while," Ben said. "But I do need to make a quick run out to that boat."

"Is that smart? You have your hands full here." Hansen specifically glanced at Ruthie, who was busy arguing with Captain Rogers when he tried to move the crime tape back. "People are going to get nervous. She already looks ready to explode."

"No choice. And there's one more thing." This time Ben turned toward her.

Tessa thought they were already dealing with enough things and about a million unasked questions. "Uh-huh."

"Even though he likely wasn't killed here, your house is a crime scene."

She took in the mud on her porch steps and the pebbles kicked up everywhere. "You mean outside."

"Do you want to sleep near this?"

Her mind raced to the blood and the noise at the door last night. "I kind of want to leave the entire island behind."

"It's okay." Hansen's fingers tightened against her back. "She can stay with me."

Ben smiled. "She can?"

"I can?" Yesterday she would have jumped at the chance. Now she was too busy fighting off a mix of confusion and queasiness to enjoy the idea.

Ben's smile only grew wider. "What exactly happened with you two last night?"

How in the world did she answer that without breaking her temporary promise to Hansen or sounding like she'd lost it? "I . . . uh . . ."

"Okay, I was kidding but now I really do want to know." Ben pointed at Hansen's shirt, then at her legs. "Especially since you're wearing the same clothes as yesterday, and honestly, I'm not sure what you're wearing."

"Pajamas." She realized for the first time she wasn't wearing much and how all of this must come off. She clearly was not far out of bed and Hansen was right there, at her house, looking scruffy and sexy and more than a little dazed.

The Whitaker gossip circle would rev up to high speed now.

Ben nodded. "Of course."

"It is seven in the morning." She was not sure what that proved, but she said it anyway.

Hansen cleared his throat. "Is our dating life relevant to the murder investigation?"

"I'm not sure what's going on or what's relevant right now, but since you just admitted you're dating, I'll let it go." Before she could debate the word, Ben started talking again. "But I'll need you to come to my office in an hour to answer some questions and sign a statement."

Hansen finally let his arm drop to his side again. "Sure."

He agreed like none of this was a big deal, which only made her more dizzy. She forced her mind to focus on Ben. "Can I get some clothes first?"

He nodded. "I'll take you inside."

"Thanks." Then she took off toward the house because she didn't want to go in, but she didn't want to be out here either.

HANSEN NOTICED BEN didn't immediately run after Tessa. Leaving her alone right now seemed like a bad idea but he had to stand there and accept it. They had enough of a circus to deal with without adding to the dating gossip.

"Well." Ben stared at the front door of Tessa's house as he talked. "We've known each other for a while now. We're friends."

That didn't sound good. "What's your point?"

Ben turned. Put his body between Hansen and the house and forced Hansen to look at him. "I wanted you to remember that when you think about lying to me in an hour."

"What are—?"

"Cut the shit."

Ben was too smart. He noticed too much. The Whitaker board might not appreciate the professional they had on their payroll, but Hansen did. "It's not what you think."

"We have a dead guy on her lawn. Someone put him there, in the same house where you also happened to be. You're both whispering. You look like garbage. Not in an I-had-sex-I'm-tired kind of way, but actual garbage." Ben put his hands on his hips. Took on that law enforcement watching-you stance. "Whatever is going on, I can't help unless you're honest with me. And I can help. No matter how bad it is."

Denial wouldn't work, so Hansen didn't hedge. "Got it."

"I hope so."

CHAPTER 7

Tessa changed into slim jeans and a T-shirt but even that outfit and how good she looked in it couldn't drag Hansen's mind from the past. It didn't make sense for the man he hated most to be on Whitaker, let alone dropped dead near her front door.

The annoying blowhard lived a life filled with business parties and thousand-dollar-a-plate dinners thousands of miles away in Washington, D.C. He talked big, played hard, and believed that only the East Coast stretch from Connecticut to Virginia mattered and wrote off the rest of the country. He was a lawyer and an asshole and now he was dead.

"We agreed."

He was barely listening, but Tessa's voice brought him back to the present. He knew he needed to respond. If she wavered or started talking before he could think it all through, he would be in huge trouble. "We will tell the truth. I promise."

"You mean not all of it." She snorted as she pushed open the door to the Whitaker police station, once part of the library but now broken off into a tight, almost-suffocating space, consisting of the outer reception area, Ben's office, and a conference room with no windows next to a set of jail cells.

The furniture looked old and on the verge of breaking apart. The chipped green paint on the walls didn't help the needed-to-be-updated atmosphere. Compared to the charm of the rest of the island with its cottages and open vistas, this was not the most welcoming place. That likely explained why Ben spent most of his days roaming around the island and checking in with the answering service every few minutes.

Hansen caught the door and held it open for her to go inside first. "I'm only leaving out one part of the story."

"It's kind of a biggie." She walked into the center of the room, then turned around to face him. "Don't you think?"

She had every right to be ticked off. He was asking for her to exercise a great deal of trust and even he could admit he hadn't done much to earn it. "I just need time."

"You already said that." She fingered the pamphlets spread out on one of the tables, ferry schedules and healthcare information for the island's clinic, before looking up at him again. "Are you ready to tell me how you know the guy? Knew. Ugh, this is awful. The man is dead and was found on my lawn, and I don't even know his name."

"Judson."

"Is that a first name or last?"

"Judson Ross."

"You know him well enough to be on a first-name basis?" She rolled her eyes for what had to be the tenth time in two minutes. "This just gets worse and worse."

"Tessa."

"Fine." She held up a hand in fake surrender. "I'm giving you a short reprieve but dial back the disapproving tone. You do not have the high ground right now."

"Fair enough." He'd never admit it, but he loved this side of her. The part that didn't take any shit. She came off as light and friendly, almost carefree, but her mood shifted when she thought someone needed her protection or that she needed to stand up for herself.

"If you knew how difficult it was for me to do this . . ."

He had no idea what that meant. "This?"

Every now and then she'd provide a brief and confusing glimpse into her past. Whatever drove her here, it was not to find a place with fresh air while she worked. That's the story she told but he didn't buy it. Everyone on Whitaker, except for the rare few like Cliff who were born and raised here and never left, had a story they fought to hide. Him included.

"Bury information. Lie. Provide a fake alibi." She repeatedly ran her finger along the edge of the table next to her thigh. Back and forth along the hard seam. "That's what you want from me, right?"

The way she talked tipped him off that there was

so much more to know about her. So much deeper he could go if he were willing to take the risk.

He fought back the need to take the peek she offered and ask her to share more. He could not afford the time—not now—so he tried to shift her focus. "We were together last night. There is nothing fake about that."

"You're playing verbal gymnastics." Her hand dropped to her side again as phones rang out around them. "Hiding important information still counts as lying."

"Everyone on Whitaker is covering up something." He thought about moving in closer but stayed right where he was instead. He didn't want to crowd her. "I'm assuming that includes you."

"Is that a threat?"

"No, it's the reality."

"Oh, really?" Her face flushed and those hands at her sides curled into tight fists. "Because I can start talking. Who knows what I'll say by the time I stop."

He'd said the wrong thing . . . again. He did not like being on the wrong side of her but he sure spent a lot of time there. "Okay, you win."

"Good of you to admit that."

The door opened behind them and Ben stepped inside. He didn't bother to shut it as he headed through the reception area to the desk in his office. After a quick check of his cell, he looked at them.

"Thanks for coming in." His smile switched to Tessa. "And thank you for finding clean clothes."

That was enough about that topic. Hansen tried to push them toward another. "Everyone on the island must want your attention right now."

Ben nodded. "Let's just say it's been a rough morning."

"No kidding," Tessa said as she leaned in the doorway, not quite stepping inside.

"The statements and the nine hundred questions I planned to ask—"

"Please be kidding." Hansen couldn't imagine a worse afternoon.

"—need to wait." Ben opened his top desk drawer and dumped a set of keys inside. "I have to get out on a boat, check the yacht, secure it, and tow it back. There's another line of storms rolling in, so I need to do it now."

Hansen had been itching to get on that boat. Now that he knew Judson had stayed on it for some period of time, even if just for a short leisure ride, Hansen wanted a look around. Something on there might explain Judson's presence and eventual murder. "I'll come with you."

Tessa raised her hand. "Me, too. We all know I'll be more careful than Hansen."

"No." Ben drew out the word. "You are not coming along because you're a civilian."

She pointed at Hansen. "So is he."

"Even though he grumbles about it, he's one of the volunteers who helps me from time to time with police duties. The other two are clearing trees and checking property, along with Captain Rogers and his crew, to make sure everyone is okay. I need Hansen with me in case there's trouble on the boat." Ben swapped out one coat for another from the rack behind him. Every time the phone rang he looked at the buttons, but he never answered it.

"Are you expecting a stray octopus or something?" she asked.

"I'm ignoring that comment." Ben stopped moving around. "But I do need to do a quick check-in with the doc before we go because if we do have a primary crime scene that's not your house, Tessa, then I need to find that and fast."

"Doc?" Tessa asked.

"Lela Thomas is examining the body. She helps out with forensics in police matters, which doesn't happen often." Ben delivered the information as he walked back into the reception area.

Hansen could hear the clock ticking in his head. He couldn't hold back the truth from Ben for very long. Hell, he shouldn't be doing it now, but his past was such a mess. People heard the truth, then they saw him differently. With most people he might not care but that wasn't the case with Ben and Tessa, which meant he needed a bit more time to figure this out. "You see Doc Lela. I'll line up a boat to get out to the yacht."

"Then we'll call the others and put a search together for blood or anything else that would indicate where this man was actually killed."

"And I'll sit, I guess." Tessa dropped down into the

nearest chair and picked up the ferry schedule brochure.

She pretended to read but Hansen sensed that subterfuge wouldn't last long. She'd made it clear she had no intention of being left behind or missing out on her chance to look at the boat. She viewed the boat as her "find" and acted like that gave her some rights to it.

He disagreed. "Don't move."

She didn't even look up as he headed for the door. "Don't boss me around."

SEVEN MINUTES AFTER sitting down, Tessa was ready to get back up. The phone in Ben's office would ring once and then stop. She assumed he had the answering service on. But that didn't stop people from sticking their heads in the door, looking for him.

After directing residents back out again and collecting messages for Ben, Tessa was ready for some fresh air, especially if they were going to get hit by another storm. She also needed to check on her house, move the generator, and pack to go stay with Hansen.

The only good part of any of that was that she finally would get to see the inside of his cabin. That wouldn't be a hardship, so long as he didn't talk. His grumpy muttering tended to interfere with his hotness.

"Good morning." Ruthie issued her greeting as she shut the door to the street behind her and entered the small waiting area outside of Ben's office. It consisted of a few chairs and tables and, now, one self-appointed town matriarch.

Tessa exhaled. She did not have the emotional strength for this showdown today. "Is it? I'd rather go back to last night and start over."

"Good point. Is Mr. Clifford in?" Ruthie didn't bother to wait for an answer. She opened Ben's door and stuck her head in before popping out again.

It took Tessa a second to catch up with the conversation because no one called him that. "You mean Ben?"

"It's best if we keep the relationship formal."

That sounded friendly. "Why?"

Ruthie dragged the empty chair closer to Tessa's and sat down close enough for their legs to touch. "Frankly, Ben is little more than a security guard on Whitaker."

"Have you tried to tell him that?" Tessa decided right there and then to apologize to Ben for being crappy to him. Now that she heard someone else do it, and for no apparent reason, she knew she'd been out of line. Frustration was fine. Doubting his competency wasn't.

"He understands the limits of his position. The state police should be handling this, not him."

Tessa crossed and uncrossed her legs. Something about having Ruthie this close, being all snotty and superior, made Tessa want to stand up and get out of there. But she had to provide a defense first. "Isn't Ben retired military police?"

"May I be candid? You know, woman-to-woman?"

As if she could stop Ruthie if she wanted to. "Sure."

"Be careful who you trust on Whitaker." Ruthie shifted in her chair until she faced Tessa. "I know you're new here and things can be confusing." She shook her head. "Heaven knows Sylvia doesn't always play by the rules."

First Ben and now Sylvia? Nope. That was one step too far. No one made fun of her friends. "Don't take a shot at Sylvia."

Ruthie kept right on talking as if Tessa wasn't ready to pounce. "You're friendly with everyone and you're spending more and more time with Hansen."

Well, this took an interesting turn. Now she was taking on Hansen. Ruthie had balls. Tessa had to give her credit for that. "Your point is?"

"Let's just say not everyone is who they pretend to be on Whitaker."

Yeah, no kidding. And Ruthie's handsy, totally inappropriate son who pretended to be a choirboy fit that category as well.

"But people *are* entitled to privacy," Tessa pointed out.

"It's my responsibility to know what's happening around here so I can keep people safe."

Tessa was pretty sure that was not her actual job description. "I thought Ben was in charge of that."

"You want me as an ally, Tessa."

"Okay. Sure." Her mom had taught her to protect her friends and watch over her enemies in case they made a move to start more trouble. That adage seemed to apply here.

"I want you to be happy on Whitaker. You're a great asset to the community."

She had no idea how that could be true since she

didn't really contribute much to Whitaker other than to buy things. "That's good to know."

"You're friendly and people trust you." Ruthie reached over and squeezed Tessa's hand. "I'm sure I can count on you."

Tessa looked down at her lap and tried not to flinch. She hadn't given permission to be touched but the other woman didn't seem to care about that. She operated by her own set of rules.

"To do what, Ruthie?"

"If there's something I need to know, I hope you'll tell me." The older woman leaned in as if they were sharing a big secret. "Not Ben, me."

Wrong. She'd probably tell Cliff and maybe even walk down to the marina and tell Arianna before she confided in Ruthie. The woman held too much power and Tessa was not about to give her more. "I doubt I'll find out anything that rises to that level."

"Don't underestimate yourself." This time she patted Tessa on the knee.

She fought the urge to move her leg. She might not like Ruthie, but the woman did like to talk, and that meant she might spill something worth knowing. "I'm not."

"Excellent." Ruthie stood up and slipped a hand over her hair as if to make sure nothing fell or leaked out or otherwise moved during her impromptu exercise. "I knew we could come to an understanding."

Oh, Tessa understood the older woman just fine. "I haven't seen Doug in a few days. How is he?"

Some of the tension left Ruthie's shoulders. "Very good."

Tessa guessed that huge smile, the one reserved only for her son, was the first genuine emotion she'd ever seen from Ruthie. She might be a mini-dictator and difficult and far too invested in her Madam President role, but she loved her boy.

Having been raised by a doting single mother herself, Tessa appreciated the bond. For so long, she and her mom moved through life as a unit. They conquered and survived. They fought and disagreed, and Tessa remembered more than one teen tantrum that ended with a door slam and her mom threatening to remove it if she ever tried that again. But heaven help anyone who tried to bad-talk the other.

She grew up in a tangled mess of family dysfunction thanks to her idiot biological father, but she knew unconditional love. It was the greatest gift her mother ever gave her. That continued to this day with her Sunday phone calls and concerned texts.

"In fact," Ruthie continued, "my son will be working here soon. Not my first choice, of course, but it's a school credit sort of thing. As a side benefit, I figure Doug might also be able to keep me updated with any concerns about what happens in this office."

Man, the woman just did not quit with the anti-Ben rhetoric.

"Isn't that interesting." And damn Ben for not telling her about the office work thing. Of course he'd tried to rein in Doug. It would have been nice if he had told her that and saved her from being ticked off for no reason.

"I'm sure you'll be seeing a lot of him very soon."

Tessa felt her insides shrivel. If Doug tried to touch her again, she was throwing a punch. He'd had his one warning. "I can only hope."

CHAPTER 8

Water pelted Hansen's face as they rode out to the boat; he could barely see. His glasses fogged up into a wet mess. He hardly noticed. Too many thoughts ran through his mind.

The fights and the threats. Without Judson, Hansen would be back in Washington, D.C., attending meetings and cursing the commute home from work. That would mean no Whitaker. No Tessa. That last thought sent a sharp pain stabbing in his chest.

The roar of the engine cut off as they pulled beside the yacht. Hansen got a close-up of its size—maybe sixty feet or so. It towered over the water as it bobbed.

He was about to comment on the lack of movement inside and the deathly quiet except for the waves lapping against the boat. Even this close to shore, it rocked up and down and the storm churned the water and the waves began to crash.

"You ready to tell me?"

Ben's comment broke through Hansen's mental wandering. "What are you talking about?"

"Not sure how long we're going to play this game, but okay." Ben secured their small motorboat, the one provided to Ben for business use only—Ruthie had made that clear. He tied it off to the back lower deck of the yacht, then turned to face Hansen again.

"Are you talking about me spending the night with Tessa?" Because as far as Hansen was concerned, that topic was off-limits. Sure, nothing happened but he *really* wanted it to. So much that the idea of kissing her, touching her, refused to leave his thoughts. He dreamed about her. Hell, his mind wandered to her on and off throughout the day even though she'd stood a few feet from him for most of that time.

There were so many reasons nothing could happen between them. His mess of a past and bad choices being the biggest. But it was more than that. Her sweetness. His mood would kill off the best part of her in a matter of weeks. And Judson. Alive, he had been a constant reminder of all Hansen had lost. Dead proved to be an even bigger nightmare.

Hansen tried to conjure up a speck of sympathy for him and couldn't do it. That likely made him an asshole. Even if what he and Tessa could share would amount to a pleasant fling and mean nothing to either of them except a much-needed release, Tessa deserved better than that. Better than him.

"Please tell me the weirdness between you two isn't because you had sex." Ben made a strangled noise. "Oh, shit. You did, didn't you? Was it bad?"

"Stop talking."

Tessa and sex. A man could only take so much temptation. And the sex would be great. He'd bet his life on it.

Ben shrugged. "Fine."

"You say that, but I know you don't mean it." Hansen knew better. Ben had never just let a subject drop. Once he got something in his head, it would linger there. Pop up at the worst times.

"I'm here if you need to unload."

"Got it."

"Right, work now. You can fill me in on your love life later." Ben glanced up at the threatening sky before stepping onto the back of the yacht.

"There's nothing to tell."

Ben shook his head. "If that's true, then I really don't get you."

"Meaning?"

"Tessa."

Hansen felt like he missed part of the conversation. "And?"

"Forget it. You need to figure it out yourself." Ben reached for his side, where he'd once strapped a gun.

Hansen knew the move was born of instinct and all those years as military police. He also knew Ben had firearms locked in a safe in his office. One of the many Whitaker board rules was that Ben had to remain unarmed while on duty, which was usually not an issue because crime on Whitaker rarely rose above fights between neighbors over "missing" newspapers.

As Ben stepped toward the cabin, he stopped Hansen from following with a wave of his hand. "I don't want any more contamination of the scene than necessary. You stay there."

Hansen waited until Ben disappeared into the cabin to step onboard. He glanced around the sundeck. Nothing there but towels, now soaked from last night's rain and plastered to the cushions. He didn't know what he expected to find or what might help his case, but the idea of taking a peek into Judson's life proved too tempting to ignore.

"Shit!" Ben yelled and kept on yelling. "Hansen, get in here."

Without thinking, Hansen darted through the doorway, then into the plush living area filled with overstuffed chairs, through to the kitchen area. "What's going on?"

But Ben didn't need to answer. Hansen saw her. A woman, petite with sandy blond hair hanging in clumps covering her face. Her wrists were tied together and her arms outstretched where a rope held her tight to a hook on the wall. Blood streaked her skin and was stained and smudged on the floor. The bruise under her eye seemed to darken by the minute.

"Kerrie." The name escaped Hansen's lips before he could call it back.

Ben's head shot up and he pinned Hansen with an angry glare. "Who?"

"Is she alive?" Trying to step around the splatter and the mass of papers and pots and every other kind of kitchenware strewn all over the room, Hansen kneeled at Kerrie's side. He lifted his hand, but he wasn't sure where to touch her or how to help.

Ben alternated between taking photos with his cell and checking her pulse. "Breathing but not conscious." Ben shoved his cell in Hansen's direction. "Snap as many photos as you can. Get her and the boat."

Hansen's stomach rolled. "What the hell?"

"No choice." Ben checked her arms and legs for injuries. "I need to untie her, but we also need to preserve the evidence as much as we can."

That's what she was reduced to—evidence. Logically, it made sense, but Hansen's brain rebelled. He forced his muscles to move but every shift took effort.

Ben kept working. He took care and was gentle.

"Hey." Ben waved a hand in front of Hansen's face. "Call for the ambulance. They should meet us at Stark's Marina."

The steady tone got through. Hansen jumped to his feet, careful not to touch anything. He dialed but his gaze kept returning to Kerrie. To her face and her swollen eye. Over her ripped shirt and the dried blood circling a cut on her arm.

She'd been attacked, probably by Judson. That's the only explanation that made sense.

The idea of Judson hurting her . . . Hansen almost lost his balance, but he somehow made it back to the doorway. Fresh wet air slapped him in the face just as he thought he might double over with the need to get sick. He dropped his head back and inhaled as he waited for Maddie at the answering service to pick up.

"And Hansen?"

He spun around to face Ben again. "Yeah?"

"I fucking heard what you said."

THE RAIN HELD off until the rescue boat arrived at the yacht but no longer. The mist gave way to a steady downpour. Not violent or rough but not great to stand in either.

Tessa waited on the dock with Sylvia and stared out over the water, waiting for the boats to appear. A few minutes later, they rounded the curve from Throwaway Beach and came into view. The smaller one towed the yacht.

Finally. Tessa let out the haggard breath she'd been holding. "There they are."

It took a few more minutes for Ben to steer the yacht toward the slip reserved for town use. It sat at the end in the locked section of boat slips, which meant it would take a little bit longer for Hansen to get over here.

The combination of the storm, the scare with the knocking last night, and finding the body had her on edge and jumpy all day. She'd been shaking on the inside while fighting to present an outward calm.

Rain fell harder now as gray clouds tumbled and rolled. Outside it looked like sunset instead of the middle of the day—very little light along with the thundering sound of wind. This storm could whip through the island and cause some damage. No wonder Ben made recovering the yacht the priority.

"Lela is only going to have an hour or—" Sirens

drowned out Sylvia's voice. She yelled the rest. "What is this about?"

The ambulance raced into the parking lot. A second later, Captain Rogers and two of the volunteer first responders, both full-time fishermen, jumped out. The three of them scurried around, collecting equipment and grabbing the stretcher.

Tessa tried to inhale but suddenly she couldn't catch her breath. "Do you think one of them got hurt on the boat?"

Her mind flipped to Hansen. He went out there distracted and frustrated about this guy Judson. He could have lost his balance or . . . anything.

She started forward to check, but Sylvia grabbed her arm and tugged her out of the way. Footsteps thudded on the dock as the crew zipped by them. Tessa could hear voices on the radios they carried. Very loud voices.

People started to gather. Some came off their boats and others ventured out of the marina's clubhouse. A few cars pulled into the lot behind the ambulance. The siren going off happened so infrequently that some of the nosier residents used it as a summons to chase the ambulance and see what was going on.

"I don't think I've ever seen Captain Rogers run," Sylvia said.

"There's Hansen." A whoosh of relief ripped through Tessa. Her knees threatened to buckle but she forced her body to stay still. But confusion quickly replaced any ease she'd experienced. "He does not look happy."

Sylvia made a humming sound. "Ben looks worse."

They were arguing. Ben shouted directions, something Tessa couldn't quite hear. The rain and wind drowned out everything, but she could see their stiff poses and Ben barking to the crew, then turning to yell something at Hansen.

None of it made sense. "What happened out there?"

"Huh." Sylvia frowned. "Looks like Ben is ordering Hansen out of the slips."

Tessa saw Ben point. The showdown continued for a few more seconds until Ben disappeared back on the boat and Hansen stormed down the walkway that connected the public part of the marina slips to the ones operated by Ben.

"Here he comes." But Tessa wasn't convinced that was a great thing. Something had gone sideways out there.

Right before she could call out to Hansen, Ben appeared again.

"Don't go far." This time his low angry voice carried over the edge of the storm.

"They're fighting?" She didn't mean to ask the question out loud, but the idea seemed so strange to her. Ben's personality never wavered. He didn't get upset and never took a shot at Hansen. Not that she'd ever heard.

"Hansen . . ." He walked right past her, ignoring her outstretched hand. "Hansen!" She looked at Sylvia. "Where is he going?"

"That was rude even for him."

She heard the ding of metal from the boats bobbing in the water. Captain Rogers issued orders as the wheels of the gurney rumbled against the wood dock, coming toward them.

A person? "Who did they take off the boat? It looks like someone got hurt."

"No idea." Sylvia sounded as confused as Tessa felt.

"We need answers. I'll go get him." She looked around, trying to figure out which direction Hansen had stomped off to.

"Maybe wait." Sylvia bit her lower lip. "Tessa, he's not great with empathy. You go talk to him now and he could say something you find unforgivable."

He was going to act like an ass. She knew that. He could be testy even when he was in a good mood, and he seemed anything but that right now. But she'd taken a chance on him. She deserved some answers. "He's not a child."

"No, but he has a temper and I don't want you to be the target of it."

"Well, he doesn't have a choice. I'm living with him, remember?" She threw that out there.

"Stay at the lodge. Give him some time to calm down."

The advice made sense, but Tessa wasn't thinking about bedrooms and greeting Hansen over coffee in the morning right now. "I can't let this go."

"Why?"

"We have an agreement." That idea kept bouncing around in her mind. He'd promised her. "He's stuck with me. At least for now."

CHAPTER 9

Hansen got as far as the parking lot before he remembered he'd caught a ride to the marina with Ben. He flattened his palms against the car's hood and inhaled. The questions screaming in his head refused to quiet down. Thoughts bombarded him. Judson dead. Kerrie injured. They must have followed him here, but why? Judson had won the battle and the war. Literally drove Hansen out of town.

Those days, all those months ago, replayed in Hansen's mind. Rage he couldn't control or redirect overwhelmed him. He could trace his personality flaws now to his obsession back then. He'd always been predictable and short-tempered. He couldn't lay the blame for that on Judson. But the explosion, his inability to find steady ground again, tied right back to Judson.

As the anger grew, his work had suffered. His younger brother, Connor, finally begged for him to go away for six months or a year, however long it took to regain his focus. Hansen was pretty sure that goal would never be obtained, but at least here he could wrestle with his anger in peace. Shut himself off from most people and stupid arguments.

He tried so hard to clear his mind and tuck the debilitating grief for Alexis away. But the guilt kept swamping him, as did the need to balance the scales. If Judson had walked up to him in town two days ago and said hello . . . Hansen didn't know what he would have done. A month ago, he would have unleashed. Now, maybe, but the idea of never letting Tessa see his feral side started to matter to him, too.

So many conflicting emotions. That last confrontation with Judson. The satisfied look on his face as he wiped the blood from his nose after being on the receiving end of the punch. How quickly Judson called the police.

Hansen had gone too far, and it hadn't done anything but scare his parents. Connor meeting him at the police station. The untethered fury and pain that nearly doubled him over. It had subsided to a dull ache that never fully eased. Seeing Judson and Kerrie brought it all back.

The rain fell harder, soaking Hansen and streaking his glasses. He felt as if he hadn't been dry in days. The second time he took the glasses off to wipe the lenses he saw her, standing just off to his right.

"Not now." He couldn't deal with her questions and doubts on top of everything else. He needed her on his side and the only way to keep her there was to not tell her one more sentence of his twisted story. It was manipulative and shitty. She didn't deserve to be used but some days she was the only light spot in the darkness that fell over him, and he wasn't ready to give that up.

She walked over to him. Stood next to the car, only a few feet away. "You don't get to make that rule."

She didn't back down or scare easily. She took him for who he was, full of attitude and sarcasm, and didn't hesitate to shovel either back at him. Usually that was enough. He'd snap out of it when he saw her smile or they launched into verbal banter. He actually craved both at this point, but he couldn't rally for her. Not today.

"Seriously, Tessa. I am not at my best right now. I can't pretend for you."

She pushed the wet hair off her face. Tucked it behind her ears. "You pretend with me?"

"I try to be civil with you." Wrong words. He couldn't find the right ones, so he let those sit there.

"Since when?"

And he sure didn't have the energy to fight. If they started, he feared he wouldn't fight fair. "Not. Now."

"We had an agreement."

She was being rational and calm, and he couldn't fight that. "Jesus, you just don't quit."

"You know how careful I was with the few answers I gave Ben before. I have no idea what I'm going to say once he finally has time to formally question me. Lying is not something I do but now I'm worried about you and how what I say might impact you, and it's making my stomach twist. So you owe me. You just do."

The words sliced into him. All he'd wanted was an

hour or two of breathing room. If he could go to Ben with a reasonable explanation, he'd save them all a lot of trouble. But that couldn't happen now because telling the whole story meant making himself the number one suspect in a murder. The stakes had risen. Kerrie's injuries could be serious, which put him at the wrong end of the firing line again.

"Tessa." When she started to tremble he almost went to her. She had to be cold and frustrated. She needed a shower and warm clothes and to be at least two states away from him. "Don't do this."

"I'm trying to help you." The pain, genuine and immediate, echoed in her voice.

"I don't want your help." But, God, he did. Some days carrying all the baggage dragged him to his knees.

"Yeah, you've made that clear." She crossed her arms in front of her. "For the record, maybe if you let someone in, shared some of the weight, you wouldn't be so damn angry all the time."

Without another word, she turned and started walking. Her shoes squeaked with each step. Stiff shoulders but her head down.

He felt like he kicked a puppy. "Wait."

She didn't face him. Just gave him a short wave and shouted over her shoulder. "You want to be alone, you got it."

Hurting her just added to his guilt. "Tessa, please."

At his begging, she stopped. This was becoming a habit. He'd push her, and she'd finally draw a line and leave . . . and then he'd falter. Watching her as she walked away from him knocked into him like a kick to the gut. He shouldn't care, but he did.

Finally, she turned around. "Just tell me what happened on the boat."

Her expression didn't give anything away as she stood there, dripping, seemingly oblivious as the rain pelted her in the face.

He swiped at his glasses but finally gave up the losing battle against the rain. Maybe it would be better to face her through blurry raindrops. "There was a woman on the boat."

"How is that possible?" Her eyes widened. "Wait . . . is she okay?"

Exactly the response he'd expect from her—a mix of caring and wanting to know more. She didn't just accept what people told her. She investigated. She was a technical writer. He couldn't remember that term before but did now. For the longest time he thought that meant she spent her days researching, because that fit with who she was, until she explained that she created and reviewed manuals and online guides. She literally made sure documents that explained how to do things made sense.

He wished she could explain what was happening now. "She was tied up and unconscious, but Ben said her breathing sounded steady."

Tessa swept her hair back again and moved in closer. People milled around and several residents crowded the ambulance as the back doors slammed shut.

"How long has she been on there? Was she attacked or did—?"

"She's the wife of the man we found on your lawn."

Tessa blinked as she fell silent. "What?"

"You heard me." He could almost see the information click together in her head. One piece, then another. Any second now she would step back, move away from him. Fear would cloud her vision and he couldn't blame her.

"Then you know her, too."

"Yes." There wasn't any reason to deny it, so he didn't try. Already wet and miserable, he turned and leaned against the front of Ben's car in a relaxed stance that didn't give away anything about the energy pinging around inside of him.

She took another step until she stood between his outstretched legs. "How bad is this going to get for you?"

"I have a history with this couple. A bad history." He glanced around but no one was standing near them. The crowd huddled closer to the marina building, though more than one onlooker spent a lot of time watching them. "When the facts come out . . ."

"Did you hurt them?"

Just as some of the tension left his body she asked that and the adrenaline surged through him again. "What?"

She rested a hand on his thigh. "I'm asking one time only and expecting you to tell the truth."

The soft touch comforted him when he thought nothing could. More than anything he wanted to slide his hand over hers, but he held back. "You think that I would do that?"

"No."

The tension spinning around and ratcheting up inside him broke. "Then why ask?"

"I knew you'd assume I was interrogating you and I wanted you to hear my answer. But I still need to hear yours." She slid her hand to his knee, until she barely kept contact. "I saw your face when you recognized the man this morning. You were stunned."

This time he reached out. Rubbed his thumb over the side of her index finger. "I didn't know they were here. I didn't touch them."

Her gaze searched his face for a few more seconds before she nodded. "I believe you."

"Thanks." The small word didn't do justice to how he felt.

He continued to skim his fingers over the back of her hand. Her soft skin and the tenuous connection grounded him. The way she turned her hand over and let her fingertips wander over his palm reeled him in.

"Hansen."

He picked up on the question in her voice. He claimed to need space, but he'd forfeit it in a second for her. That realization scared him more than the prospect of jail.

He dropped his hand. "This can't be happening."

"We need to go to Ben's office." She looked up, closing her eyes as the rain fell on her face. "And maybe find a towel."

Some strands of hair stuck to her shoulders, but the rest cascaded down her back. If the rain truly bothered her, she hid it well. The chill wind turned her cheeks pink, but she didn't complain. She rarely complained.

She had the kind of open personality, warm and giving, that would be so easy to fall into. Except for the questions. She seemed to ask whatever popped into her head. But here, watching the ambulance speed away and the crowd start to clear, she didn't go there.

He didn't know if he should be nervous or not. "You're not asking for specifics. Why?"

"I plan to be standing there when you tell Ben. Maybe not this second because his attention is scattered in a million different directions, but we both know you're going to do it and not wait." She threw him a look that suggested he shouldn't argue with her. "He's your friend and you're not a jackass. You're not going to put Ben in a terrible position."

It made sense . . . right up to the part where the truth made him look pretty guilty. "Telling him will do that. He'll have to arrest me."

"Maybe it's your turn to have a little faith in him." She sighed at him. "As you pointed out, we all have secrets. Yours are about to be splashed all over this island."

"So?"

She sighed. "You need one person on your side who's not bombarding you with questions or doubting you right now."

He didn't say it but it sounded like he didn't have to. Ben would do his job. Tessa would support him. That was a gift he might not be able to repay. "And that's you."

"Me and Ben, once he stops being super lawman.

And hopefully not just us." She sighed. "People are going to talk. Say things."

It would all start again. The rumors, the staring. It was one thing to be considered the mysterious loner on an island filled with people harboring secrets. It was another to be the target of a murder investigation. "Shit."

"Yeah, exactly."

SYLVIA DROPPED THEM off at Ben's office an hour later. Hansen wanted to head home, but Tessa knew that would only raise more questions. No matter how hard and emotionally exhausting the next few minutes might be, he needed to get to the other side of it. The only way to do that was to go through it.

Ben lifted his head as they stepped into his office. "Tessa, I need to talk with Hansen alone."

"She can stay," Hansen said in a tone that sounded flat and lifeless.

"It doesn't work that way." Ben leaned back in his chair. "But she's not going far because I need to talk with her, too."

Tessa dreaded what would happen *later* and what he might ask. But at least he hadn't sent her home . . . yet. "Then we're good."

Ben's gaze shifted between her and Hansen. "Friends or not, we need to play this by the rules."

The tension snapping across Hansen's shoulders and down his back pulled his posture even straighter. "I've already told her most of it."

Most? True, she still hadn't heard a word about his

past and whatever trouble he'd gotten tangled up in. It would be so easy to throw up her hands and walk away. Let Hansen clean up his own mess.

But curiosity nagged at her. *He* intrigued her. She'd been sucked into his life and caught up in his past. Bad moods, grumpy disposition, and all.

But he wasn't a killer. She didn't fear him. She knew to her soul that he hadn't left her house for a few minutes to step outside and kill his one-time nemesis in a flash or wander over to the beach and hurt a woman on a boat. Even if the timing worked and all those noises she'd heard outside that night related to the murder and not him pleading for help as she'd assumed, she couldn't make a man who killed and attacked in such a cold rage fit with the man who agreed to be dragged out to the beach with her to look at a boat.

"Huh." Ben's eyes narrowed. "Interesting how you think 'most of it' is enough."

"He didn't—"

Ben held up a hand. "You don't need to rush to his defense, Tessa. If you think you can stand there and not say a word, then fine. I'll ask you both about the body this morning and wait to go over your movements last night in more detail after I put you in separate rooms later."

"Lucky us." She hated the idea of *later* and *questions*, but she understood. Whitaker might be relaxed, but murder was murder. The good people of this island would be on edge and snapping at each other until Ben figured all of it out.

"Do you know where the primary crime scene was?" Hansen asked.

Phones rang nonstop, but Ben didn't bother to answer. He didn't argue with them either. "Shut the door. We'll need a bit of privacy."

Hansen nodded and closed it. Leaned against it, either to keep anyone from barging in or because he needed the extra support; Tessa wasn't sure which.

"A fight or something happened on that boat but there's no blood trail, no pool. Nothing points to the stabbing taking place there. The blood on Tessa's lawn wasn't consistent with him being stabbed there either." Ben exhaled. "Which means he was most likely killed at another location on the island, one we haven't discovered yet."

"That sounds ominous." When neither man said anything, she guessed she'd picked the right word.

"Judson and Kerrie Ross." Ben dropped a file on his desk. "They live in Alexandria, Virginia. He's a partner in a law firm in Washington, D.C. Specializes in something called complex civil litigation, according to his bio. It looks like she designs interiors for high-end boutiques and small hotels in the area."

Hansen closed his eyes for a second, then reopened them. "All true. Yes."

"They're well-off. No kids." Ben flattened his hand on the top of the file. "But you know all of that, too."

"I do."

The information didn't change anything for her. Made the couple more human, maybe, but she didn't need a reminder of that. She saw Judson's face every time she closed her eyes. She knew that would happen for a long time. Killer or terrible husband or just unlucky, the end result was the same. She'd come face-to-face with death, right there where she planted her flowers and raked leaves, and that would linger.

"They don't own the yacht but the identification and paperwork I found provided the basics about them. Makes me wonder what ten minutes on the internet will show me." Ben's tone didn't threaten but it didn't waver either. Gone was the usual joking between the men. Ben stayed focused, his frustration with Hansen very clear.

Tessa tried to change the subject to give them both some breathing room. The question picked at her and she needed to know the answer anyway. "Is Kerrie okay?"

"Unconscious. She has a head injury and bruising. She's dehydrated from being on the boat alone for at least a day." Ben glanced at Tessa, but his focus mostly stayed on Hansen. "The doc said she should be fine physically. But who knows what she saw or survived."

The news sounded good, but the timing didn't make sense to Tessa. Not at all. "She was there this whole time?"

"Apparently." Ben opened the cover of the file but closed it without really checking inside again. "It looks like she was punched. Knocked around." Ben stared at Hansen. "Any of this sound familiar to you?"

Without even thinking, Tessa shifted. She went

from standing beside and a little in front of Hansen, to putting her body in front of his. He didn't need a shield, but her feet had a mind of their own. "You can't think Hansen did this."

Ben finally looked at her, really looked. That's when Tessa noticed the fatigue. The tugging around his eyes and flat line of his mouth. He wasn't enjoying this interrogation any more than Hansen.

"I need to ask him, Tessa."

But he couldn't believe this. There was no way. "Do you?"

Hansen pushed away from the door and came to stand beside her. "Yes, he does. He's doing his job."

Some of the tension around Ben's mouth eased and he nodded. "Tessa, I'm guessing by this time tomorrow everyone on Whitaker is going to think Hansen did this. I'm not going to be the only one searching online. Once the names go public, Hansen's entire life will be fair game. All of Whitaker is going to know."

Without specifically saying it, it seemed like Hansen and Ben had found some common ground. She still blustered and wanted to stomp around, asking questions and demanding answers. But they were much more realistic about Judson and Kerrie and Hansen's past spilling over into everything. "That doesn't mean—"

"I knew them." There wasn't a surprised reaction to Hansen's admission. More like a shared understanding in the room. "Ben knows because I said Kerrie's name the second I saw her on the boat."

"And the gossip mill's been churning since Judson

was found on your lawn and Hansen was standing right there." Ben stared at the phone for a few seconds when one of the calls went longer than the usual two rings.

When he glanced over at them again, some of the exhaustion had vanished. He looked more like the Ben she knew. The one who would calmly weigh the evidence but be ready to charge into battle if needed.

Well, he wasn't the only one who could fight. She refused to wait on the sidelines. "He was with me last night."

Hansen started to talk but Ben put a hand up to stop him. By some miracle, that move worked. "Were you close enough to him *all night* that you would have known if he'd gotten up?"

"Okay, yeah." Hansen scratched the back of his head. "We should talk about this alone and then—"

Tessa caught Hansen's arm before he could bluster his way into a jail sentence. "I'm his alibi."

He looked at her hand, then at her face. "Tessa, you don't want to be in the middle of this. Trust me."

"It's okay to say he was right there and you think you would have heard him leave. No one is going to blame you for falling asleep or for anything that happened before he got to your place," Ben said.

Okay, that was exactly what happened, but it left an opening for doubt and she hated that. "Hansen didn't do this. We both know that."

Silence filled the room, but it didn't last long. Ben's cell started buzzing. He glanced at the screen and immediately answered. "Yeah? Coming."

"What now?" If anyone else from Hansen's past jumped up, she might just lose it.

"I need to go help Lela." Ben winced as he glanced over at the door leading to the cells.

He had to be kidding. For the second time, she stepped in front of Hansen. This was starting to be a habit now. "You are not putting him in there."

Hansen laughed, but it sounded hollow. "It's fine."

She was two seconds away from smacking their empty heads together. Since Hansen had shifted into full-on guilt mode, she tried to reason with Ben. "This is an island. A storm is coming. He can't go anywhere."

"But you two can work on your stories if I don't separate you."

She had to give the man credit. But he missed his chance. "Don't you think we would have done that already?"

Ben's exhale cut through the incessant phone ringing and Hansen's dramatic sigh. "Good point."

It was about time she found an argument that worked. Her back ached from standing there, so stiff and ready to fight off anyone who touched Hansen, and a puddle surrounded her feet. "Thank you."

"For the record, I don't think you killed anyone, but we both know you're hiding details because you think they matter, which means they're bad." Ben glanced at Hansen before grabbing a dry coat from the rack. He seemed to have an endless supply, but if the storm lasted as long as predicted, he'd need a few more. "As soon as I'm done, I'll be at your house and you'll need to come clean on everything. Not just the pieces that are easier to tell."

"Got it." Hansen hesitated for a second. "And thanks."

Ben nodded as he walked past them and opened the door. He was out of the office and through the reception area in less than five seconds. A man on a mission.

Tessa vowed to make sure that Hansen didn't become Ben's next target.

She looked at him, saw all the horrors of the last few hours mirrored in his expression. "What happens when Kerrie wakes up?"

"With our history? Ben will probably arrest me."

That would teach her to ask. "That won't happen this time."

"We'll see."

CHAPTER 10

Hansen opened the front door to his brown shingled cabin. Locking it hadn't been an issue . . . until now. Until they settled whatever was happening, he'd have to make a habit out of using the dead bolt.

Unspent energy still bounced around inside him and he had to move. He walked across the room to the leather ottoman he used as a coffee table and set down Tessa's gym bag with the few belongings Ben let her grab from her house this morning.

The cabin consisted of the main floor and a bedroom loft. The living area amounted to little more than a twenty-by-twenty square with a kitchen against one wall, a bathroom at the other end, and a sofa and chair in the middle. It was small and tidy and perfect for him. He didn't own much, at least not here. Back home he had a condo and a closet full of suits. Here, no.

"This isn't what I expected." Tessa delivered the comment from the doorway as she dumped her raincoat on the hook by the door and toed off her shoes.

He got it. She'd expected an easy day and he'd

plunged her into a nightmare. "To get sucked into my messed-up life?"

"The throw pillows." She walked over to the sofa and ran her fingers over the braided edge of the blue one. "You don't seem like a throw pillows kind of guy."

One smart-ass joke and she broke the tension that threatened to suffocate him. "Who doesn't like pillows?"

She hummed. "I would have guessed you."

"I am human, you know." Though most days he felt as if he were held together with rubber bands and little else.

"I'll take your word on that." She slid her hands up and down her arms as she scanned the room.

"Want to change?"

She reached for her bag before he finished the sentence. "That would be great."

"You can take a shower." Making the offer almost killed him. She'd be in the shower and he'd be out here squirming. *Great idea, Hansen.* He wanted to kick his own ass.

She shook her head. "Just a change of clothes and a towel are fine."

He pointed toward the door to the bathroom. "Extra towels are on the shelves."

"Excellent." She stepped through the door and out of view, then popped her head out again. "This is a real test, you know?"

Did she think he'd spy on her as she changed? "How?"

"Once I go in here I'll see how messy you are, look through your cabinets. That sort of thing."

"Are you really going to look in my medicine cabinet?"

Her eyes sparkled with mischief. "You'll never know."

"Take the wet clothes off before I have to take you to the clinic for pneumonia."

The second she disappeared again, his spirits dipped. She worked like a light switch for him. With her there, his mood stabilized. Without her, the anger seeped back in.

Rather than analyze her impact on his life and what that meant, he took the opportunity to find some warm, dry clothes for himself. He rummaged through the closet area beneath the loft ladder and found his softest and oldest pair of jeans. He pulled them on, along with a long-sleeve T-shirt, before she stepped into the room again. Once she did, her outfit made him yearn for a cold shower.

A thin tie held the relaxed sweatpants on the top of her hips. They balanced there, just touching the bottom edge of her I Trust Dogs More Than Men T-shirt. When she moved, a sliver of skin peeked through and his stomach flipped over.

And she did move as she conducted an informal surveillance of the open room. She walked around the small space and skimmed her fingertips along the top of the sofa. Looked inside the lampshade from above. Even went over to the window and shifted the curtains to glance outside.

She hypnotized him. The slight shift of her hips. Soaked to the skin from the downpour or dry didn't matter. She calmed him. Made his world tilt right again.

For the first time in hours he felt like he could breathe. He hated that he needed her, but he did and that meant fighting every instinct to build his defenses even higher and being honest with her instead. "Ask me."

She ran her hands through her hair, fluffing it up from underneath. The strands straddled the line between damp and mostly dry. She must have used a towel to take care of the worst of the rain damage.

"It's frustrating that after everything, including me dancing around the question about how much I slept when you were at my house to avoid lying but still cover your butt, that you don't trust me enough to just tell me whatever I need to know without me begging for answers." Her tone carried a hint of not-sure-what-to-do-with-you frustration.

But man, did she read him wrong. "I do trust you."

"That's the only part you heard me say?"

"It's a big point." He saw her shrug. Then came the smile.

"True." She walked around the sofa and sat down. Not at either end. No, she planted her impressive ass in the middle, which meant if he wanted to sit with her, they'd be up close and very personal.

She folded her legs in a pretzel position he couldn't achieve even after a full day of stretching. The move showed off her fluffy white socks. The casual look worked for him. Made him want to snuggle in next to her and close his eyes. Forget this day and the fact he still had to talk with Ben.

But he needed to make her understand one very big fact first. "It's important to me that you know I do." Her eyebrow lifted but she didn't say anything, so he kept going. "You and Ben are the two people, other than my brother and parents, that I do trust right now. I've put you both in a tough spot, and that sucks."

"To be fair, you haven't had the easiest time of it."

He turned on the coffeepot, thinking the caffeine might help with the adrenaline burn-off he suspected was headed his way. "It's been a pretty shitty year and a half."

"I'm trying to figure out if I'm more surprised that you have parents or a brother."

The scent of brewing coffee floated through the air. He sat down next to her, going slow and giving her a chance to scoot over and avoid him. But she didn't move. By the time he slouched down on the sofa her knee pressed against his outer thigh and only a few inches stood between them. "Doesn't everyone have parents in some form? Maybe they don't know them, but still."

"You seem like such a loner."

He folded his hands and rested them on his stomach. "My mother is part of a big Korean family. The youngest of six kids, which means I spent most of my youth and a good chunk of my adulthood, actually, visiting with aunts and uncles. They have managed to produce about three hundred cousins between them, or it feels that way when we're together."

"Wow."

He rolled his head on the cushion until he faced her. "Being alone isn't exactly a choice you get in my family. They get together often—weddings, celebrations, or just because it's Tuesday—to make food, then eat it all."

She shifted a bit, turning her body until her legs curled under her. "I didn't see that coming."

"What?"

"You offering up so much personal information."

They were whispering and he had no idea why. "Want more? If that's what it will take to prove I trust you, I'll keep going."

She lifted her hand, and when it fell again, the back rested against his arm. The position, close enough to hear her breathing and see every thought as it swirled in her head, was so unlike anything he'd experienced. The intimacy froze him there while he savored it.

"My brother's name is Connor. He's younger and brilliant. He also insists he's the pretty one."

Her eyes widened. "Do you have a photo? Maybe I could call him."

Hansen decided to take that as a compliment . . . and vowed never to introduce her to Connor. "Funny."

"And you're stalling." She rubbed her thumb back and forth over his biceps. Her soft tone matched the soothing calm of her touch. "Not that I don't love the information dump, because I do. It will take me days to make the idea of you hanging out with a big, loving family fit with the man I see grumbling around town if someone dares to say hello to you."

"I'm not sure what 'grumbling around' even looks like." But he feared that was a pretty accurate description of the man he'd become. He'd gone from outgoing and sure of himself, to dedicated to his work—possibly too much so—but still able to have a good time, and finally to this: constantly angry and on edge.

Fucking Judson Ross.

She smiled at him. "Still stalling."

The combination of her gentle encouragement and the brush of her hand against his arm did him in. She didn't insist or raise her voice. She coaxed the impossible out of him and he wasn't even sure how. Just by listening, maybe. He always had the sense with her that there was no ulterior motive. Her desire to help, to make him a better man, grew out of genuine concern.

"My sister's name is Alexis. Was." He stared up at the ceiling, unable to look at Tessa for this part. "Shit, I still don't know how to refer to her because it's just not real."

She wrapped her fingers around his arm and pulled her body in closer. "What happened?"

The words that had been dammed up inside of him for so long started to break free. "Nineteen months ago, she was hiking with her new husband during a weekend away in West Virginia. She fell and died."

Tessa's hold tightened. "Oh, Hansen. That's awful. I am so sorry."

Needing to touch her, he rested his hand on her leg. That final connection between them made it possible to go on with thc awful story that haunted him. "Her husband insisted she was taking a photo and slipped."

"Oh . . . you don't believe him."

"Fuck no." He watched his hand flex against her thigh. "My sister was an avid hiker."

"It could still have been an accident though, right?"

He tried to inhale a deep cleansing breath but couldn't drag enough air in. "She confided in me just a few days before they left that she might have made a mistake. It was a whirlwind romance. He was loving and sweet and then the honeymoon ended and things changed." The words tumbled out of him now. Memories flashed in his mind. He could hear his sister's voice. "I begged her not to go, but she hated to fail at anything. She thought she might be able to save the marriage if they talked it through."

Tessa put her head on his shoulder. "I don't know what to say."

"She was the middle child and used to whine about how our parents ignored her. Of course, they didn't, but it was the family joke. The forgotten child. Beautiful, smart. So fun and strong. She thought she could take on any challenge and conquer it." Only one thing stopped her and now he was dead, too.

"You think he killed her," she said in the same steady, caring voice.

"Judson Ross pushed my sister off that trail."

Her head shot up. "Judson . . ."

Hansen knew Tessa had put those pieces together. She was too smart not to, but she didn't flinch or pull away from him. That didn't mean he knew the kind of thoughts traveling through her mind, because he didn't. But he was desperate to hear and know how she viewed him now.

"Kerrie is his second wife. They got married three months after we buried Alexis."

"And now Judson is here, on Whitaker, this remote place where you are, and he's dead."

Her thumb kept rubbing against his arm. He had no idea what to make of that. "You see my problem."

She whistled. "Damn."

"Feel free to use a stronger word."

"Why was he here? They could have gone boating anywhere, but right where you are? That can't be a coincidence."

Typical Tessa. She jumped right to analyzing. To needing to know the answers and run the calculations to turn the situation into something that made sense. He understood the desire, but he'd learned that life didn't always work that way. Sometimes you put the pieces together and the puzzle still refused to make any sense.

"Judson isn't the type to take a vacation. He cut the honeymoon with my sister down to a weekend at a beach because he had billable hours to meet at his law firm. He was afraid he'd fall behind." Hansen tried to ignore the growing ache in his chest. "There was nothing coincidental about where he docked that boat."

At first Tessa didn't say anything. She didn't stop

cuddling in close or freeze or try to inch away. She just sat there, focused on some distant spot in the kitchen.

It only took a few minutes of quiet for Hansen to break. "Tessa?"

She stood up. "Okay, so, I want to pelt you with a million questions."

Not sure what was going on, he got up, too. "I'd be stunned if you didn't."

She went over to the kitchen and poured each of them a steaming cup of black coffee. When she returned, she held both mugs and nodded toward the sofa. "You need to sit back down."

"Why? How hard are these questions going to be?"

She laughed, and the rich sound filled the cabin. "I mean that I'm going to refrain from pouncing on you with an interrogation. Somehow tamp down on my natural nosiness."

None of this made sense but he followed her suggestion and took one of the mugs when she offered it to him. "You, Tessa Jenkins, who asks a million questions about everything, are going to let me off the hook without more explanation?"

"For now." She sat down next to him again, just as close as she had been before.

He started to drink the coffee, then stopped. He put the mug on the ottoman and faced her instead.

"I didn't kill Judson." That was not even what he expected to say, but the words slipped out and he didn't regret them.

She might not be asking but he needed her to

know. This time he made the admission without being drowned out by the rain or the ambulance or the other people stumbling around the marina. This moment belonged to them. Right now. She needed to hear truth and be able to see his face and assess the words, so he gave her that.

"You don't have to—"

"I admit I wanted to hurt him and thought about it more than once, but I didn't do it. And I would never touch Kerrie. My real fear was Judson one day would turn on her like he did on Alexis."

"You were worried about the woman who, I assume, Judson was cheating with while still married to your sister?"

"That does seem to be the timing, yes." His grip tightened on his mug. "But that doesn't mean she deserves to be another one of Judson's victims."

Tessa took a sip of coffee. Made a cute slurping sound as she did it. "He could hardly kill two wives without calling attention to himself."

Wrong answer. "A guy with his ego could."

"But it's so risky."

"She was tied up and injured while he was walking around Whitaker. He sure as hell did something to her."

Tessa slowly lowered her mug again. "Huh."

He figured she was mentally working through the horrors of what Kerrie went through, and he caught glimpses of that in her sad eyes, but something else lingered there. A question. "What are you thinking?"

"Judson was on the island. She was trapped on the

boat. That means she didn't kill Judson in self-defense or any other way."

He could see her working the pieces in her mind. "Right."

"Neither did we."

Relief surged through him again. She didn't even hesitate as she said the words. "True."

"So who did and why bring him to my house?"

Excellent questions. He'd been turning the possibilities over in his head and none of them fit. Kerrie's brother, Allen, had called him right after Kerrie and Judson got married. He seemed worried about his sister's safety. Asked for all sorts of details but then he stopped responding to texts and eventually blocked Hansen's number.

Allen and Connor both had an interest in what happened to Judson, but they lived thousands of miles away. As far as Hansen knew, no one else on the island had any connection to Judson.

Hansen knew that made him the lead suspect. The *only* suspect.

"My guess is Ben will ask that exact same thing as soon as he gets here." But that would only be the beginning. Tessa might be cutting him a break. Hansen expected the opposite from Ben. He had a job to do.

She leaned back until both of their heads rested against the sofa cushion. Their bodies barely touched. Her gaze wandered over his face and hesitated on his mouth for a few seconds before traveling back to his eyes. "You look exhausted."

It was as if her saying it touched off a decline. Fatigue pulled at him and suddenly he wasn't so sure he could get back up off the sofa without some help. "Again, it hasn't been a great day."

She slipped her hand over his. Threaded their fingers together. "It's probably a good thing you stick to water."

Nothing in her tone suggested she was poking around for more information but he gave it to her anyway. His drinking occupied the prime spot in the island's rumors about him. That would change very soon. "My father is an alcoholic, but with a lot of coaxing and a few threats from my mom, he learned how to not take a drink. About ten years ago, on the anniversary of his sobriety, Alexis, Connor, and I took a vow of solidarity to give it up."

She trailed a fingertip over his bottom lip. "You're a good man, Hansen Rye."

Screw the cons of trying to figure out what that gesture meant. "I'm really not."

"Hush, I know people. Trust me when I say you are."

"I'm tired and angry and everything is about to explode again." He blew out a long breath. They were close enough that he could see a few strands of her hair move in response. "You should run away from me."

"I'm not going anywhere." She lifted her head. Not far and not away from him. Watching him every second, she slipped in closer until her mouth hovered over his. "Yes?"

The word blew across his lips on a whisper. He

should shout *no* and get up . . . He leaned in. His mouth slipped over hers, light at first. Exploring. Then the need to know more, taste more, bolted through him.

His fingers slipped into her hair and her scent wound around him. A buzzing started in his head as her mouth slid over his. Every worry fell away until all he could feel and see was her and the heat threatening to overwhelm him.

Worried he'd go too far too fast, without thinking it through, he pulled back. Every muscle screamed at him to dive back in. To kiss her until his need for her erased everything else. But that was about his needs and he needed to remember hers.

Unable to fully break contact, he balanced his forehead against hers. "Tessa."

"Close your eyes." She shifted until her back rested against the sofa and guided him down to put his head against her lap. "We'll deal with the world later."

BEN TEXTED. SHE'D been dozing when the buzzing started. First it came from across the room, then stopped, so she ignored it. Less than two minutes later, her phone started.

Between lifting her butt to retrieve the cell from the small space between two cushions and shifting and sliding until she wrenched out from under Hansen and landed on the floor on her knees, she was sure she'd wake him up, but no. Hansen had drifted off, becoming boneless as he slept across her lap.

She glanced at him now, finally at peace after a day

of backbreaking emotional blows. The story about his sister still shook her. She'd tried to listen and stay calm, not let the horror of it bring her to tears. He'd needed a friend and comfort tonight. She'd offered both, but that kiss had been for her.

The desire to touch him drove her until finally she'd reached out, half expecting him to pull away. When he didn't, when his lips touched hers, at first soft, then more insistent . . . excitement had exploded inside her. The heat and the need. She wanted more. So much that when he'd pulled away her lips chased his.

She opened the door to Ben before he could knock. He stepped inside, clearly ready to call for Hansen, before his gaze went to the sofa. Some of his bluster vanished and the frustration pounding off him eased at the sight of Hansen sleeping on his side.

Ben's shoulders unclenched as he looked at Tessa. "How is he?"

"Kind of a mess." She hadn't mentally prepared for the answer, but she had to ask. "Any news on Kerrie?"

"Still out, but Lela thinks she'll be fine." Ben shrugged. "Who knows what she'll say when she wakes up."

"You can't believe Hansen would hurt her."

Ben didn't hesitate in his response. "No, but people will say anything under stress."

That horror hadn't even occurred to Tessa. Now a new wave of panic moved through her, shaking her right down to her bones. Chilling her from the inside out. "You believe she'll blame him? That's a stretch, don't you think?"

"Did he tell you how he knows Kerrie?" Ben finally dragged his gaze away from Hansen and back to Tessa. "They have a pretty sordid history. I found the connection between them after just a few online searches."

Everyone would know. On an island filled with secretive people, Hansen coveted anonymity more than others. He was about to lose all of that. "The connection is Hansen's sister. Her marriage. Her death." The weight of all Hansen had been through hit her. "What a mess."

Ben shook his head. "This looks bad, Tessa."

"He didn't do it."

"You're his alibi for a period of the night, but not all of it."

She tried to figure out what that comment meant. Nothing in Ben's tone gave him away, so she tried to match that flatness. "I know."

"Be careful about overstating or drawing conclusions. It's safest for you, and for him, honestly, if you stick to the facts."

Ben made it sound so easy, as if the wrong word or a few minutes of unaccounted-for time couldn't hurt Hansen.

"I would have heard him if he'd engaged in some sort of battle before he came to my door, or if he got up during the night." When Ben continued to stare at her, the words fumbled in her brain. "Come on. He's your friend, too."

"This is about to get rough. Us trying to fill in the blanks for him invites trouble."

His words stopped whatever had been jumping around in her stomach. "I hear you."

"As soon as you two are awake tomorrow, come to my office. We have a lot to discuss. Facts only, got it?"

"You're not going to talk to him now?"

"Be there by eight." He shot her a knowing gaze that made it clear he was granting a reprieve. "Whatever his story is, he needs to have it straight and be ready by then."

CHAPTER 11

Hansen managed to sleep with Tessa—on her, actually—and not kiss her again. He chalked up the glaring oversight to yesterday's shit show. A testament of how debilitating and all-consuming a mix of grief and worry could be.

He looked at her now as she closed the passenger side door of his car. She shot him a big smile before trotting across the parking lot toward Ben's office. She looked ready to pick up a shield and sword and do battle for his honor. She'd said as much this morning over coffee as she prodded him to get dressed and get moving.

Sexiest. Woman. Ever.

She hesitated right as she got to the door. Being only a few seconds behind her, he almost ran right into her but still didn't know what stopped her short. Sure, more people than usual milled around. A few glanced at him, then looked away instead of holding eye contact. He assumed that's how life would be here now.

He followed her gaze until it landed on Doug, the

kid who'd touched her and just happened to be the pride and joy of his mother, Ruthie. Doug didn't look very tough right now. His mouth opened and closed a few times as his wide-eyed gaze traveled from Tessa to Hansen and back again.

Tessa's eyebrow lifted. "Problem, Doug?"

The tone would crumple lesser men. Doug stood there and took it, even though he did look like he wanted to scream and run.

"Nothing." Doug shuffled, smartly not turning his back on Tessa. He put about three feet between them before banging his thigh on the bench outside of the office door. He fell in a heap into the seat.

Tessa shook her head. "Smooth."

"Anything we need to talk about, Doug?" Hansen figured he might as well use some of his newfound dangerous reputation on the island to make this kid understand there were consequences to his actions.

Doug shook his head hard enough to injure himself. "No, sir."

Tessa snorted.

"I'm just waiting." Doug nodded toward Ben's office. "My mom's inside."

Not what Hansen wanted to hear. Talking with Ben—fine. He'd be fair. Getting debriefed by Ruthie? No fucking way. He seriously considered getting back in his car.

"Don't even think about bolting." Tessa didn't give him a chance to disagree after issuing the order. She opened the door and went inside, leaving Hansen standing in the doorway with Doug.

"She scares me," Doug said under his breath. He kept staring after her. Sat up straighter in his chair to look through the window on the top part of the door and watch her.

"Remember that next time you try to touch her."

All of the color drained from Doug's face. "I didn't mean—"

"Apologize to her, not me. And do it soon." Feeling as if he'd at least accomplished something today even if he did end it by getting thrown into a jail cell, Hansen let it go . . . for now.

He walked inside, expecting to see Ben and Tessa and now Ruthie, but Sylvia paced around the outer office as well. He guessed she showed up as backup support against whatever idea or rule Ruthie might come up with to screw him.

"Maybe we should do this outside so everyone on the island can watch," he said dryly.

Ben looked up. "Lock the outer door. There are too many of us for my office. We're using the conference room."

The logical solution would be to remove a few of the people present, but Hansen chose not to point that out. He figured Ben had his reasons for wanting a display.

"Arrest him," Ruthie said without waiting for the conference room door to close behind them.

That explained Ben's reasons. Ruthie had taken on

the roles of cop, judge, and jury. Hansen sat down. He should have seen this coming.

Ben gestured for the rest of them to fill in the seats around the table, then looked at Ruthie. “Calm down.”

“Like, way down.” Sylvia rolled her eyes. “Good lord, woman.”

“He’s a killer.” Ruthie stayed on her feet. She hovered in the small area between the end of the table and the door, crowding in closer to Ben than Tessa.

Tessa shook her head. “What is wrong with you?”

“Apparently, Ruthie went on the internet last night and now thinks she knows Hansen’s life story,” Ben said.

Sylvia reached for the coffeepot in the middle of the table and started filling the mugs. “And wants to talk all about his supposedly scandalous past. As if she doesn’t have one.”

“I don’t.” Ruthie managed to gasp and sound horrified at the same time.

Sylvia glared at her. “Do you want me to start talking?”

“How dare you suggest that—”

“You’re so busy poking your nose into other people’s lives. Is it because Daniel is away?” Sylvia asked, clearly wanting to land a shot. “He’s been on that business trip for, what, three weeks?”

“You have no right—”

“Enough.” Ben raised his voice and drowned out the arguing. “Everyone has secrets. I’d prefer if we didn’t vomit the irrelevant ones out here. Let’s stay focused and respectful.”

Hansen was starting to wonder if he even needed to be here. Ruthie had condemned him. Sylvia and Tessa took turns defending him. Ben pretended to be Switzerland. It sounded like something was going on with Ruthie and her husband, and Hansen didn't want to know a single detail about that.

It wasn't as if he could deny the basic facts of what Ruthie may have found on the internet. He had screwed up back then, all those months ago. He did threaten Judson and he absolutely did know the dead man no one else on the island seemed to have a relationship to.

Ruthie turned on Tessa. "Do you know what you're sleeping with?"

When Ruthie grabbed Tessa's arm, Tessa jerked out of the hold. "First, don't touch me without permission. That's a thing in your family and I don't like it."

"What?"

"Second, Hansen is a *who*, not a *what*. And, yes, I do know him. A lot better than you do."

Ruthie's hand dropped to her side in a balled fist. "He's a criminal."

"I'm sitting right here. Maybe don't talk over me." Hansen had been willing to act all nice and quiet until Ruthie touched Tessa. She wasn't the only one who could act like a shield.

Ruthie kept her focus on Tessa as if Hansen wasn't even in the room. "That poor man had a restraining order against him. So did his wife and now she's in the hospital."

Sylvia whistled. Made it last a pretty long time, too.

"Wow. You must be exhausted from all that conclusion jumping."

While he appreciated the backup, Hansen had a question he needed an answer to because she knew more than the few basics someone might find on a quick internet search. "How do you know about the restraining order, Ruthie?"

She finally treated him to eye contact. "It's public record."

"Maybe." Ben leaned back in his chair and looked up at Ruthie. "But it's one you would have to dig to find and you haven't had much time."

"Do not play into this nonsense. Just because he's well connected he gets to keep his violent nature quiet? No scandal for Hansen Rye?" Ruthie scoffed as she looked at him. "Well, you deserve whatever happens to you now."

"Okay, really. That is enough." Ben stood up.

Hansen wondered if Ben intended to escort Ruthie out. Some island rule probably prohibited such a thing, but a man could hope.

"You're pretending to be a handyman but that's a lie, too." Ruthie's smile turned feral. "You've been found out. All that money and prestige didn't save you back in D.C., did it? Well, it won't here either."

That accusation hit harder than it should have. Back when everything happened in D.C., Hansen's brother had stepped in and offered support and explanations. Some of his friends rallied. The expensive lawyer he hired insisted the situation would work out, and in a way, it had. They ended up reaching an agreement to spare everyone a hearing, but Hansen got the impression Judson didn't want peace.

Ben held up a hand. "Everyone be quiet. Last warning."

"He means you," Tessa said to Ruthie.

But Ruthie had stopped listening. She lifted her chin and shot them all an I'm-superior-to-you glare. "I'm calling an emergency meeting of the board to resolve this matter. A vote of no confidence. Then we'll bring in outside investigators and figure out how to contain Hansen until they can get here and take over."

"What's wrong with you?" Tessa wrapped her fingers around the mug in front of her. "Let Ben work."

"It is raining, and the outer bands of the kind of storm that blows roofs off buildings have landed," Ben said. "It's not a great time to gather people across the island."

Ruthie pointed at Hansen. "Then arrest him and put him in a cell. That's the only way to know we'll all be safe until the real police can get here."

Ben shook his head. "I don't arrest people based on an internet search."

"We vote tomorrow morning. The storm should have died down by then." Ruthie clearly had made up her mind and switched to dictator mode.

"Which will give you just enough time to tell everyone on the island what you think you know about Hansen and what the outcome of the vote should be." Sylvia sighed as she stood up again. "You are tiresome."

"If you're so horrified, feel free to skip the meeting." Ruthie opened the door and started to leave, but not before glancing at Ben again. "Do your job or be prepared to lose it."

She slammed the door behind her hard enough to cause the wall to shake. Then the silence descended. It lasted until Tessa's confused expression gave way to a question. "They can vote to have someone arrested?"

"She's ridiculous." Sylvia took a long sip of coffee, emptying the mug, before setting it back down again.

Wrongheaded and over-the-top, yes. But Ruthie had reason to be concerned and Hansen recognized that much. "She's not totally wrong about me."

Tessa put her hand on his knee. "Hansen, stop talking."

"Hansen, she's right. You probably should have counsel," Sylvia said.

"I talked with my lawyer this morning. No one can get here because of the damn storm, but—"

"Then ask one of the lawyers on Whitaker to help or pretend I'm your lawyer and listen to me," Tessa ordered. "Mouth closed."

She rose to his defense just as he knew she would. That kind of faith was humbling and, he feared, not totally deserved. Still, he couldn't deny the warmth that spread through him when the we're-done-here tone moved into her voice.

He slid his hand over hers. "I didn't kill anyone. Hell, I didn't even know they were on Whitaker. It makes no sense that they're here, but that's beside the point. They do have a restraining order against me because I didn't back off. I wanted to make Judson's life miserable."

Tessa shook her head. "That's no one's business on Whitaker."

"It's sort of mine." The chair creaked under Ben as he sat down again. "Keep going."

"I'm guessing the court order is about your sister?" Sylvia asked, then shrugged when Tessa shot her a look that suggested she wasn't helping the situation. "I have the internet, too. Or I did until it went out five minutes ago when the wind kicked up."

Hansen studied his friends, and that's what they were. They'd come to the part of the story when he needed to fill in some details. His lawyer had cautioned him to stay quiet and let him handle everything with Ben. Right now he likely was trying to call in and getting the answering service.

Smart advice. Solid. The same thing he'd tell anyone in his position—shut up and stay out of the way. But the details mattered, especially since he had no idea what Kerrie might say when she woke up. He wasn't sharing anything that wasn't in a court record back home. Every word he said now could be traced back to what really happened back then.

And none of it meant he'd killed Judson.

He'd spent months trying to forget but for a few minutes, at least, he needed to remember. "I went after Judson to get him to tell the truth about what he did to my sister. But, really, the other reason for hounding him was to warn Kerrie. She needed to know how dangerous he was. Admittedly, I was very . . . energetic about it. They filed for protective orders to get me to leave them alone."

Sylvia hummed in response. "Kerrie, too?"

Lying didn't make sense and Hansen had no interest in trying. "I can't be within a hundred feet of either of them."

Tessa squeezed his hand. "And Ruthie somehow found all of this out."

"It looks that way." Sylvia tipped her mug to look inside, then shook her head. "The gossip hounds are going to go wild once they know about the court orders."

Nothing new there. The last time he'd heard the thunder of whispers, he left his job, his family, and moved thousands of miles to Whitaker. "Believe me, I know how this game is played."

"Okay." Sylvia put both hands on the table and pushed up. "Let me go do some damage control and try to head off Ruthie's mess tomorrow."

"Why?" That was the part he never understood. He crossed a line back then, more than one. No matter what Judson had done, he wasn't the only one at fault for the position in which Hansen now found himself.

She froze in the middle of standing up. "That's really your question?"

"A protective order isn't a joke." The words jammed in his throat. He had to clear it twice to get them out. "I'd understand if the information about the restraining orders changes things. Changes how you view me."

"Hansen, while it's true you try very hard to push

people away and act as if you can't tolerate anyone, I know the act is bullshit. You're a decent guy, better than I think you even know, and Ruthie is a pain in the ass. The no-confidence vote for Ben and throwing her weight around to have you arrested . . . it's all bullshit." Sylvia winked at him. "I'm siding with you on this one."

She nodded to Ben, then walked out of the room.

Another vote of support. Having people get it, get him, proved to be a humbling experience.

Tessa smiled at him. "She trusts you."

He was starting to believe they all did, if only a little. After months of solitude and refusing to get involved, trying not to care, they reeled him in. The distance he put between them and him shrank. Being vulnerable, part of something—knocking down the last defenses he threw up against Tessa—scared the shit out of him. But truth was he needed them to believe in him. To fight for him.

He released Tessa's hands and flattened both palms against the table. Drew in a deep breath before he started the apology tour.

"Look, I'm sorry for all of this. For not warning you." He stared at Ben until he nodded, then turned to Tessa. "And I'm sorry for putting you in the position of keeping the details from Ben."

Ben groaned. "I'll pretend I didn't hear the last part."

Hansen appreciated that, but the situation had grown past anything he or Ben could control. "This really could blow up."

Tessa shrugged. “We’ll figure it out.”

“Always do,” Ben said.

They stayed so calm. So dedicated. “Are you two being nice to me because you think I’m a mess right now?”

“Of course,” Tessa said.

Ben nodded. “Clearly.”

The tension that had been pounding Hansen into the chair vanished. “Thanks.”

CHAPTER 12

After many hours and rounds of questions, reviewing internet information and island maps, Ben finally let them leave his office. He made it clear he didn't intend to arrest Hansen right then because there was no evidence to support it, but he would if Hansen didn't stay out of trouble. The good advice and friendly warning saved Tessa from having to say the same things.

Still, from all the talking and worrying about what surprises Ruthie had planned for tomorrow, Tessa had worked up an appetite. Being on edge and ready to do battle seemed to work like a fat-burning tool for her. Coaxing Hansen to join her at the lodge took another twenty minutes. At this rate they'd be eating lunch after two.

When they entered the main dining room, everyone—absolutely everyone, and for some reason there were four times the usual number of people in there—turned to stare. Two older ladies whom Tessa recognized from the craft shop gave Hansen a thumbs-up. Tessa vowed right then and there to learn to knit as a thank-you.

"This is awkward," Hansen said under his breath as they walked over to the bar.

"And it's only the first day." She couldn't imagine what the response would be after Ruthie's sham of a hearing . . . or whatever she had planned.

Sylvia worked behind the bar, pouring drinks and writing up orders. "Thought you two might stumble in here eventually."

Hansen sat on one of the open stools. "I was okay with soup from a can."

"Canned food?" Sylvia snorted at him. "What's wrong with you?"

Tessa loved Sylvia, enjoyed talking with her and the way she offered support without asking any questions or expecting anything in return. But she was surprised to see Sylvia here right now. "Thought you'd be working the board members for votes to help Ben and, by extension, Hansen."

Sylvia smiled. "Don't worry, hun. That's happening behind the scenes."

Dishes rattled as a person from one table knocked into another table. The hushed apologies quickly died out and a strange silence fell over the room again.

"Do people not know it's pouring out there and they should stay home?" Hansen asked as he cleaned his glasses.

Tessa shrugged. "We're here."

"Neither rain nor snow nor dark of night will keep

them from collecting interesting intel on one of their neighbors." Sylvia plopped a copy of the island's weekly newspaper on the bar in front of him. "In this case, you."

Tessa leaned into his side to get a better look. The headline about Judson's death jumped out. "The Ruthie Gossip Network moves really fast."

"It's not as if she's the only one with the internet." Sylvia put a mug of coffee in front of each of them. "From what I've been able to pick up from the whispers around here, the reporter, Lin, was on the scene at Tessa's house and again at the marina, taking notes and photos. I'm sure he researched Hansen's past for the article."

A warning bell went off in the back of Tessa's mind. Newspapers meant photos. Photos led to being discovered. "Let me see that."

She paged through and there it was, a photo of her and Hansen at the marina. She had no idea how anyone got the shot. They stood in the parking lot, away from the ambulance and the crowds.

Her throat began to close as that familiar sensation of being hunted, tracked down, and threatened swamped her again. "We're in here."

Hansen took a quick look. "I made the paper . . . again. Great."

"Be positive. It's your first time on the front page of the *Whitaker Express*." Sylvia turned the paper around to stare at the photo of Hansen and Tessa. "It's a shame this one is buried inside where no one will see it. You two look good despite the rain."

"I feel much better now. Thanks." Sarcasm vibrated in his voice.

Tessa tried to ground herself by focusing on what Sylvia said. *Buried.* Yes, that meant not easy to find. Someone would have to be searching weekly newspapers from across the United States in order to track her down this way. Even then, the blurry photo didn't give away much. A side view. Her name, but that shouldn't matter.

She blew out a long breath, trying to get her jumping nerves to settle. She felt the heat of Hansen's stare and rushed to cover the panic that had bubbled to the surface with a lame joke. "There is some good news. You might not have to worry about people calling you all the time to fix things." When Hansen's eyes widened she assumed she'd missed the mark. "What? I'm searching for a silver lining."

Sylvia made a groaning sound. "That's not the way."

"Good afternoon."

Hansen cringed at the sound of Ellis's voice floating up from behind him. "Have we found that silver lining yet?"

Arianna shoved her way into the small space between Tessa and Hansen, ignoring the fact the barstools were bolted to the floor and there was only so much room between their bodies. "We hear you had a busy night."

Ellis crammed in on the other side of Hansen. "And a nice little boat trip."

"We had a view of the recovery from our house,"

Arianna said as her gaze bounced between Hansen and Tessa.

The rapid-fire questions made Ruthie's company seem like a fun time. Tessa tried to peek around Arianna to see Hansen. "I'm getting dizzy."

Ellis picked up the paper Hansen had abandoned and paged through it. "Look, we want you to know we don't believe the rumors."

"Excellent. That's very neighborly." Sylvia pointed toward a table on the other side of the room. "You two ate an hour ago and left. Now that you're back, why don't I bring you some dessert menus to a table?"

"I mean, we all have trouble now and then, right? Maybe the man . . ." Ellis dropped the paper against the bar with a thwap. "The dead one. What's his name?"

"Jackson," Arianna said.

Hansen rubbed his forehead. "Judson."

"Maybe he got a little too familiar with Tessa, here." Ellis made a tsk-tsk sound.

Okay, that was enough of that. "Please don't spread that rumor about me. It's not true."

"It would explain the fight he and Hansen got into by Cliff's place." Ellis looked over Hansen's head to talk directly to Arianna. "The folks around here understand jealousy. Protecting your own and such."

Tessa ignored the backward comment. It was either that or yell and make a scene.

Hansen swore under his breath. "None of what you're describing ever happened."

"We didn't know Judson was on Whitaker until we

found him outside of my house." Tessa felt the need to make that clear even if the only people listening were the eavesdroppers staked out around the room.

Arianna looked at Tessa, eyes glowing with excitement. "I thought you talked to him on the beach."

Ellis leaned on his elbows on the bar to stare at Tessa, who sat two people away from him. "And there was blood."

"What is going on right now?" Hansen slapped his open hand against the bar with a smack.

"Nothing that apple pie won't fix." Sylvia scooted around the edge of the bar. She slid her arm through Arianna's and pulled her away from Hansen's side with a firm tug. "Let's take a seat and let Hansen and Tessa drink their coffee alone. They've had a rough few days."

Hero. Tessa didn't think she could love Sylvia more. She was wrong.

Hansen didn't say anything for more than a minute. He concentrated on drinking his coffee with his gaze locked on the shelves on the wall behind the bar. Sylvia guided the unwanted couple away, then stayed in the dining room taking orders and talking to customers.

He exhaled. "This Tuesday sucks."

Tessa could feel people staring at them and hear the rain pelt the floor-to-ceiling windows out to the expansive lawn. It was as if the entire room held its breath, waiting to see what happened next. She had no intention of feeding that beast.

"It's Wednesday, and yes." She followed his lead and

took a sip of coffee. Tried to give off an outward appearance of calm while the newspaper photograph and what it could mean for her by being out there in public kept running through her head. "Any idea what the fight talk is about?"

"Cliff insists he heard something but I'm doubtful. He's not exactly the best witness."

"Maybe he likes the attention." He was older and probably lonely. She couldn't really blame him for trying to be part of the conversation.

"What Arianna and Ellis were saying . . ." Hansen let the comment trail off as he made a groaning sound.

Yeah, she got it. The headache from that back-and-forth would take hours to go away. "The most annoying couple ever but go on."

"Well, it's tough to admit but I haven't really given you a reason to believe me."

They'd been through this. They'd kissed. Slept together on the sofa. Shared breakfast and survived the meeting with Ruthie. Man, he was not picking up on the clues here at all. "You are desperate to have me not trust you."

He shrugged. "I haven't always been . . . as friendly as I should with you."

"Understatement. You've been either demanding or snotty, sometimes both together, not to mention overly sarcastic and a bit of a dick." She refrained from continuing the list because she'd never get lunch.

"It's like you had that comment ready and were waiting to use it."

Something like that. "Look, you're difficult. That's just a fact."

The stress finally left his face. He almost smiled. "I've been called worse."

"*I've* called you worse. That's my point."

"Yeah, well. You scare the shit out of me." He went back to drinking coffee.

The comment ran all the other thoughts about her life before Whitaker and being discovered right out of her head. She struggled to get over the shock and ask a profound and reasoned question. When that didn't work, she fell back on a shortcut. "Me?"

He slowly lowered the mug and shifted on his stool to face her. "I wasn't supposed to meet you."

The conversation grew more and more interesting. She almost felt bad that the rest of the room couldn't hear his deep sexy voice . . . no matter how much they strained to do so. "What were you supposed to do?"

"Come here. Get my head together. Figure out a way to move on from what happened to Alexis, then go home."

Made sense. Even though she couldn't imagine his desperation and despair at losing his sister, she knew what it was like to be forced to set everything aside and regroup. "Your family's idea?"

"Mostly Connor's. We're business partners in a design firm."

That sounded like code for something. She had no idea what. "So, like paintings?"

"Engineering, building design, and construction."

"A bit bigger than paintings then."

"Paintings are cool. We commission murals sometimes, but yeah, we took over for Dad. He retired, which means he only comes in four days a week instead of six, or he did until I took a hiatus and he stepped back in to keep Connor from working twenty-four hours a day."

"He's a workaholic?"

"Yeah, but he's also pretty great. Don't tell him. It will make him intolerable."

Pride laced through his voice. She could hear it, see it in his eyes. The man loved his family and that was a pretty sexy thing.

"Right. That explains Ruthie's comment." Powerful . . . Tessa's least favorite type of person. She'd had her life turned upside down by one of those. But sitting there, hearing Hansen talk, gathering all she knew about him and all she'd seen, she knew he wasn't anything like the people in the life she was running from.

"Which? I try to ignore most of what she says."

"About you being well connected and using that leverage to stay out of trouble. Even though I think she's confused because you didn't do that from what I can tell. You accepted responsibility. There *is* a protective order."

Tessa hadn't really thought about how odd it was that he could pick up his life without a financial strain. She worked from home, took contract assignments. But most people didn't have that sort of work freedom.

She didn't know what to do with the information now that she heard it. Wealthy men who could weasel their way out of anything had chased her out of town. She was here on Whitaker because of them. Because of one, really, and Hansen was nothing like him. But still, powerful D.C. men were a type and she was not a fan.

"She . . . I do fine. It's really my dad . . ." Hansen spun his mug around on the bar. "And we're . . . not . . ."

Good. Lord. The fumbling was new and adorable. Combined with the limited eye contact and slight blush, it held her fascinated.

The cool and detached attitude he usually carried had vanished. This version of Hansen grew wary when an uncomfortable topic arose rather than his usual grumping his way around it and walking away. He spent a lot of time pushing up his glasses and fidgeting. She liked that money was the type of topic to turn him into a bit of a blubbering mess rather than something he wore as a sort of shiny honor.

But that sound. She put her hand over his to stop the thudding of the mug against the wooden bar. "I don't need your résumé right now. Later? Yes. But let's stick to this topic."

"Right." He set the mug aside.

She slid it even farther out of his reach. "Right."

"I moved here for a break. Connor's words, not mine."

"Was he worried keeping you out of jail would become his full-time job?"

Hansen reached for the mug but dropped his hand

before touching it. "He worried Judson would set me up for a really big fall."

She hadn't thought about that. Now that she did, a wave of queasiness rushed through her. "Damn."

"Exactly."

Her stomach continued to roll. She slid a hand over it to try to settle it down. "So, you think Judson was here to . . . what?"

"Frame me."

She had no idea what to say. "Hansen."

He stole a quick glance at the rest of the room. "And from the way the rumor mill is working, he might have succeeded."

CHAPTER 13

Hansen walked into the cabin later that evening. He hated leaving Tessa at the lodge after their late lunch. A part of him worried she'd decide to grab a room there instead of staying with him. Sylvia twice offered her a room. Both times Hansen changed the subject.

Not that separating wouldn't be smart. He could avoid sleeping on the couch. But the bigger issue was that he had a target on his back and a head full of confused thoughts. He couldn't shake the sensation that someone aimed to take him not just down but out.

Even with Judson dead—maybe because Judson was dead—the little bit of calm Hansen had been able to establish on Whitaker evaporated. He morphed back to being frustrated, like he was swimming through slime and couldn't get clean. This wasn't the first time. Ever since his sister's death he'd been treading water. Barely making it through.

Connor figured out within months how to compartmentalize his nonstop anger. He put it in a neat box somewhere in the back of his mind and only took it out and examined it when he had to. He funneled all of his energy into work and running. Hansen let it fester. He refused to forget Alexis or the awful thing that happened to her.

But now, as he shut the front door to his temporary home and saw Tessa wrapped up in a blanket on his couch, paging through a book with a steaming cup of tea right next to her, he wanted more from his life. He'd become so accustomed to suffocating darkness that he didn't even know he wallowed in it until she burst into his life. All sunshine and light. Trusting and open. Part of him wondered how she survived this shitty world this long.

"Hey." She smiled at him. "How did the second round of questions go? I'm hoping having your lawyer call in kept things calm."

"It's been a long-ass day." But the night was looking up. "I had to wait while Ben and Captain Rogers searched Whitaker for the location where Judson was killed. They didn't get far before the thunderstorm started and they came back in."

"You didn't go along and help?"

"I'm the main suspect, so no."

"Right." She glanced at the clock on the wall. "Well, while you had a boring four hours in Ben's office, I had time to take a shower, change, and relax a bit."

Thinking about her in his shower would lead to interesting places, none of them *okay*. "Ben didn't seem to feel bad about wasting my time."

Hansen slipped off the wet coat and shoes and disappeared into the bathroom for a few minutes. When he stepped out again, he had switched out the damp jeans for dry lounge pants. His stomach made a noise and he thought about his late lunch and skipped dinner but quickly dismissed the idea of food. What he wanted sat on the couch. He joined her, sitting close, letting her knees balance against his thigh.

"I had to walk him through my activities of the last few days, while he and my lawyer went back and forth on speakerphone about every detail. It took forever before I could sign a formal statement and get out of there." He slipped his hand under her legs and lifted them until they rested across his lap.

The position, all warm and bound together, struck him as domestic and wildly unfamiliar. He had dated on and off, preferring to pour his time and attention into the job as he and Connor built on the impressive foundation their father and the people who worked for him had built.

Long hours. Lots of takeout food. Sex here and there. Dating when he found someone interesting but never serious and never for long. He'd only ever brought a few women home to meet his parents. They were great—smart, dedicated, caring, pretty—and he should have been hit by the *she's-the-one* sensation at some point, but it eluded him. He didn't go hunting for it either, much to his mother's chagrin.

His mom always made it clear she wanted her kids happy and hoped that meant marriage but understood it might not. At least that's what she used to say until Alexis walked down the aisle to Judson. After she died, his mom didn't say much at all.

He lost focus due to the constant crash of guilt for not doing enough and frustration over not getting answers. She grew quiet, wistful. Hansen's father could coax her out, but she now wrestled with a sadness that could never really be healed.

Tessa set the book down and relaxed into the cushions. "You okay?"

He touched her because he couldn't *not* touch her. Ran his hand up and down her leg over the blanket. Let the thumb on his other hand skim over the back of her fingers where they rested on her stomach. The moment felt right. *She* felt right.

"I told him the truth, Tessa."

She tilted her head to the side and her long hair fell over her shoulder. "Which one?"

The words sliced through him. He hadn't expected the body blow, but it landed. "Yeah, see, I don't like that I put you in the position of having to ask that question."

"I volunteered to act as alibi. No one forced me. And even then, I avoided any details so I didn't *really* lie."

It humbled him that he'd earned her loyalty when he hadn't acted in a way to deserve it. "That's not really the point."

"You were right there in the house, and that's what I said."

He massaged her calf. "I filled in all the pieces for Ben. Every little detail, no matter how frustrating and infuriating. He knows about my sister, her murder, the way the justice system failed, and my reaction to Judson getting away with it. It's not information I normally spew like that, but I don't want you to be in the position of covering for me."

"Careful, your decency is showing again." She lifted her hand. Skimmed her fingertips along his chin, over the ruff scruff he now wore. "You're going to ruin your grumpy-old-man reputation."

"Old?" She made him feel powerful, capable. Not like someone who lost his way and couldn't figure out how to get back.

The sheer force of how much he wanted her scared the hell out of him. He didn't come to Whitaker for sex or a girlfriend, not that he knew exactly which, if either role, she wanted to fill. But the days of pushing her away and using sarcasm as a weapon to fight her off seemed like they happened years ago. When it came to her, his defenses slammed down, and he couldn't yank them up again even though he'd tried.

Her thumb traced his mouth and slipped over his bottom lip. "Don't worry. You look like you can still move."

This sounded like flirting and he should end it, but no way in hell was that going to happen. If one of them planned to throw the brakes, it would have to be her. He didn't have the will to avoid her. Not anymore. "Oh, really?"

"I mean . . ." She drew out the phrase. "I'd have to test the theory to see, but sure."

Heat shot through him. Raced from his head to his lower half and pooled there. Mind-blowing heat that could get them both in trouble if they weren't careful. "You're walking a dangerous line."

"I'm not afraid of you."

"That's because you don't know what I'm thinking right now." Her naked. Under him. And that was just the start. He'd been dreaming about her for weeks. If he were being honest, he'd admit it started the day they met six weeks ago.

"Give me a hint."

The husky edge to her voice made him ache to say the words. The way the light bounced off the lighter streaks in her hair. This close, he could smell his soap on her skin.

She was one hundred percent pure temptation. Had him running in circles and mentally shouting for more. But he had to at least try to exhibit some control. "That wouldn't be smart."

"What am I wearing in this mental picture?" Her hand slipped down, trailed along his neck before settling at the base of his throat.

"Nothing but me."

She made a low satisfied sound like a mix between a moan and a hum. "I've had the same dream."

Every argument left his head, the logical and the illogical ones. He could almost feel the words tumble out and scatter on the floor. "You . . ."

Her fingers slipped back and forth, under the neckline of his T-shirt and across his collarbone. "Do you think you're the only one who's been thinking about us getting together?"

The few remaining words he did manage to remember how to pronounce jumbled together and his brain refused to sort them out. "Maybe."

"For a very smart man, you can be kind of slow to pick up on obvious clues." She gathered up the blanket and dumped it on the floor.

Bare legs. That fact hit him first. A solid slam to the gut that had his breath stuttering in his chest. His gaze wandered over her, up those sexy legs to the shirt. *His* shirt. The worn chambray one he liked to put on at the end of the day after a shower. It only reached to the top of her thighs, exposing miles and miles of bare skin.

He was so screwed. "You know if we go one inch past that kiss . . ."

"Things will get messy. Yes." She shifted to her knees. Threw one long leg across his lap until she straddled his hips with a knee on either side.

Hot. Damn.

He tried to gulp in air. Find one last shred of reason. "Neither one of us wants a relationship."

"Very true." Her fingers speared through his hair.

"We both have a lot of baggage." He had to swallow a few times before he could continue because she massaged the back of his neck with a touch both gentle and insistent. "You haven't shared, but I'm guessing from the way you tensed up when Ruthie talked about my family's connections that I am not the only one dragging a rough past behind me."

"I'm not denying it."

She didn't offer up any details, but this was *not* the time for an interrogation. "So, it would be smart to not even think about us doing anything."

His hands slipped up her bare thighs. Caressed and memorized every inch of her with his fingertips. Her skin was as smooth as he thought she'd be.

"Absolutely." She nodded as she nudged his lips with hers. Not kissing. No, this was some sort of sensual torture she'd devised that included the brush of her mouth over his nose and chin. A dart of her tongue over his top lip. "Not smart at all."

He was all in. "We're ignoring that, right?"

She leaned forward until her breasts skimmed his chest and her mouth hovered over his ear. "Yes."

The heated whisper and puff of warm air sealed his fate. "Thank God."

His hands went to her face and his mouth covered hers. The kiss hit him with an explosive bang. Heat rolled over him. He couldn't get close enough, pull her in tight enough.

Still cradling her with their legs and arms entwined, he lowered her down until her back hit the couch. His lips trailed over hers, then moved to her neck.

She slipped his glasses off and curled her fingers around them. With the glasses in her hand, she stretched, head thrown back and hair spilling on the cushions, giving him room to worship her.

The fire he'd banked for so long roared to life. Energy sparked in every cell. The mix of hands and lips.

The warmth of her mouth. The way she clamped her thighs against his leg, trapping him there while desire ramped and revved inside him.

She smelled of his shampoo, and with every blinding kiss, the hold on his control loosened. The rest of the world faded away as he trailed his tongue down her neck to that soft divot at the base of her throat. He licked her there once, then again. She moaned and shifted, her body restless underneath him.

Her fingers pushed under the edge of his shirt and shoved it higher. The edge of his glasses, still in her hand, scraped against his side but he didn't give a shit. He lifted off her, leaving just enough space for the two of them to yank and tug and nearly rip it off. Then he eased on top of her again, his body melting into hers. Her back arched off the cushions as his hand inched higher on her leg. Her skin, so smooth under his fingertips.

One elbow hit the back of the couch and his foot fell to the floor. They were making out on the couch when a perfectly good bed sat right upstairs. He wanted room to explore her, nestle between her legs. Lick her.

Out of a desperate need to bring every fantasy he'd ever had about her to life, he broke off the kisses and lifted his head. Staring down he saw her puffy lips and pink cheeks. She got sexier by the second.

"Bed." That's all he could get out.

Her gaze shot to the ladder. "Once I'm up there I'm not going to want to come down for a very long time."

The words sent a renewed flush of heat racing through him. "And we're moving."

He balanced a knee on the cushion and sat up. Wrapping an arm around her waist, he took her with him. One swoop and he had them on their feet. Unsteady and still intertwined. Her ankle hooked around the back of his calf and she balanced on her tiptoes.

"You're wearing my shirt."

She leaned in and kissed him under his chin. Gently sucked on his neck, then licked the spot. "It smells like you."

Damn. "Now it will smell like *you.*" So did he. His whole house did. She used his soap and his shampoo, yet on her, mixed with her skin, every scent took on a new dimension.

"I can take it off." She tucked his glasses into the front pocket and her fingers went to the top few buttons. That sexy eyebrow lifted in question.

"You definitely should do that."

She unfastened the rest of the buttons one by one. Bare skin peeked out from the gap she created. The deep shadowed vee grabbed his attention and wouldn't let go. The tops of her breasts and the strip of flesh she'd uncovered. She didn't stop until the sides hung open and her fingers wrapped around each side, holding the shirt not closed but not open either.

It was a seductive tease that called to him and he didn't hold back. His finger trailed over her body, starting at the base of her throat and skimming with the barest touch down her chest. The plump sides of her breasts brushed against his hand, but he forced his arm to keep moving in a straight line. Over the sexiest little swell of her stomach. Then he stopped. Hesitated, craving an invitation until the need pulsed inside him.

He glanced down, letting his gaze follow the path his finger just traveled. She'd left the bottom two buttons fastened and the material blocked his view. "Are you wearing anything under there?"

"I guess you'll see in a second." She dropped her hands to her sides. The material draped over her breasts, hanging there and hinting at so much more.

"You should show me now."

"I will." She winked at him before heading for the ladder. After two steps she shot him a look over his shoulder that issued the invitation he'd been wanting. "Follow me."

He nearly tripped over the couch to get to her.

She got to the base of the ladder and turned to face him. "Will this hold me?"

Every syllable she uttered sounded like a seduction. The husky voice and the barely there shirt.

"I'll be here to catch you."

Without breaking eye contact she peeled off her socks. Treated him to a peek at those toenails painted a deep red that glowed almost black in the low lighting. Then she started up, taking the first rung backward, while still facing him. On the second step she turned, flashing him the full length of those made-for-sex legs.

The last of his calm broke. She took a step and he inched up right behind her. Her butt wiggled in his face and he had to fight the urge to give it a nip. He settled for sliding his hand up her calf. When he reached the back of her knee, she stopped climbing.

Heavy breathing echoed around them. He didn't know if it was his or theirs and he didn't care. Heat had settled over the room, and the tension ticking up had him wanting to grab her and race up the ladder. But the smooth silk of her inner thigh silently begged for him to wait, draw this out.

With one leg stretched straight and the other bent on the rungs above, she leaned into his touch. Taking that as a call for more, his fingers edged higher until he found the elastic band at the bottom edge of her underwear. "Yes?"

She balanced her forehead against the rung above her. "Please."

Need thrummed off her until it thickened her voice. He identified the sensation, hot and ready and itching to peel the rest of her clothes off, because he felt it, too.

His finger slipped under the band and over her ass. The touch of skin against skin made his hand shake. They needed to get to solid ground, but one more thing . . . His finger brushed over the plump globe, then down. Tracing just outside the place he most wanted to touch. Heat and wetness greeted him.

"Inside."

She whispered the word, but he picked it up. Knew what she wanted. He ached to plunge inside, first with his fingers, then his body. He tightened his grip on the ladder with his free hand. It didn't move but he couldn't take the chance of it wobbling while they were so vulnerable. And he wanted to see her. All of her. Laid out, legs open, hands over her head, every inch of her welcome to his touch, his mouth.

"Keep walking." His finger kept slipping over her, around her outer lips, but depriving them both of the final satisfaction.

She still hadn't lifted her head. "I can't."

"Pink."

She shifted her elbow and looked down at him through the small space she'd made. "What?"

"Your underwear. Sexy, little, pink." He pulled at the top edge, dragging them over her ass cheeks, then kept going.

"Hansen."

"I want to see all of you."

"You're killing me." Her head fell back now. She would have enjoyed a perfect view of the beamed ceiling, but her eyes stayed closed.

"Let's take these off." He glided the bikini bottoms over her ass, taking his time to reveal inch after inch of the body he fantasized about every night. When he dropped them down to her ankles, she hugged the ladder and stepped out of them. He rubbed the soft cotton against his palm before letting it fall to the floor. "You're not going to need those tonight."

"We need to get to the bed."

She moved now. Her bare feet thumped on the rungs as she climbed. With each step she flashed him a sexy peek of that ass. Tempted him with glimpses of her naked body as the material billowed around her.

At the top, she stood there, looking from the ladder to the bed. Her chest rose and fell on harsh breaths and she balled her fists, clenching the bottom of the shirt in both hands.

"You could take a better look now." She sounded out of breath and so ready.

"I was hoping you'd say that."

He didn't wait another second. His arms wrapped around her waist and he lifted her off her feet. One hand tapped against the back of her thigh and she took the hint. A second later her legs clamped against his waist and her hands dangled down his back.

Somchow he managed to hold her, walk, and not crush his glasses. Good thing he didn't have to go far. The loft held the bed and a small dresser and little more. He maneuvered them to the end of the mattress and dropped down. He had her out of the shirt and completely naked before her back hit the comforter.

Then his mouth was on hers. Bold and demanding, fierce with need. His muscles shook from the force of holding as he savored the taste of her lips against his. He dreamed about curling her body around his, but he'd never imagined the smell of her, the heady excitement he would get just from his lips touching her.

The woman knew how to kiss. She dove in and devoured. Her tongue swept over his. She didn't hold back or hide. She knew what she wanted and grabbed for it, and he loved that. Loved meeting her halfway, as lost as she was.

The curves of her body proved too inviting to ignore.

He slipped down, trailing his mouth from her cheek to her neck. He lavished every inch of skin he discovered. His tongue swept over her nipple, then around it. When the nub puckered, as if begging for more, he did it again. One, then the other, he sucked and caressed her breasts. Inhaled her fragrance.

When his mouth moved lower, her fingers speared through his hair. She held him, guiding his mouth where she wanted it to go. Between her legs. He ended up sprawled there and couldn't think of anything he wanted more. Trailed a nibbling line of kisses along her soft thighs. Tormented her with soft touches, his thumb brushing back and forth over the very heat of her without slipping inside.

Her fingers tightened in his hair. "Now, Hansen."

He couldn't deny her. Braced between her thighs, his tongue rubbed over her. Back and forth. Circles. He treated her to the most intimate touch. Loved how she lifted her lower body, meeting him partway. He opened her with his fingers, diving in deeper, hitting that spot with his tongue that made her heels dig in to the mattress.

When he slid a finger inside her, those tiny muscles clenched, pulling him in deeper. She moaned as her head thrashed on the bed. She grabbed him and brought his face closer to hers. One leg fell to the side while the other curled over his shoulder.

She didn't hide her pleasure, wouldn't let him ignore her needs. If he pulled back, she pressed forward, keeping the solid connection. He caressed her with his mouth and hands. Traveled over her, learning every curve.

"Now." Her voice sounded rough and husky.

He balanced on his elbows and started to shove his pants down when reality hit him with a cold smack. "Wait. Shit."

"What?" She lifted her head and stared down at him.

"Condom." *Damn it.* "I don't . . . I haven't slept with anyone on Whitaker. Didn't think I would and then more recently I thought buying them at the store might end up as front-page news."

Her arms sprawled out to the side as she panted, clearly trying to regain her breathing. "That would have been a better way to make the paper."

"We can do other—"

"Unzip the side pocket of my bag."

The edge to her tone had him glancing up. He took in the length of her body. Yeah, he could think of all sorts of things to do with her tonight. Then her order hit him. "What?"

She waved her hand in thc air. "On the floor."

Hating to leave her but *really* hating the idea of not being inside her, he shuffled to the side of the bed and lay on his stomach. The stretch let him grab the handle of the gym bag and pull it in closer. His brain and muscles fought each other but he managed to shove his fingers into the pocket and pull out the package.

The woman brought condoms.

So fucking sexy.

He ripped the box to get to what they needed. "Impressive."

"Sylvia gave them to me."

He laughed as he opened the wrapper. His pants were in the way, so he shoved them down on his hips and rolled the condom on. A few kicks later he was as naked as she was. "Sylvia might be my favorite person on Whitaker right now."

"She's first?" Tessa asked in a playful tone.

"Well, second favorite."

"Better." She opened her arms.

He didn't wait. He slid over her, rubbing their bodies together. Loving the friction and the way they fit together. He wanted to be smooth, draw this out, but his control was shot. The ladder, her stripping off his shirt . . . The combination did him in. He was hard and ready and fighting the instinct to plunge inside her.

"Yes?"

She ran her hands over her breasts in what might have been the sexiest come-get-me gesture ever. "Do I look like I'm not with you on this?"

"I need to be sure." Because once he was inside her he doubted he would want to leave.

Her thighs dropped open. "Now, Hansen."

He didn't need another invitation. He slipped into the space she'd made and lifted her legs until they pressed against her stomach. This is what he needed. Her open and clawing at him. The way she raked her fingernails down his arms before grabbing his wrists and tugging him closer.

She chanted his name. The pleading was right there in her voice.

He rubbed his hand up and down his length. When heat sparked in her eyes, he did it a second time. Then he pressed his tip against her, teasing and waiting as she squirmed beneath him.

The first plunge had him trembling. He fought back the churning inside him. Forced his tense muscles to hold on as the voice in his head screamed for more. A pullout, then another plunge. Slow at first. Calculated to steal their breath. Then his control snapped. The steady pumping sped up. Adrenaline swamped him as she tugged at his hair to bring him down for another soul-shattering kiss.

He got lost in the feel of her mouth and slip of her tongue until she lifted her hips off the bed. "Faster."

He pumped in and out. The tension whirled inside him. His legs shook with the need to end this. But he had to touch her one more time. He reached between them, and his fingertip brushed over her where his body moved inside her. The combination had her gasping. Her body shook and those delicious thighs flexed.

Her head tilted back and a rough sound echoed in her throat. He wanted to watch her lose it but the short tether he held on the last of his control snapped. Lost now, he moved inside her. Felt her orgasm sweep through her and let it touch off his own.

They panted and moaned. His head filled with strings of words, none of which made sense, but he didn't hold them back. His focus centered on her need, her satisfaction, and the orgasm pounded him into submission.

WHEN HANSEN OPENED his eyes again, some time had passed. He lay sprawled over her with his head on her stomach. Her fingers flipped through his hair, raking through it in a gesture so soothing he almost drifted off to sleep.

He knew he should check on her, mention food. Be chivalrous and not a dick.

The wind still howled outside, and the rain pelted the window, but he hadn't heard any of that for probably hours. Now, resting there, loving the feel of her body under his, the sounds of the outside came rushing back. So did the mess he was in.

"Tessa, we should—" The buzzing sound stopped him. It took him a second to place it, then he remembered sliding his cell into his pocket when he came out of the bathroom.

He scanned the area for his pants. Before he could ask, her voice, all tired and mumbling, reached him. "Floor at the end of the bed."

Without looking at her, because he knew the need to check that call would be forgotten if he did, he slid down the mattress and reached over the side. The name and number . . . Yeah, this spelled trouble.

"It's Ben." Hansen put the phone on speaker so they both could hear. "What's going on?"

"Kerrie's awake. Get here now."

CHAPTER 14

The walk from the parking lot into the medical clinic took two years, or it sure felt that way. Tessa battled the rain and wind, gathering the hood of her raincoat tight around her head and ducking to keep from getting a direct hit of water in the face. With each step she cursed her choice of jeans. They stuck to her legs and weighed her down. Keeping up with Hansen's long-legged stride was tough enough without being at a speed disadvantage.

He didn't seem to notice the weather. He zipped up a thin running jacket and threw on a baseball cap. Tucked his glasses in his pocket.

He wrapped an arm around her and guided her through a rush of water that threatened to turn into a river if the storm didn't move on soon. The closeness, so different from the last few hours spent wrapped around each other, didn't slow the fine tremor running through her.

The dark of the early morning closed around her just as he opened the door of the clinic and ushered her inside. The smell hit her first. A mix of disinfectant and staleness. The noises—talking, the beeping of a nearby machine of some sort, shoes squeaking against the linoleum floor—bombarded her. Bright lights bounced off every white surface.

People bustled around. Two nurses, only one she recognized, and the fisherman who also played the role of volunteer on the ambulance crew talked in a corner on the side. In the middle of it all, Captain Rogers spoke on the phone. He waved hello as they passed him and headed for Ben, who stood at the end of the hall, gesturing for them to join him.

Hansen didn't say a word as he slipped his glasses on. He ignored the controlled chaos around him. If people staring or the constant pulsing of noise and activity bothered him, he didn't show it.

"How is she?" Tessa asked as soon as they reached Ben's side.

"Awake and doing well. Cuts and bruises mostly."

On the outside. Ben didn't say the words, but Tessa heard them. Ben picked an odd time to keep his responses short, but it had been a tough few days, so Tessa cut him some slack. "What is she saying?"

"Nothing."

Hansen frowned. "What?"

"She refused to talk until she saw you." Ben's expression stayed unreadable. "She provided her name, got teary, and asked specifically for you."

"So, her being here is not a coincidence," Tessa said.

Ben shook his head. "Clearly not."

Hansen's frown only deepened. "There's a protective order."

Yeah, no way. Tessa didn't trust anyone on Whitaker right now except Sylvia and the two men in front of her. "She could set him up."

The blank expression faded as Ben held up both hands. Tessa could see the emotions whirling through him now. The clash of friend and professional. The mix of wariness and concern as he looked at Hansen. The carefully banked frustration he excelled at keeping under control.

"We'll all go in. In case anything goes sideways, I'm the witness that she asked to see him. I'll take responsibility," Ben said, his voice understanding but firm as he eyed them. Then he pushed open the door to the private room. "Ms. Ross?"

The other woman looked so small. So lost. With hunched shoulders and her hands curled into the blanket beneath her, she sat on the bed with her legs dangling over the side. She wore hospital scrubs that dwarfed her.

At the sound of her name, her head shot up. Her eyes went from unfocused to wide and shocked, then tears spilled over her cheeks.

She hopped off the bed and headed for Hansen. Her arms wrapped around his waist and she buried her face in his chest. "Hansen. Oh, thank God."

Hansen didn't touch her. He stood there with his hands in the air as if he had no idea what to do. "I . . . uh . . ."

The sight froze Tessa. She stood there, watching this woman crumble with relief. Kerrie didn't sound scared of Hansen. Even now, she gathered his wet jacket in her fist as she held on to his back. Held on to him in a death grip as if he were her rescuer, not the one she claimed to fear.

Tessa had no idea what was happening. She'd read about abuse and the cycle of violence. She didn't know if this scene fit that or if this was something more sinister. From the way Hansen stood there, unmoving and stunned, he didn't get it either.

After a few minutes, Hansen gave Kerrie an awkward pat on the arm and gently pried her hands away from his back. The move put some distance between them and let him look at her. "Why are you on Whitaker?"

"He's here." She wiped at her tears as they fell. "He found out where you were and insisted we come here. Said he was hunting."

Ben shut the door behind them, giving them all a bit more privacy. "Wait a second."

"I don't understand any of this." Hansen looked to Tessa, then to Ben. He seemed unsure of his next move.

Tessa couldn't blame him. The weeping woman in front of him had filed for a protective order against him not that long ago. Now her voice shook in terror, but not about Hansen.

"Ms. Ross, I have some—"

She shook her head at Ben. "Kerrie."

Ben hesitated. "Okay, Kerrie. About your husband."

The harsh reality of what Ben had to say punched

Tessa in the stomach. This poor woman didn't know about her husband's death. Asshole or not, she must love him to be married to him. At least on some level. She was babbling and panicked, and it sounded as if her life had been turned upside down. Ben's news would flip it again.

"Did you stop him?" She grabbed on to Hansen's forearms, her voice pleading. "Did he hurt you?" She glanced at Tessa. "Or you?"

Ben took over. "Ma'am, I think you should sit down."

He pulled Kerrie away from Hansen, careful not to hurt her, and set her back down on the edge of the bed. After looking around, he grabbed some tissues and handed them to her. She wiped at her shirt, now wet from hugging Hansen, and dabbed at her big blue eyes, one of which was still swollen.

Kerrie's gaze darted from person to person. She rubbed her hands together on her lap until her pale skin turned red. Despite the strange sense that something didn't fit, Tessa's heart ached for her.

"I need to get out of here." Kerrie shook her head as she looked first at the floor, then to Hansen. "You were right. I only filed for the order because he made me. All those threats about me ending up like your sister if I didn't obey."

Relief washed over Tessa. She sensed that might be the case but to have it confirmed meant everything. This information might free Hansen. Give him a chance to move forward. "He admitted his claims against Hansen were fabricated?"

Kerrie nodded before glancing at Ben. "Please tell me you have him in custody."

"I'm sorry . . ." Ben struggled as a range of emotions raced across his face. He even glanced over his shoulder at the door. Voices floated inside the room from the hallway, but no one came inside. It took another few seconds before Ben looked at Kerrie again. "Your husband has been killed."

The last of the color ran out of her face. All life, all expression vanished, and she seemed to list to one side. "What?"

"He was attacked." Ben shook his head. "We don't know why or by whom."

"Here." Tessa sat down next to the other woman, not knowing what to say or what could possibly help her right now.

Kerrie visibly swallowed. "Hansen, you didn't . . ."

He shook his head. "No."

"He didn't." Tessa needed her to know that.

"Did he touch you?" Kerrie asked Tessa.

The question slammed into Tessa like an icy cold hand. "Hansen?"

"My husband." Kerrie grabbed for Tessa's fingers and held on. "He was furious that Hansen started over. Talked about him dating and having a life."

"Dating?" The word just sat there. Tessa wasn't quite sure what to do with it or how information like that could have wound its way to Judson thousands of miles away.

Hansen cleared his throat. "Kerrie, who tied you up?"

"Judson." Her grip tightened on Tessa's hand. "We fought about his plans for you. I refused to help and he . . ."

"Help him what?" Ben asked.

"He wanted to set up Hansen. Make it look like he lured us here by pretending to be someone else, then lie . . . again."

Hansen blew out a long breath. "He wanted me in jail this time."

"For hurting me. That's why I was tied up." She continued to cry, quietly sobbing as she told the story. "Once he hit me, he realized he could say you did it. He went to the island to talk with the police. He had this whole scheme, complete with fake emails and documents, saying you lured us here by pretending the trip on the yacht was a gift from one of his big money clients."

"You picked up the yacht in Seattle?" Tessa had so many questions that they tripped over each other in her head. That was the only one she could get out in a reasonably coherent way.

"Yes. We have a much smaller speedboat at home. Judson took a coast guard course and the required safety courses. He went out with a guide for a refresher when we picked up the yacht. We've been in and around the area for more than a week and . . ." When Kerrie's gaze landed on Hansen again, she stopped talking.

He didn't look even a bit surprised. "He's been spying on me?"

"Collecting information, yeah." She wiped at the

last of her tears. "He wanted to come here, cause a scene, get people's attention, and then . . . ruin you."

Hansen nodded. "Sounds like him."

"He was convinced the police would have no choice but to throw you in jail for violating the protective order if he said you tricked us into coming here and then attacked us."

"Definitely," Ben said.

"After that, with Hansen in jail and the police investigating, Judson thought he'd have time to get to your house and find something of yours, like a shirt or glass, to plant in this cabin he has set up on Howard Island to make it look like you were using that to launch your plan against us."

This was no joke. Tessa tried to imagine what could have happened if Judson had gotten to Ben before the whole scheme blew up or if Kerrie had gone along with the plan. "He should have put that much effort into his actual job and stayed at home."

"I agree." Kerrie's gaze skipped around the room. "But what happened to him once he was on the island? I don't understand."

"We're not sure but he never came to my office." Ben didn't provide any details or mention that Judson likely died before he could hatch his elaborate plan to take down Hansen.

Tessa thought waiting to deliver the entire story was the right call. Kerrie had been through so much and Tessa assumed she'd only told them a fraction of the horrors. The dazed expression and the haunted sound to her voice suggested Kerrie needed time and rest. Even then, Ben would need to be careful about what he asked so as not to trigger more despair.

"Where did he go?" Kerrie seemed determined to clarify that point. Whatever fear she once had or didn't have for Hansen didn't matter now. She looked to him before every answer, acted like she wanted to reach out to him. They had some bond that she was desperate to hold on to.

"That's what we're trying to find out." Ben nodded. "Tell me when you last saw your husband."

"On the boat. He'd been on the island before that and saw Hansen working the yard. Alone, which meant he didn't have an alibi. Between that and seeing someone watch the boat on and off from the beach, Judson thought he had to move." Kerrie looked at her hand and Tessa's. "He must not have tied the dinghy tight enough when he came back because it floated away."

"I was the one watching." The man-in-a-business-suit piece of the puzzle finally made sense. Tessa struggled to figure out how that fit in but now it sounded like it was part of some bigger, more elaborate plan. "I guess without a dinghy he had no choice but to swim."

"It also explains why he didn't stop or say anything on the beach." Hansen slid his hands into the front pockets on his jeans. "He likely recognized me and that's why he disappeared."

"I can't . . ." Kerrie burst into tears. Cried so hard her shoulders shook.

Tessa wrapped an arm around her and pulled her in

close. The vulnerability ate at her. She tried to imagine being thrown into such a desperate situation and surviving it. Her troubles with her father—the man she had spent most of her adult life avoiding—struck her as tame by comparison. "Okay, I think you should crawl back into bed."

"I can get the doctor," Ben said. "She should check on you before we run through too many more questions."

"I can't stay here." She reached out for Hansen then. "The person who killed Judson is out there."

He held her hand but didn't step closer. "He can't touch you."

"I'm so sorry." She pressed their joined hands to her cheek as the tears continued to fall. "The things I said. I should have fought back. You tried to help and I—"

"Okay, rest time." Tessa decided to save both Kerrie and Hansen. He looked ready to bolt, half drawn in by Kerrie's pleading yet totally confused about how the last half hour unfolded. Kerrie just was not in any condition for questions or talking. The woman needed to calm down and begin dealing with the horrors of her marriage and what Judson's death meant.

Ben nodded. "I'll get Lela."

Tessa helped Kerrie get into the bed. Shifting her and peeling back the covers proved to be a bit of a struggle since Kerrie wouldn't let go of Hansen's hand.

"Please forgive me."

Hansen waited until she lay down, then with the utmost care placed her hand on her stomach. "You need to concentrate on getting your strength back."

"Reception is spotty because of the storm, but do you need me to call anyone?" Tessa asked. Kerrie might view Hansen as her lifeline but Tessa could tell he was not comfortable with the role.

"Maybe your brother?" Hansen suggested.

"What's his name?" Tessa was making small talk now. Anything to ratchet down the anxiety and stop those tears, at least for a few seconds.

"Allen Bernard." Kerrie took a deep cleansing breath as her head dropped back into the pillow. "But I'll call. He needs to hear this from me."

Made sense. Tessa didn't have any siblings—well, sort of, but not really—but she always wished she'd had someone there to share the load, who understood every good and warped thing that happened in the family. "Are you sure?"

"Yes, thank you." Kerrie finally focused on Tessa. "Who are you? I'm so sorry I didn't ask before."

"My girlfriend, Tessa." Hansen sounded so clear and sure on that one point.

That made one of them.

Kerrie tugged at Tessa's hand again. "I said terrible things about him to get that order but none of it was true. He was nothing but decent and concerned. He never would have hurt me."

That part Tessa did get. "I know."

Ben opened the door and poked his head in. "Let's step out so Lela can come in."

They almost reached Ben before Kerrie spoke again. "Hansen? Who would do this to Judson?"

That's the question that had the whole island buzzing. Tessa wished she knew the answer.

"We'll find out," Ben said before pulling Tessa and Hansen into the hallway with him.

Once outside the room, Hansen leaned against the wall. Bent over with his hands on his knees, he drew in a few breaths before standing up straight again. "That's not how I expected that to go."

"I'll stay with her. You two need to get to the board offices," Ben said.

Hansen frowned. "What?"

Between the hot sex that left her breathless and meeting Kerrie, Tessa had forgotten all about the big news of the day. "The vote is this morning, which means soon."

Hansen's frown only deepened. "I was planning on ignoring it because for her to fire you then try to perform some sort of citizen's arrest against me is ridiculous. She's wasting both of our time."

She understood the sentiment. There was only so much a person could process, but his freedom and name mattered too much. Plus, now they had ammunition to stop the mess. "No, you were ignoring it back when you were being railroaded."

Hansen snorted. Actually made the annoying sound. "And?"

He needed to take this seriously because if Ruthie had her way, Ben would be taken off the case, possibly lose his job, and the board would put Hansen in a cell until reinforcements arrived on the island. Tessa wasn't sure why he didn't get that. "Kerrie is pretty clear you didn't touch her."

Hansen shot her one of those you're-not-making-sense expressions. "Judson is still dead."

"But half of Ruthie's story fell apart," Ben pointed out. "There's no reason for you to be in a cell, which means there's no reason for me to arrest you or lose my job for not arresting you."

Hansen sighed. "Right."

Tessa had one more reason. "And I really want her to know all of that."

HANSEN WANTED TO be anywhere—literally, anywhere else on the planet—but in the Whitaker board offices right now. Not that Tessa gave him that option. She'd taken his hand at the clinic and escorted him back to the car. Even insisted she drive, and now they stood outside the double doors to the meeting room.

She smiled up at him. "Ready?"

"No." Because why lie?

Tessa opened the doors anyway. Not just one. She went for the much more dramatic throw-them-both-open approach. Of the many things he liked about her, this was near the top. This move, coming with him, insisting he stand his ground, was about loyalty. It ran bone-deep through her.

He tried to imagine being in her position. His past forced her to choose a side, and she picked his. Other than his family, that hadn't happened a lot since Alexis died. Sure, some of his friends had stuck around and fought for him. But when Judson exerted his pressure, even Hansen gave up trying to defend himself. His sole focus had been on getting answers about his sister and keeping Kerrie safe.

That was the mess he'd plunged Tessa into. The friendship, the sex, sticking by him. She took on each new role as if she were born to play it.

The first thing that struck him when they got into the room was its size. Ben's whole office, the inner private one and the outer one for the public, could fit in half the space. Nothing like sticking him in the crappy area while Ruthie presided over the fancy room with the dark wood paneling and plush leather chairs.

Hansen's gaze wandered over the five members sitting on one side of the table as if they were holding a hearing without anyone being in the room. Ruthie, of course, and Sylvia. Tim, the real estate guy on the island who sold insurance on the side. Sid, a lawyer who was born and raised here. Only left to get his degree, then hurry back. The one on the far end was Paul. He was retired and pushing eighty and that was the extent of what Hansen knew about that guy.

Ruthie barely spared Tessa and Hansen a glance. "This is a closed meeting."

Tessa rolled her eyes. "It's about him and you using him as an excuse to go after Ben."

"We have rules and protocol and—"

"I'd like to hear from Hansen," Sid said as he tapped his pen against the desk. "He fixed my porch a few weeks back."

Ruthie leaned forward and glared down the table. "What does that matter?"

"Fixed the staircase to my upstairs. Doesn't creak anymore." Paul nodded. "That was good work."

"He probably came to the house to see what you had inside." Ruthie wrote something on the notepad in front of her. Scratched it in with enough force to tear the paper.

Hansen assumed that anger was aimed at him. "So now I steal things?"

She finally focused on him. "We don't know anything about you. That's the point."

Tessa walked up the aisle to the table, ignoring Ruthie's sputtering and the empty chairs lining each side of the room. "Kerrie Ross does, and she says Hansen didn't touch her—never did. He actually tried to save her, which ruins Ruthie's theory about Hansen being this violent killer who needs to be locked up."

"She's awake?" Sylvia asked.

Hansen didn't bother answering. He did follow and stand beside Tessa so he could enjoy the front-row seat to her temper. She was in public-defender mode and he sat back and drank it in. On fire and sexy, ready to talk Ruthie down. It almost made him feel sorry for the board for holding this ridiculous meeting . . . almost.

Tessa nodded. "About an hour ago. She told us her husband attacked her."

"And he's dead." Ruthie smiled. "That's part of the reason we're here. The poor man had a protective order against Hansen and it looks like Hansen violated it."

Tessa treated the board to a second eye roll. She'd perfected the move. "You're making things up."

"Including the part about Judson being a 'poor man' because the guy was a piece of garbage." Hansen could only take so much when it came to the art of making Judson a victim, even though, in this case, he was. He'd treated people like shit. *And he killed Alexis.*

Tessa held out her hand. The back of it rested against Hansen's chest. "Don't help."

"She's right, Ruthie." Sylvia spun her chair around to face her nemesis. "You said Hansen hurt this woman. He didn't. You were wrong and Ben was right not to rush ahead with an arrest."

"That order against Hansen sounds like garbage to me," Sid said as he folded the paper in front of him with the agenda on it in half and slid it down the table toward Ruthie.

Tim stood up and stretched. Looked ready to head back home. "Me, too."

The tension spinning inside Hansen broke. He didn't understand what had happened with Kerrie or the change in her—any of it—but watching Ruthie lose control of the meeting filled him with a deep satisfaction.

The paper could print its stories. Folks were forming opinions and those opinions didn't match the one Ruthie held. She hated him, and he didn't know why. In many ways, he didn't care. He never bothered to ask and didn't plan on starting now. But disbanding this meeting and taking the target off Ben's back mattered to Hansen. Tessa forcing him to come here had been the right answer, but then she didn't make many wrong turns.

Ruthie smacked her palm against the table. "You two need to leave so the board can deliberate."

"On what?" Sylvia asked.

Ruthie spoke over the shifting in the seats and the screech of chair legs against the floor. "You are not in charge here."

"Your initial accusations were wrong. Before we go around blaming an innocent man and impugning his character, we need more facts. Ben understands that, which is why he's the law enforcement here, not the board, and we need to let him work without interference." Sylvia folded her paper and sent it Ruthie's way as well. "You can keep your agenda."

"Exactly." Tessa's voice stayed steady and calm. She didn't get fidgety or angry. She held it together and commanded the attention of the rest of the board. "It's what you all voted for when you hired Ben. Let him do his job."

Ruthie's face flushed red. "Nonsense."

Sylvia stood up next to Tim. "I don't think we need a vote, but we can take one so that it goes into the newspaper as a loss for you."

The throat clearing at the end of the table grabbed everyone's attention. Paul stood up with a soft groan. "It looks like you have a brief reprieve, Hansen."

Tessa smiled at Ruthie. "It sounds like you overplayed your hand."

"The meeting is adjourned." Ruthie banged her little gavel, then gathered up her things in silence. She was up and around the table before anyone said a word.

"I'm pretty sure we need a vote to adjourn and . . ." Sylvia called to Ruthie as she walked around the outside of the room, avoiding the aisle where Tessa and Hansen stood. "Okay, yeah. Just go."

The rest of the board members filed out of their chairs and around the table. Most headed out, but Paul stopped. "Hansen, my back door keeps sticking."

One of the benefits of living on an isolated island: people needed things done. Hansen appreciated Paul's practical nature in making sure he was at the head of the list. "After the storm passes, I'll call and we'll set up a time for me to come over."

"Good man." Paul patted him on the shoulder, then nodded to Tessa before joining Sid at the back of the room.

Sid shook his head. "Can't believe she brought us out in this weather."

The voices faded as the room emptied out except for the three of them. Hansen wouldn't have bet money on the morning ending on this note.

He glanced at Tessa, not even trying to hide his gratitude. "Impressive."

"Is Judson's wife really awake and okay?" Sylvia asked.

Tessa laughed. "You thought we lied about that?"

"I thought about making up a story that she woke up just long enough to clear Hansen." Sylvia shrugged.

"Half of them would have bought it. Ruthie is not exactly an island favorite right now."

"Was she ever?"

Tessa asked the question before he could, but he thought he knew the answer. Despite everything, Ruthie did love the island. The way she went about showing it was the problem. She'd changed over time. All the residents talked about it. She'd become difficult and determined to model the entire island the way she wanted it, even if that meant stomping all over due process and fairness.

"At one time." Sylvia put on her raincoat. "She's now more on edge than usual. Not sure if it's because her husband is away or if it's the reality she's losing control of the island."

"Either way, I'm happy you were here." Hansen meant that. The women had saved him this morning. Kerrie coming forward. Tessa defending him. Sylvia lending her support. Together they were formidable, and he benefited from that collective might.

Sylvia waved him off. "This is what we do around here. Support each other."

"Judson might not agree," Tessa said.

"Sounds to me like that guy checking out is not a big loss for the world."

Tessa's smile grew wider. "Don't let Ben hear you say that. Or Ruthie."

Hansen could hear the amusement in their voices, but he wanted to add one serious note. "Thank you both. Truly."

Sylvia winked at him like she usually did. "Go prove who did it and your position on this island will be secured."

That sounded ominous. "What position?"

"As the guy who can fix anything."

CHAPTER 15

Hansen managed to get through the whole day without getting into more trouble. He texted Ben on and off to check on Kerrie. Her turnaround made zero sense to him. The way she clung to him . . . not what he expected.

At lunch, Tessa had explained the pressure Judson exerted and how Kerrie likely felt trapped. Hansen listened, half understood. Mostly, he stared at Tessa. Watched her talk and gesture. The energy. The memory of those little moans that vibrated in the back of her throat when she came.

Sweet hell, he needed to get home to her.

He swung through Ben's office for one last check. The storm had blown north of Whitaker. Rain pummeled them, and winds howled, but the damaging center of it missed them. The gray sky still shrouded the island in darkness, but lights flickered on across the island as the electricity rebooted.

Ben glanced up from the stack of papers in front of him as Hansen walked in. "Where's Tessa?"

"Home."

Ben stood up and went over to the whiteboard he'd set up on the side of his office. "Do you realize how easy you say that word?"

Realized. Panicked about it. Tried to pretend he didn't say it or feel it. Now planned on ignoring it. "She's staying with me. You're the one who kicked her out of her house."

Ben shot him a satisfied smile. "Uh-huh."

"You know we're grown-ups, right?"

Ben froze in the middle of attaching Judson's photo to the top of the board. "You know you're defensive, right?"

Well, shit. Hansen dropped into the chair in front of Ben's desk. "It's too easy having her there."

Whatever Ben had planned on doing, he stopped. He leaned against the board and watched Hansen. "I'm confused. You're saying that's a problem or no?"

"You know my plan was to come to Whitaker, recuperate, calm the fuck down, then go back home." It sounded so easy broken out like that. It proved to be anything but.

"You never specifically said it, but it was clear to me you were trying to get over something." Ben didn't sound like he bought into the concept.

Unspent adrenaline poured through Hansen. He tipped his chair to balance on the back legs. It was either that or get up and pace around.

This confusion, muddying everything, adding in feelings, he knew it would all lead to a bad place. The kind of place where he stumbled around and fought to stay emotionally closed off but failed, and Tessa got hurt. That was the one thing—the only thing—he couldn't tolerate. Causing her pain. But he felt pulled and what he wanted got jumbled up with the fact he planned to leave.

What a mess.

"Where does Tessa fit in?" He asked because he really wanted to know.

Ben's eyebrows lifted. "You're asking me?"

Yeah, good point. Hansen groaned as he rubbed his hands through his hair and linked his fingers behind his head. "Things got complicated. I wanted easy."

"Life doesn't work that way." Ben dropped the papers back on his desk and went around to his chair. But he didn't follow up his comment with more.

"If that's some sort of man-to-man wisdom . . ."

After a good deal of huffing and some get-your-shit-together glances, Ben leaned forward, balancing his elbows on his desk. "You don't get to decide who and how you fall in love. It happens. It's a spark. You get plowed under. You hope like hell you can keep the spark alive."

"You sound like an expert."

The phone rang and Ben reached to turn the volume down. "A long time ago."

Hansen lowered the front legs of his chair back to the floor and dropped his arms. "You fell?"

Ben never talked about it but it made sense. He'd had a career in the military. Moving around sucked, but Ben would make it work. That was who he was. Solid and smart. He was the one person, before Tessa, who kept Hansen tied to the island.

They'd become friends almost immediately and at a time when Hansen didn't want any. Ben insisted when he sat down next to him at the lodge and started talking. He didn't make demands or ask about the past. He just let the friendship and who they were start from that point, which explained why Ben hadn't shared this news flash before now.

"Got married. Got divorced."

Okay, that was big. Not just an unrequited love thing or a crush. "Oh, shit."

Ben stared at his hands while he talked. "I was barely out of my teens."

"You're, what, thirty-four or so now?"

"That's close enough. Point is, we were too young." Ben acted like it didn't matter but his voice said otherwise. A sadness lingered there.

Maybe it was nostalgia, but Hansen wondered if the emotion loomed larger than that. "You're older now. You never know."

"Her husband, our former neighbor, by the way, and their son might mind. That's the point. I was the wrong guy for her, but she found the right one. Not even that long after me. Right time. Right guy. Huge spark."

She did. Hansen noticed Ben didn't fill in the blanks about how he survived the whole breakup. "You're not angry?"

"I spent a long time being upset for me, but I've always been happy for her." Ben glanced to the side and didn't say anything for a few seconds. "I'll always love her, but I stopped being *in love* with her a very long time ago. She deserves to be happy. We all do."

"That sounds healthy."

Ben leaned back in his chair. "You should try it."

That was nothing but an invitation to needless heartache as far as Hansen could see. Which reminded him of the one point he needed to clear up. "I didn't use the word *love*."

"I did." Ben pointed at him. "About you."

Time to divert and ignore. "Back to Judson."

"Look at you wallowing in denial."

Absolutely. Thinking about Tessa made his mind spin. It would be so easy to get caught up in her and the possibilities and forget how unfair it was to drag anyone into his mess.

"So, the murder." It was a sad statement on his love life that he'd rather talk about death.

Ben's amusement disappeared in a flash. "You didn't kill him, unless you somehow figured out he was trying to set you up, tracked him down, killed him, then, for some odd reason, dumped him on Tessa's lawn even though that choice pointed the spotlight right at you because you were at the house."

"That sounds exhausting."

Ben shifted in his chair for what felt like the hundredth time. "Kerrie was beaten up and tied to a wall, so she didn't do it. Judson didn't kill himself."

"So, we have nothing."

"You're not in my cell tonight. Count that as a win."

"Would you have arrested me?" It was more curiosity than anything else. Hansen didn't view the answer as a loyalty test. He understood Ben had a job and an island to protect.

"Only if I thought you did it, which I don't."

Exactly as he expected. "You're a practical guy."

"Now, about Tessa."

Hansen groaned. "You're killing me."

"That's kind of my point. Someone on this island is a killer. Until we know who, I feel better knowing she's with you than sleeping alone somewhere else. And her house is still out, so keep her with you. And, this is my real point, keep her close to you in general."

That was his intention, but Ben had his full attention now. "She spends time with Sylvia. Do you think Berman's Lodge isn't safe?"

"It is, but we both know she's the type to go around asking questions. If it weren't for the unending rain over the last few days and people being on edge, she'd be out there."

"True." He could visualize it. The idea of her knocking on the wrong door. Of someone deciding the way to resolve the case was to drag her into it.

"Instead, she's inside with you." Ben looked as if he were biting back a smile. "Earning your trust . . . or whatever it is she's doing there. Keep doing that."

Hansen ignored the nosiness and repeated girlfriend talk, which she might be. Hansen didn't know despite what he told Kerrie. But he was sure of one thing. "I'm not great with trust."

"Are you good at listening?"

Not on this topic. "Doubtful."

"Tessa is probably the best person on this island and for some reason she chose you."

Hansen couldn't circle back to the subject again. He never really escaped it. She stayed on his mind all the time now. Since the sex—touching her, kissing her—he ached to do it again. So, he didn't need a reminder from his supposed best friend. "This is a very moving speech."

"My suggestion?"

He hated to ask but did anyway. "Yeah?"

"Don't fuck it up."

HANSEN EXITED BEN'S private office with too many ideas swirling in his head. What he owed Tessa. How Kerrie attached herself to him. The way Ruthie wanted to go after him.

The women in his life were confusing the hell out of him.

"I hear that you and Tessa . . ."

At the sound of Arianna's voice, Hansen looked up. He immediately regretted it. She sat there in one of her long dresses with her raincoat folded on the chair next to her in the reception area rather than on the coat hook. Because of course.

She smiled and . . . Wait, what had she said? "Excuse me?"

"Oh, it's not a secret. You and Tessa."

"Our relationship is private."

"On Whitaker?"

Well, he had to agree with her there. For an island that prided itself on privacy and being the last resort for so many, people sure craved gossip. He was not one of them, except for the questions he had about Arianna right now. "What are you doing here?"

"Ben insisted I come without Ellis, so he's getting coffee. Then it's his turn." She glanced at her nails, which were painted light blue. "Ben has talked to us, but I think this is the formal interrogation."

"I already had my time. I'm thinking we'll all be questioned eventually." To the extent that made Ben's life easier and eased Arianna's mind, Hansen wanted her to know. "It's a formality."

With that done, he headed for the door, grabbing his coat as he went.

"Tessa doesn't think so."

That stopped him, but he guessed that was the point. "Why do you say that?"

"She's the kind of person everyone trusts." Arianna smiled as she examined the nails on her other hand. "Of course, in the movies those are the ones you need to watch."

"This isn't a movie." The comment came out sharper than he intended, but it was out there now.

Arianna looked up. "Of course not. We all know Tessa is innocent. She's not the suspicious type. I mean, she kind of is because she's always digging around and asking questions, but she isn't the one who draws suspicion. She quietly investigates and thinks we don't know."

Arianna bobbed her head and twirled her hands in the air as she spoke. It all looked casual, as if they were having a friendly chat. But Hansen knew better. This was a carefully calculated move. He just didn't know why Arianna would take a shot or shine the light on Tessa. "Uh-huh."

"I'm saying that's why she's so effective. Everyone likes her." Arianna gestured in his direction. "Including you."

"Right." Knowing he wasn't going to get the answer from her, Hansen filed the conversation away and shut it down. He had better places to be and only one person he wanted to talk with. "Enjoy your night."

CHAPTER 16

Tessa killed a few hours doing some work. She wrote and revised the user manual for a rainwater recovery system. The topic interested her. The idea of being productive didn't. But she needed something to keep her hands busy and her mind off Kerrie.

She'd been attacked by her own husband. Used. Forced to tell lies about Hansen. Tied up. And now she'd be expected to mourn that asshole Judson. Part of her probably did love him despite everything.

Tessa knew from experience how difficult it could be to separate what you wished could be from the reality of what was. Her history was nothing like Kerrie's, but she felt a strange kinship.

She felt something else, too, and she feared it made her a pretty shitty person. She knew about the ties and the bruises. About Judson being awful. But something nagged at her. This uncomfortable sensation that Kerrie told part of the story but not all of it. If the scene in the clinic was a performance, then she was quite the actress. No, Tessa believed every word but she felt as if there was some question she should ask that would have cleared up the residual confusion.

What she really needed right now was a sweater. She'd only brought a few pieces of clothing over to Hansen's place from her house. Thanks to the rain, she'd run through those pretty fast. Her jacket hung on the hook by the door. She'd draped her jeans over the back of a dining chair. She wore sweatpants and a slim-fitting T-shirt and needed more. This clearly called for a second raid on Hansen's closet.

She tucked her pen behind her ear, abandoning all of her paperwork on the ottoman, and stepped into the closet area. He had a dresser upstairs, but this was where he kept the bulk of everything from extra napkins to towels to some clothes. Everything had a place and he kept it all neat and tidy. One set of shelves held the sweaters and sweatshirts. The few shirts he owned were lined up on the opposite wall with shoes on the floor beneath them.

She peeked in, thinking to count his sneakers because he seemed to have an endless supply. Each day he kicked off a soggy pair. The next morning he'd appear with a new pair.

She pushed the clothes to one side and smiled as his familiar scent hit her. All those soft plaid and denim shirts. He owned about twelve shirts and ten of them fell into that category. When she moved in for a closer look, her foot smacked against something hard and she glanced down. Looked like a safe of some sort.

The pen slid from behind her ear and bounced with

a clink before disappearing into the darkness. She flicked on the light and sunk to her knees.

With her body half in and half out of the small space, she patted around with her hand. She almost screamed *gotcha* when her fingers grazed the tip of the pen.

"What are you doing?"

At the sound of his voice she squealed in surprise and smacked her shoulder off the closet wall. She dropped the pen, but it didn't roll or bounce this time.

Spinning around, she landed on her butt on the hardwood floor and looked up at him. "You're home."

"Surprise," he said in a flat, lifeless tone.

The severe frown. That voice. "What's wrong?"

"You're snooping."

She rubbed her sore arm. "Sure, I'm . . ." Then she froze. "Wait, are you serious?"

He nodded toward the inside of the closet. "What are you looking for?"

A thin thread of anger played right there on the edge of his voice. She could hear it but she had no idea why he aimed it at her. "You think I'm going through your stuff?"

"Like you did with the medicine cabinet."

For a second she didn't know what he was talking about. Then she thought about the first night and the bathroom. "That was a joke."

"Then tell me what you're doing." His frown didn't ease and he held his body stiff. He couldn't look less open to reason if he tried. "Hell, Tessa. I've told you everything. You know shit no one else on the island knows. All about Alexis."

Okay, they'd taken a weird turn. Everything had been fine earlier. Kerrie cleared him. The board meeting was resolved without too much yelling. She laughed with him at lunch. Now this bullshit.

She stood up, forgetting all about the thumping in her arm and focused on him. And tried to get through this before he said something he couldn't take back. "What happened to you tonight? You were fine when I last saw you, happy even, because the investigation against you was shut down. Now you're—"

"What am I?"

The snap in his voice should have given him a clue. She drew a few conclusions from it. "Acting like an ass."

"We're back to that." He glanced away for a second as he shook his head. When he faced her again, the old Hansen had returned. The one that held her away and was dismissive. "Tell me what you think you're going to find while poking around in my private things. Be honest."

"I *am* honest."

"Says the woman who hasn't told me one thing about her life. About the secret that dragged you to Whitaker."

The force of his words nearly knocked her over. If he wanted to land a shot, he'd done it. That had been her plan for tonight. To fill him in. She knew about him and she wanted him to know about her. The things *no one* but she and her mother knew.

Forget sharing. Forget dinner. Right now she didn't even want to be in the same room with him.

"I was looking for this." She reached down and scooped up the pen. "I dropped it."

"In the closet?" His tone suggested he thought she was lying.

"I wanted a shirt. Like before." She swept her arm around the room. "Most of my clothes are wet."

His expression changed. Showed a hint of confusion. "I don't get it."

"Apparently." She pushed by him and left the closet. A quick look out the window showed the steady beat of rain had morphed into a serious downpour. It could be a blizzard out there and she would still leave.

She went to the ottoman and stacked her papers. Stacked them against the leather to make a trim pile, then held them up. "Want to look through these? It's part of a manual. It's what I do."

"No, I don't—"

"Whatever." She scooped up her possessions and cradled them in her arms. She tried to remember where she'd thrown her bag. Her gaze landed on the ladder and the answer hit her—up there. No way was she going up those rungs.

She walked into the kitchen area. Slammed every cabinet door while he called her name. He could talk to himself for all she cared because she'd found the random paper bag she sought. That would work for now. She just needed to get the papers into her car and she could wrap them in her coat to make it happen. Who cared if she got wet.

"What are you doing?" he asked.

Talk about being clueless . . . "Leaving."

"Where are you going to go?"

"Wherever you're not." She scurried around, collecting the few things she could find. She'd convince Ben to let her back into her house to replenish whatever else she needed and couldn't borrow or buy.

Keys and coat. Everything else could wait or be replaced.

"Okay, shit. Stop." He stepped in front of her before she could make a beeline for the door. "It's been a shitty few days."

"For both of us, Hansen." She pivoted around him and grabbed her coat. "I was there when you found Judson's body. I've been with you through all of it, and you go off on me?"

He held up both hands in mock surrender. "Let's calm down."

Now there was the wrong thing to say. "Don't pull the hysterical-woman thing on me. You did this."

"What?"

"I'm calm. Clear even." She wrapped the stack in her arms in her rain jacket. Tucked everything in to keep it dry.

"What are you doing?"

She picked up the keys and reached for the doorknob. "Going to the lodge."

"Because we had one fight?" He sounded stunned by the idea.

But he didn't get it. She pulled for him, supported him, and he continued to see the worst. She was done. "Because you don't trust me and, honestly, Hansen, I've earned it. So, this is on you."

"What does that mean?"

"You want to strike out at someone? Pick another target." She threw open the door and left. Kept going when he called her name. Didn't stop until she pulled into the parking lot at the lodge. Then she closed her eyes and let the sadness overwhelm her. "The dumbass."

SYLVIA DIDN'T ASK any questions. That made her the best kind of friend—the type with a good sense to know when not to talk. Now was not the right time. Tessa needed to fester and be pissed off. Later she'd think things through and figure out if she matched his over-the-top reaction with one of her own. Right now she felt secure in being pissed.

"We're not the same size, but you don't need to be anything but comfortable tonight and my roomier sweats will do that for you," Sylvia said as she typed something into the computer behind the main check-in desk.

Some people, like Sylvia, lived in the lodge full-time. Others used it for guests and relatives. Every now and then the random tourist would stop in. Tessa bet she was the first one to stand in the lobby dripping wet, holding a stack of soggy paperwork.

"I forgot my wallet at Hansen's house." She just remembered that annoying fact. "If you don't mind waiting until I can get it from him? I really don't want to go back and ask now."

"Or you can look at this as a gift and never again offer to pay me."

"Sylvia."

"Tessa."

"Thank you." The longer she stood there, the more her anger morphed into something almost intolerable—self-doubt. She questioned why she'd kept pursuing Hansen over the last few weeks . . . not really pursuing but asking him for coffee and having him come over and work on the house. Taking him out to the boat.

Okay, she had pursued him and now she wondered why. She wasn't looking for a relationship when she came here, and *grumpy* was not her thing. There were easier men. For some reason she picked hard.

"Get settled in and then I'll bring up some food."

She needed a shower and a few minutes to decide if she wanted to stew or cry over stupid Hansen Rye. "You don't have to—"

"You're starting to tick me off." Sylvia sent her an I'm-not-kidding glare. "Let people take care of you. And by that I mean me, your friend."

"I'm not great at accepting help."

"Then practice."

The door opened and a cool wet wind blew through the lobby. "You look ridiculous standing there like that."

"Always nice to see you, Ruthie." Tessa mentally

searched for a well of patience. This was not a time for a Ruthie battle, if there ever really was a good time for that nonsense.

Ruthie walked over until she stood next to Tessa. Gave her a quick up-and-down glance that made it quite clear she was not impressed before looking behind the counter. "I'm here to see you, Sylvia."

"Well, I'm helping someone else right now." Sylvia pointed to her right. "You can have a seat in the dining room."

Ruthie being Ruthie, she ignored the well-meaning suggestion and turned on Tessa instead. "Why are you here? This is not the best weather to be moving around."

"Honestly, Ruthie, that's none of your business." The final countdown on Tessa's patience started ticking down toward zero. She could feel her frustration rising. If this went on too long, she just might provide Whitaker with the type of scene people would remember for decades.

"It's not a surprise." Ruthie wore what likely qualified as a smile for her. "You finally realized he's trouble."

"Who?"

"Hansen." Ruthie leaned against the check-in counter, ignoring the couple that came in and headed straight for the dining room without saying hello after seeing her. "Look, he might be handsome but, trust me, looks fade. Then you're left with a guy who wanted something else and you're miserable."

Some of Tessa's simmering anger evaporated. Those

words sounded personal, painful, so she treaded carefully. "Are we still talking about me?"

After a sharp inhale Ruthie blinked a few times. "My point is that judges don't just hand out protective orders."

Sylvia sighed at her. "Ruthie, not now."

"She needs to be smart and not get turned by a pretty face."

Just as Tessa's sympathy floated to the surface, Ruthie torpedoed it again. She made it so difficult to cheer for her.

"I'm not a child."

Ruthie stepped back and looked at the bundle in Tessa's arms. "You look like one right now."

That's it. "You know what? Shut up."

"Excuse me?"

Sylvia gestured for the woman heading for them to make a U-turn. She smartly did.

But Tessa didn't care if they had an audience. She'd tried so many times to understand Ruthie. To tolerate her. To make excuses for her behavior. Not this time. "I'm sorry that you are in pain."

Ruthie shook her head. "I'm not—"

The sounds of muffled voices and clanking silverware from the dining room faded. Tessa no longer cared who heard her or what they thought of her. She'd spent her entire life following the rules and not drawing attention to herself. It was time to stand up and be absolutely clear about her position.

"We both know you are. Or maybe I'm giving you

too much credit and you really are always mean and nasty for no apparent reason." Tessa's voice rose. She managed to keep from tipping over into all-out screaming but just barely. "Honestly, I don't care about being nice to you anymore. I'm sick of it. My private life is not your business."

"I am trying to help you," Ruthie shouted back.

"No, you hate Hansen and that colors everything."

Ruthie glanced at Sylvia, but Sylvia refused to jump in and resolve this. Instead of taking the hint, Ruthie continued. "If he's so great, why are you here and not there with him?"

Because it was either leave his cabin or throw her pen at him. "We had a fight. He's difficult and annoying. He's also caring and charming and would never hurt Kerrie or Judson, though heaven knows Judson deserved it."

Ruthie's mouth dropped open. "That's a terrible thing to say."

A crowd gathered now. Some physically moved in, but others listened from the other room. Diners actively watched them, not trying to hide their interest. A couple stood unmoving on the stairway to the second floor.

Fine with Tessa. They all needed to hear this part.

"Maybe you should get your facts straight before you demean Hansen. He's a good guy even though he tries very hard some days to fight his decency." She leaned in closer to Ruthie and emphasized each word. "Leave him alone."

When she finished, silence screamed through the lodge. It bounced off the walls.

The chandelier bathed the area in a soft light, so Tessa could see she had everyone's attention. Then she heard shuffling at the door and realized Ruthie never closed it.

"Thank you."

She heard his deep soothing voice before she turned around and saw him. "Hansen?"

"You forgot your wallet." He didn't move any closer, but he held out one hand. "I also know you like these socks and my shirt." He lifted up the bag in his other hand. "And you were reading a book, so that's in here, too."

Seeing him stopped some of the thunderous anger rolling through her. Bringing the socks earned more of her forgiveness than an immediate apology would have, though he could make one of those later. The whole bag of goodies and coming here, where he had to know Sylvia would be waiting to unleash on him, was a pretty ballsy choice . . . and pretty adorable.

Ruthie treated him to a tsk-tsk sound. "She left you."

Hansen nodded. "I deserved to be left."

A soft sigh floated down from the couple on the staircase. Tessa kept her focus on Hansen. She could see his regret. It was written all over his face. Little did he know he'd inched even closer to crawling out of trouble.

She no longer felt like yelling. "It was just a stupid fight. Not a big thing."

Tension pinged through the room. Not the angry kind. The building-up-to-something good type.

He threw Tessa a lopsided smile. "Any chance you'll let me apologize? Public or private, it's your choice."

She was halfway to forgiving him already. And, if she were being honest, they'd both been wound tight tonight and lost it. Blamed each other when the real issues were so much more complex than anything either of them said or did.

But he did need to know she had her limits. "Depends. Are you going to stop being an ass?"

Someone in the dining room laughed. Another person started coughing.

Hansen ignored all of it. "For you, I'll try."

"About time." Sylvia slid a key across the counter. "Take room ten."

CHAPTER 17

Hansen didn't exhale until Tessa opened the door to her room and let him follow her inside. He took a minute to look around. The suite was about as big as the bottom floor of his house and spanned the entire side of the lodge. He pulled back the curtain and saw the lights from the Yacht Club in the distance. In the bright sunshine, the water view had to be spectacular.

The fancy blue-and-beige wallpaper surprised him. Nothing about the decor reminded him of Sylvia. He expected clean lines and muted colors, but given the age of the building, how it was one of the first on the island and used to be someone's house, the antique furniture fit.

A soft thud shifted his attention from the pencil drawings of flowers framed on the wall back to Tessa. She unloaded her paper bag and her jacket-roll of possessions on the desk with the spindly legs in the corner. The wood made a creaking noise despite the low weight of the package.

But the decorations were not really his concern at the moment. He'd lost his temper back at his house.

Let all his insecurities and confusion grow into a huge ball of fury. Then he aimed it at her, the one person he didn't want to hurt.

He set the bag of her things he'd brought on the floor near the king-size bed. "I'm sorry."

For a second, she didn't say anything. Didn't even turn around to face him. When she did, the anger he expected to see wasn't there. Her expression bordered on curious, as if she were assessing him. If she planned to test him, he feared he'd fail. His instincts had misfired earlier, and he could only hope they worked now.

She tilted her head to the side like she often did when she asked a question. "How often do you admit that?"

"Never."

She nodded as she made a humming sound. "What are you sorry for?"

Test time. "I acted like a jerk."

"Totally."

He bit back a smile. Tessa didn't sugarcoat anything when it came to him. He liked that about her. One thing about being the boss back home meant people listened and followed his directions, usually without question. He had their attention because he signed the checks and his name appeared on the letterhead.

She didn't let him get away with much. She set boundaries and didn't waver. She also declared her support of him to the entire lodge. Put that on the front page of the newspaper because that was the headline. She believed him. He wasn't sure when he'd earned her trust or why he'd been so irresponsible to risk it tonight.

"Instead of asking you a simple question about why you were in my closet . . ." She started to say something, but he quickly finished his thought. ". . . and listening to the answer, I jumped to conclusions."

Her eyes narrowed as if she were trying to figure out if he was selling her a line. "That's putting it mildly. You lost it."

He couldn't exactly argue with that version of the scene. Every bit of common sense had left his head. He would never have hurt her or even yelled at her, but words could cut and he needed to remember that. "Agreed."

She pushed away from the wobbly desk and stopped in the middle of the room where the bedroom and living areas met. "Your trust issues are annoying."

To him it wasn't about trust, but he had no intention of arguing with her. "To be fair, I have been accused of murder."

She shot him a look that screamed *do not go there.* "Not by me, so don't use that excuse."

"Okay." Yeah, wrong turn. Life sucked the last few days . . . all but the part that included her. She'd made that point.

"I dropped a pen."

She clearly wanted to bang on the message and he didn't try to stop her. "I know that now."

"You could have asked nicely earlier."

He didn't bother to remind her he already admitted that. Not when she was on a roll and unloading what he hoped was the last of her anger over his mistake. "My mind was a scrambled mess. Arianna said . . . It doesn't matter."

"It sounds like it did."

"This was my fault. I got off track."

"And you took it out on me."

He exhaled. "I did."

"Why?" All of the anger left her voice. She shifted back to asking questions without any edge.

"Because I'm an ass?"

After a few seconds of hesitation, she smiled. "You got that right."

The thick wall of tension between them crumbled. Her battle stance relaxed. The anxiety tumbling around in his stomach finally took a break.

He had one last thing to say, then he *really* wanted to drop this topic and hoped she did, too. "I didn't mean to make you a target."

"Don't give me that cute face."

All he did was stand there, looking at her through glasses that had fogged around the edges. But since it seemed safe, he let the smile happen this time. "Sorry."

"I should make you sleep in the bathroom."

She was talking about them and not hinting about kicking him out. He'd dodged a pretty big mess, which was why he stepped into the next question with some care. "Does that mean you'll come back to the house with me?"

"Don't push it."

He heard the amusement in her voice . . . and had

no idea what that meant. "Will you let me stay here with you?"

"Maybe."

"I'll go whenever you ask me to leave. Sleep on the floor." The need to stick close went beyond what Ben said about her safety, though Hansen would have liked to pretend that was the answer and not have to face his growing feelings for her. This was about wanting to be near her. Angry, happy, sarcastic, frustrated with him—he would take whatever she'd give him because he liked every part of her.

"Damn right." She walked the rest of the way across the room until she stood right in front of him. She unzipped his soggy jacket and helped him out of it. Whipped it behind her in a smooth move and managed to snag it on the armrest of a chair. "And we are not having sex."

Jesus, when was that back on the table? "I get that."

He waited until she wrapped her arms around his neck before he touched her. Even then, he moved nice and slow, giving her plenty of time to slap him away, when he rested his hands on her waist. Above all else, he didn't want to ruin this.

"You can't fix everything with that dick of yours, impressive as it is."

Well, now. "Is it?"

She treated him to a satisfied sigh as she pulled him in closer. "Don't play coy. You know you have skills."

"But will you let me . . . ?" No, he should stop there. Take the win.

"What?"

"I'm not sure what the right word is."

She frowned at him for a second before breaking into a smile. "Yes, you do. You know the word. Say it."

"Fine." He winced but mostly to make her laugh because the idea of touching her, wrapping his body around her and holding her, sounded pretty damn good right now. "Cuddle."

Joy bounced off her. "Maybe."

"You're a hard woman, Tessa Jenkins." He trailed his hand up her back. "But soft in the best places."

"You're trying to seduce me."

He fell into wanting her so easily. "I will give you whatever you want. Space. A hug. Other things."

"Oh?" Her fingers slid into his hair. "Like?"

Every nerve ending sparked to life. Somehow, they pulled an evening that veered toward catastrophe back from the edge. Where it went from here totally depended on her. "Things that make you feel good."

"You are not allowed inside me right now. I'm serious." She softened the demand with a quick kiss.

"Got it."

"I'm not going to change my mind on that."

But that left so many other options for them to explore. "That's the right answer."

"I'm furious with you." She nibbled a line of kisses over his chin to that sensitive space just behind his ear.

Her warm breath blew over him. Those amazing lips traveled and ignited. He had to fight to gather enough breath to answer her. "I can see that."

"But you should beg me." She licked around his ear.

His need for her pummeled him. Ground down any doubts and softened every fear. "I can do that, if you'd prefer."

She pressed a finger to his lips. "But no talking."

Damn, woman. There was nothing sexier on this earth to him than a woman who knew what she wanted and asked for it.

"Ah." He kissed her fingertip. "*That* kind of begging for forgiveness."

"You're not off the hook." She pulled away from him but didn't break contact. Taking his hand, she guided him to the bed.

When she sprawled on her back with her arms over her head, he thought he'd lose it.

"Whatever you want," he choked out.

"Good man."

TESSA HOVERED ON the brink, ten seconds away from screaming his name. She didn't care who else in Berman's Lodge heard or if she scared an old couple or even if Ruthie still lurked around. Hansen's mouth and fingers were pure magic. He played her like a virtuoso with their finest instrument.

Her fingernails scraped against the headboard as she reached out to steady herself. Her body shook as he pumped his fingers in and out of her. Back and forth, tongue, then touch, over the small spot that made her shiver.

She let out a groan as he revved her up one more

time. Scissored his fingers inside her, making room for that incredible tongue. Time blurred and minutes ticked by, but she didn't notice. Her entire world focused on him and the heat surging through her body.

Just as her toes curled and her hands balled into fists, as the tightness building inside her finally threatened to let go, he pulled back again.

"No!" she protested.

"Tell me."

She grabbed for him. Lifted her head and shoulders off the bed. She was about to tug on his hair when a puff of air blew across her very center, making every muscle tremble.

She fell back into the pillows again. "You're killing me."

"This is how I beg."

Then he rubbed his thumb over that spot. The one that had her breath hiccupping in her chest.

He repeated the process—bringing her right to the edge only to cool her back down and start all over again. He performed the move so many times over the hour that sweat had broken out all over her naked body and her bones had turned to mush.

When he pulled away from her this time, leaving her hovering on the cusp of satisfaction, her thighs actually shook with need. She glanced down, saw him curled between the juncture of her legs. His dark hair right there. His lips wet from being on her and inside her.

"Please end it." She'd never wanted to come so much in her life.

"I'm not done asking for forgiveness yet." He slipped his finger inside her again. Just one, only a short distance. Enough to send her hips arching off the bed.

After all the touching, all the licking, her body was extra sensitive. The littlest thing made her shake and thrash around on the mattress. Much more of this and she'd have a heart attack.

She curled one of her legs until her heel pressed against his back and pulled him tight against her. Anything to bring him in closer and finish this. "I'm ordering you."

"Help me."

Yes, anything. She slid her hand over his head, loving the feel of his damp hair. A sign all this touching cost him something. She peeked at him as her finger skimmed over his mouth but her eyes slipped closed when he sucked on the tip.

"Hansen . . ."

"Show me." He held her hand and pulled it lower. Rested her fingers against her own body.

She didn't hold back. If he wanted a show or help—whatever—she'd do it. "Watch."

She drew her finger inside her. The mix of warmth and wetness hit her. One press and her insides clenched. Her legs tightened against him.

"Beautiful." He bent down and licked her again.

Her finger. His mouth. That's all it took.

Her other hand went to the back of his head and she lifted her hips. His finger joined hers. Slipped inside next to hers, touching off her orgasm. It raced through her. Had her stretching her toes as every muscle tightened. She held him there with her hands and legs.

Waves of pleasure crashed over her. Her head rolled back and forth on the pillow. With each lift of her hips, the tension eased out of her. Her legs fell to the bed as the pulsing continued inside her.

Her breathing echoed through the room. It took another few minutes before she could form a sentence. "You're good at begging."

"I'm here to please." His words slurred.

She felt him smile against her inner thigh and lifted her head. Stared down at him. He'd closed his eyes and his hand rested between her legs. He was also rock hard and seemed inclined to ignore it . . . all because she asked him to.

She traced a finger over his eyebrows, loving this view of him. All soft and open. "You know . . ."

His eyes stayed closed, but his smile didn't fade. "What?"

"I think we could both use a shower."

His eyes popped open. "Together?"

"But you'll need to be naked." She tried to sound sad, but the idea had those familiar butterflies swirling in her stomach.

"How naked?"

She gave his hair a playful tug. "What kind of question is that?"

He shifted until he could look up at her. "Just wondering."

"I thought maybe you could beg again."

He dropped his head and kissed where he just touched. Watched her the whole time with those sexy dark eyes. “Done.”

“But you’re going to have to be the one doing the chanting this time.”

His eyebrow lifted. “Oh?”

She sat up, forcing him to do the same. “Let’s see how long you can last when I’m the one doing the touching and tasting.”

“Not very long.”

“We’ll time you.”

CHAPTER 18

Two hours, one shower, and one blowjob later, they lay curled around each other on her bed at the lodge. Neither of them bothered to get dressed again. Hansen possessed only enough energy left to wrap his arm around her waist and tug her close.

When Tessa slipped her fingers through his and held their joined hands to her chest, he smiled. This close he could smell her hair and see the sexy line of her neck. So kissable that he gave in and planted a soft one right where her neck met her shoulder. Enjoyed the way she pushed her back tighter against his chest in reaction.

He let the skin-to-skin contact warm the backs of her chilled thighs as he spooned her. Spooning . . . another thing he hadn't taken the time to enjoy in so long. With her, even the simplest gestures felt right.

Exhaustion weighed down his muscles even though it really wasn't that late. Still, a question nagged him. It kept swimming to the front of his mind and he couldn't ignore it even though he worried it might disrupt their current calm state. "May I ask you something?"

She groaned. "You're one of those."

"I almost hate to ask what that means."

"Get a girl all satisfied and sleepy, then fire questions at her."

He scoffed. "Yeah, that sounds like me."

She lifted their hands and kissed the back of his. "I'm kidding. What is it?"

"When Ruthie talked about me being from a certain type of family . . ." He stopped because he saw her eyes pop open. Yeah, he had her attention now. Shame he didn't know where to go next with the sentence.

"You mean close?"

"You know what I'm referring to." A topic he didn't like to discuss but it hung between them. She'd made assumptions, some of them right, but he didn't want her to connect dots that were not there and decide he was *that* guy.

He'd been lucky. The universe handed him great parents, a brother he considered his closest friend, and the ability to never worry whether he could cover a check he wrote. He knew if he failed or needed help, an entire family of aunts, uncles, and cousins would step in to prop him back up again. He knew because they'd proved it already. Some friends and business colleagues stopped texting back after the protective order. His family had stuck by him. That was a blessing he did not take for granted.

"The fact you're well connected. Powerful. Can do whatever you want? Yeah, I figured that out." Her voice lacked its usual light note.

Sounded as if she'd given him and his background some thought and saw it as a hurdle, not a benefit. "You clearly have your strength back."

"Maybe I misinterpreted." She turned over on her back and looked up at him. "Do you struggle to pay the bills each month?"

"There's probably a range of economic states between the two you describe."

"Not when you're on the side that can't pay the electric bill."

She wasn't wrong. People could pretend being financially secure didn't matter, but those without it didn't have that luxury. "Just so you know, I don't think I can have whatever I want just because I want it."

She studied him. "You can be impossible, but you've never acted superior or flashed money around expecting it to buy you respect."

"I appreciate that." And he did, but . . . "We got off track. I'm guessing that was on purpose."

She pulled the sheet and blanket up until they covered her breasts. "You were about to ruin my good mood."

He could almost see her fold in on herself. Her expression hadn't changed but she'd mentally closed a door on him. The slam rang in his head. "Does talking about your family do that? Because I can stop."

She picked at the blanket and at his fingers, which lay on her stomach. A few moments passed with nothing more than the sound of raindrops pinging on the window before she said anything. "I'm not used to sharing."

The answer filled him with relief. Instead of totally

shutting down or drifting off to sleep, at least she offered an explanation. General, but still an answer. "You're not alone."

"No, I mean I was raised not to share. My job was to keep family secrets and not ask questions." She finally gave him eye contact. "You weren't wrong earlier."

What the hell? "Tessa?"

"I've given you a hard time. Called you a big freaking jerk."

That sounded new. "When?"

"Not to your face."

She turned until they lay inches apart, staring at each other. His hand rested on her hip and she brushed her fingers back and forth over his chest. The touch, so gentle.

"The point is I talk a lot, but I try very hard to hold back info about myself. That's on purpose. A trained response developed from years of practice." She exhaled. "And while I complained, internally and to your face, about you shutting me out, I was guilty of the same thing. It's a habit I can't seem to break."

He fluffed the pillows under his head and reached for her hand. Smoothed his thumb over her palm in what he hoped was a calming gesture, because her pained expression said this was not an easy subject for her. "Your parents wanted you to keep secrets?"

"Not my mom. She's great." A small smile came and went.

"Where is she?" Geography struck him as a safe topic, but who the hell knew.

"Back in central New York, where I'm from."

The little pieces of where she grew up came together to show him a bigger picture. The bigger piece about the silence and secrets didn't, but he forced himself to move slowly. He didn't want to spook her or stop the flow of information. He hadn't even realized how much he ached to hear any tiny morsel about who she was before Whitaker until she started talking.

"Is that where you lived before you came here?" he asked.

"I moved to Philadelphia for college and stayed there." Then she stopped talking. With one hand tucked in front of her and the other cradled in his, she lay there, focusing on a spot on his chin.

If she needed the conversation to end there, he would oblige. "And now you're here."

They'd been on this emotional roller coaster ever since she took him out to see the mysterious boat in the water. Not that many days had passed but they crawled by.

Silence filled the room. Not the uncomfortable kind. There was nothing awkward about cuddling close to her in the quiet. Curiosity poked at him, but he fought back the urge to prod. She needed to come to him when she was ready.

After a few minutes she rolled onto her back again, taking his hand with her. She cocooned his in both of hers. She tugged at his arm until he shimmied in closer and his chest brushed the side of her arm.

Once they shared a pillow she spoke again. "Ask."

"What?" But he heard her. He almost sprawled on top of her. Still, he'd let her set the boundaries and then he would obey them.

She rolled her eyes. "Oh, come on."

From anyone else the gesture would have been dismissive. From her, in that moment, it conveyed amusement. Maybe even her appreciation that he didn't push her faster than she could go. "Is it that weird that I want to know something about the woman I'm sleeping with?"

"Sleeping with."

He didn't know how to interpret that tone. Flat, almost mocking. So, he tried again. Used a word that felt foreign on his tongue but fit in an odd, wasn't-expecting-that sort of way. "My girlfriend."

"Is that what I am?" She visibly swallowed. "You said it to Kerrie, but I thought you were just—"

"You are the only one I'm dating. And, yes, before you ask, that word freaks me the fuck out. Not kidding."

A smile broke out on her lips. "Not just you."

A new sensation hit him. A part of him raw and hollowed out but behind that . . . hope. "You are the only one I've dated since my sister died. You are the only one I want to date. I can't think about any woman but you."

She kissed the back of his hand. "Okay, you're officially forgiven for being an ass earlier."

"There's not a greeting card for this moment." He leaned in and nuzzled her neck. "But there should be."

"About that." She winced as she stared at the ceiling.

He dreaded whatever she was going to say next.

"I'm sorry I stormed out. I should have stayed. Thrown things. Yelled at you."

He smiled because he couldn't help it. Not that she could see it since he'd tucked his face into the fragrant space between her shoulder and neck and peeked up at her. "That sounds like fun."

For a night that started with his temper exploding and her running away from him, it had taken a good turn. It would be days before the image of her kneeling on the bathroom rug and taking him in her mouth left his head. He could still feel her hands on him. The intensity of the need that slammed into him. The way she licked over his length.

"Unlike your dad, my father is a complete ass."

The images flashing through him, all sexy and all about her, screeched to a halt in his head the minute she delivered that line. He mentally doubled back and repeated the words she just said . . . and he had no idea what to do with them. "I'm a little disturbed that you call me that, too."

She scooted even tighter against him. Rested her head against his chest. "Oh, no. You're adorable, with and without the glasses. Charming and decent and generally a good guy except when you flip into grumpy-old-man mode."

He knew she'd never admit it, but he thought she liked the grumpy side of him because she was the one person who could drag him out of that mood. "I have no idea how to respond to that last part, so I'll let you continue without comment."

"My father . . . I should say my birth father because he's not the man who helped raise me. That honor went to Ray Jenkins."

"Your mom's husband?"

"No but they've lived together for more than fifteen years. I consider him my stepdad. He considers me his daughter." She picked her head up long enough to tuck her hair behind her, then rested on him again. "He's asked Mom to marry him several times over the years but she's not great with change."

Her hair tickled his arm, but he barely felt it. Everything inside him froze, waiting for the rest of the story to tumble out of her. "What would change?"

"Nothing, but the last time she loved a guy—my birth father—he screwed her over. Part of her is afraid and Ray accepts that."

Hansen couldn't imagine living like that. Marriage might just be a piece of paper to some, but growing up he'd seen it as this amazing gift that only a few attained. "He sounds like a good guy."

"The best. A sculptor who teaches art at the local high school. That's where they met. They both teach there."

"You love them, yet you are thousands of miles away from them in a corner of Washington state." That piece didn't fit. He sensed that everything would either click together with what he knew about her or shatter completely once he understood the *why.*

"And people think I'm relentless."

Overstepping. The one thing he didn't want to do with her. "You don't have to—"

"Charles Michaelson."

The name immediately registered. Hansen could see him. Around sixty and fit. The kind of guy who pretended to be self-deprecating as he planted positive stories in the press about his olden days in college sports and that one time he helped an elderly constituent across the street while the cameras were rolling. Always on television. A blowhard asshole and the exact opposite of genuine. "He's a senator."

"Uh-huh. Put the pieces together."

He didn't get . . . Oh, shit. Now he did. He pushed up higher on his elbow. The move had her shifting to look up at him. "The fire-and-brimstone, doesn't-believe-in-birth-control-because-people-should-just-not-have-sex-outside-of-marriage guy is your father?"

"Birth. Father." She enunciated each word. Slapped a good deal of derision behind each one. "That family-is-everything attitude only applies to the family he publicly recognizes, not to the woman he got pregnant on the side and the kid he abandoned and pretends doesn't exist."

Hansen fell back into the pillows as the weight of what she said hit him. Michaelson was awful. Like, the kind of guy his own party wanted to disavow but he had a huge he-will-save-us following.

"Shit."

She leaned over him. "Yes, he is that."

A memory clicked in Hansen's head. "He's in the middle of a scandal, or he was a few weeks ago. I'm not sure what's happening now."

"That's me."

"What?"

"I was in D.C. on a temporary assignment that required me to spend my days with a bunch of engineers." She treated him to a head shake and made a noise that sounded a lot like *ugh*.

"Don't shudder. That's what I am when I'm not playing island handyman."

"Anyway, I spent the weekdays in D.C. in an executive rental and went back home on the weekends. Did this for a month. He tracked me down because he's awful and thrives on being secretive and has always kept tabs on me and Mom to make sure we weren't going to the press or going near his family. All he cares about is maintaining the false front he puts on as a senator, and I threaten that."

"He deserves to be exposed."

"Well, I don't want my life ripped apart by the press or by his people as they do damage control. But I must have stayed in D.C. a bit too long for his comfort during the job. He showed up at my apartment one day and demanded to know what I was doing. Then he insisted I leave the city." She let out a long sigh. "Did I mention how shitty he is?"

"I'm starting to get a picture."

"Someone who hates him—someone other than me, likely someone who wants him out of the Senate—followed him, got a partial photo of me, and—"

"Wait, you're the one they say he's having an affair with?" Hansen tried to hold back a laugh but couldn't. Tessa didn't deserve to be caught up in this mess, but the stupid bastard did. "There's something immensely satisfying about him getting tangled up in his own lie."

"I half wished I'd set it up."

"I bet."

Her stomach balanced against his chest. She bent her leg and her ankle bobbed in the air as she shook her foot back and forth. "So, now he needs me to come forward and lie for him."

"Why would you?"

"I wouldn't but I guess he's used to having people scurry around and obey him because of who he is and how he can *make one call and change everything.* Yeah, that's what he said to me. Made these veiled threats about Mom's and Ray's jobs and how he could turn their lives upside down. He thinks he can sell a version of the story where my mom hid me from him and that he's the victim."

"Motherfucker."

"Exactly. As if I'd turn on my mom or lie for that guy."

The picture cleared in his mind. He could see every step. Imagine her trying to duck out of the limelight. Her father did that to her . . . or the guy who pretended to be her father when it was convenient for him.

Mostly, Hansen loved how all of the stress and tension that held her in its grip as she'd started talking had faded now. She shared with him and he knew how hard unloading family baggage could be.

He felt more secure filling in the blanks now. "So, you came here."

"Yes."

"To protect your mom and the life she's created."

"And to deny the good senator what he wants."

Nice try, but Hansen knew this was really about her mom. That's who Tessa was. She protected. "Can't he just investigate and track you down again?"

"Maybe, but I tried to make it a bit harder for him to do it by using Ray's last name and dealing in cash only. The senator is being questioned and hounded, so every day I'm here makes it harder for him to keep his fake persona together." She rested on his chest with her hands propped under her chin. "Honestly, I came here to buy time, but I fell in love with the place. He needs to fix his mess without me, and the pressure is on him now."

"You want him to step down."

"I want him to go back to forgetting I exist."

"That . . . Okay, I wasn't expecting any of that." Hansen didn't fight the smile. "You're pretty impressive. Playing chicken with a powerful senator. Damn, woman. You are fierce."

She shrugged. "Learned from the best. Mom struggled to keep us out of the public eye. He never paid child support, so everything fell to her."

Of course he didn't. "There is nothing redeeming about this guy."

"Not really, no. I can only hope my half brothers, the twins he had with his wife, take after her or, frankly, anyone but my father."

"You don't know them, I guess." A state Hansen couldn't imagine. He and Connor fought, but they were dead loyal to each other. Surviving losing Alexis without having Connor? Hansen's mind blanked at the idea.

"I doubt they know about me. That's the point. No one does. Mom kept quiet. She moved out of the D.C. area, got her teaching certificate. Homeschooled me for a time just to make sure my name didn't pop up on any records he might trace."

He flipped back and forth between being sad for all she and her mom had lived through and stunned by the lightness he saw in her eyes. That spark happened when she talked about her mom. Money may have been tight, and parts sounded very odd, but her loyalty to her mom never wavered. Hansen thought that was a testament to her goodness and to the resilience of children.

"Michaelson eventually did find you." Just thinking about the senator made Hansen want to fly back to D.C. and shake the man.

"We underestimated his desire to make sure we never used his name or spoke about him. He kept an eye on Mom from a distance the whole time, which Mom knew because she'd get a warning from him right around election time to stay quiet."

"Doesn't part of you want to go on television and out him?" Hansen had to beat back the instinct to rush in and try to fix this for her. She didn't need a savior. She needed him to listen, and he concentrated on doing just that.

Her leg waved behind her as she watched him. "I toyed with that. If I thought it would end the stalking, I might. But the reality is my life would blow up. And I'd mess up his wife's life and his kids'."

Leave it to her to put everyone else's needs in front of her own. "You're one of his kids."

"By biology only."

He threaded his fingers through her hair. Loved the silky feel of the strands as they draped over the back of his hand. "Charles Michaelson fucked up every way a person can fuck up, but missing out on knowing you was his greatest mistake."

She turned her head and kissed his palm. "Sweet-talker."

"But sincere."

"Okay, I take back what I said earlier." The playful tone moved back into her voice.

That fast, she morphed from serious to the Tessa he knew. So full of life. But he saw underneath her sunny smile now. Pain lurked there. A tiny bit of the lonely and abandoned girl she once was.

But she clearly wanted to move on from this conversation, put the serious moments behind her tonight, and he didn't try to pull her back in. "Which part?"

"You can get inside me."

Air sputtered inside him and he coughed. She never ceased to surprise him. "Such sexy talk, Ms. Jenkins."

She shot him a smile filled with the promise of a very exhausting next few hours. "It's a limited time offer."

He rolled them over, putting her beneath him. "I'll take it."

CHAPTER 19

Tessa and Hansen crowded into Ben's office the next morning. Beams of light peeked through the gray clouds and brightened the plain room. Ben had stacks of files and all sorts of clippings spread out on his desk. He'd tacked a few to the whiteboard that spanned half of one wall.

"We have the pieces." Ben pointed from his seat on the edge of his desk. "Like the Taylors' stolen clothes, which might be related."

"What sort of clothes?" She didn't know if it mattered, but she wanted to know.

Ben shuffled through the paperwork beside him. "Men's gray utility pants and a black long-sleeve T-shirt."

"Not helpful," Hansen said as he studied the board. "An outfit most people on the island own. And probably not relevant since Judson was found in the same suit Tessa saw him wearing on the beach. He didn't change."

Phones rang in the background. Not in Ben's office but out in reception. Tessa counted, expecting the noise to stop at two rings, but today it continued.

"No sign Judson was attacked for money or anything else. He still wore his expensive watch and had money in a clip in his pocket." Ben kept flipping through pages, putting them in an order only he understood.

Hansen glanced at Ben. "How much?"

Ben just smiled, or he did until the phone in the outer office rang for a fifth time. "I haven't released that information."

The rough topic didn't stop her mind from wandering. Last night, she'd told Hansen things she'd never told anyone. Things she only shared with her mother because they both lived it. Maybe not the specifics about the dragging loneliness at being trapped in the house while other kids played outside. Over time, her mother's restrictions eased, and Tessa went to school and made friends, but not at first. The confusion and the weight of all the secrets, most of which she didn't understand at that young age, took a toll.

She'd locked away most of those feelings—the insecurity, the loss, the pain of being unwanted—and pretended they didn't exist. Wiped her birth father out of her mind and her life and moved on. She shared them with Hansen because she ached for someone to help her carry the emotional load.

They both wrestled with things other people had done. Those things shaped both of them. Being able to confide in someone other than her mother, someone who didn't have a list of explanations and a few excuses for past choices, lifted a pressure Tessa hadn't even realized rested on her chest.

It was gone now. And Hansen was still here.

He hadn't panicked and bolted. Hadn't acted weird or tried to defend her father's actions. He'd listened and sided with her, unconditionally. Forget not wanting to get involved or be in a relationship or insisting what she felt for him amounted to nothing more than a crush. The last few days shifted everything.

Ben glanced up at the whiteboard. "Judson was stabbed somewhere other than on Tessa's front lawn and brought there. But there are no tire marks or drag marks and no blood nearby." He glanced at Tessa. "We've done three forensic sweeps of the area around your house and found nothing to explain how Judson got there."

Right. The case. She forced her mind off the man standing across the room who blew through her control and had her chanting his name last night. There would be time for that later.

When she focused again, the photos and slips of paper Ben had collected, the heaviness of the information spread out around her, hit hard. From everything Hansen said, Judson was a terrible man. But he'd had a life and people who cared about him. Clients and a wife. Tessa assumed family. Judson deserved to be in prison, but the rest of this mysterious mess turned him into a victim. She hated that circumstances meant she should feel sorry for him when she couldn't.

She lifted her head and saw Hansen. He watched

her. His expression managed to be both knowing and soothing. Not a smile but a look that told her he understood the thoughts running through her head.

"It also rained that night, so we don't know how much evidence we lost," Hansen said.

"And someone pounded on my door." She'd forgotten to highlight that earlier. She'd been terrified that night, convinced someone wanted to break in, but now it amounted to one horrible piece of a big horrible puzzle.

Ben's eyes narrowed. "I thought you blamed the storm or—"

"It was a person." She refused to let that fact get lost. It might, or it could be unrelated. She didn't want to prejudge.

"Not Judson." Ben shook his head. "The waterlogged state of the body messed with the temperature, but Lela thinks he was killed within an hour or so of you two seeing him on the beach. That explains why he didn't come find me and set off his grand plan against Hansen. It also means he was not the one knocking at your door."

"Exactly," Hansen said.

"And that's all we have." Ben stood up and walked around the back of his desk with a hand resting on his chair.

"Plus, Cliff's insistence he heard a fight." Hansen took out a pen and wrote that on a notecard.

"Was that even the right night?" she asked.

"It was the night Judson showed up on the island."

One more round of musical files and Ben had a new one on top. "And then we have Arianna and Ellis."

After a quick glance at the board Hansen looked at Ben again. "How are they related to this?"

"They're so weird I want them to be guilty of something," Tessa said. "And they're way too interested in this case." She tried not to be *that* person, but there was something off about the couple. They were too nosy. Too quick to pop up where they shouldn't be. Too fake.

Ben held up a hand. "Some might—and don't get upset here—but there are those who would say the same thing about you."

"All that hedging didn't help you sound nicer."

Ben smiled at her but kept talking as if she hadn't dropped that. "But I do need to take a deeper look since I'm having trouble tracing their background."

"Meaning?"

"They don't have a paper trail."

From Ben's smile she guessed she'd accidentally proved his point about her being nosy as well. "The dead guy was on my lawn and my boyfriend is the lead suspect. Anyone in my place would ask questions."

A groan started on Hansen's side of the room.

Ben's grin grew. "When did you hit boyfriend-girlfriend status?"

This was Hansen's fault. He used the word last night. It rolled around in her head now. It was only logical she'd latch on to it. "Is that what we should be focusing on?"

Ben snorted. "Definitely."

"Excuse me."

They all jumped at the sound of Kerrie's soft voice. She'd tiptoed in or something because she hadn't made any noise. Tessa even stood facing the door and hadn't seen Kerrie come in. "When did you—?"

"Sorry for stopping by. I tried to call first but the phone just rang and then the answering machine picked up." Kerrie slipped into the room and stopped right next to Hansen. Her gaze went to the whiteboard, then back to him. Without any warning, she wrapped her arms around his waist and gave him a squeeze. It happened so fast, but she didn't move away from him. She leaned into him with a hand on his forearm. "It's so good to see you."

"Uh, okay." Hansen stood frozen with his arm in the air and that notecard he wrote still dangling from his fingertips.

Ben shifted around his desk and pushed the board just enough that Kerrie didn't face it head-on. The small office space didn't allow for more. "Did Lela release you?"

"She said later today and that was good enough for me, so I left." Kerrie glanced into the outer office when the phone started ringing again, then back to Ben. "Now that the rain is slowing down and the phones work, I need to make arrangements."

Tessa noticed Kerrie still touched Hansen. That seemed to be a thing with her. She also noticed Kerrie. Styled blond hair fell in waves to her shoulders. Those big blue eyes. Petite and beautiful in a way where it was hard not to stare at her. Flawless skin. Trim and compact in her slim dark jeans and dark purple V-neck tee. Perfect without looking as if she put any effort into it. Tessa had no idea where Kerrie had found clothes while in the hospital and felt a little guilty for not offering to collect some for her.

She also wore lipstick. Tessa tried to remember if she'd even brought a tube to Whitaker. "Is there anyone we can call for you?"

"My brother is on his way."

Hansen tapped the notecard against his palm. "To Whitaker?"

"There are details about releasing the body and the boat that I'd rather he handle for me." Kerrie visibly shuddered.

"No to both. The investigation is ongoing," Ben said.

"Hello." Doug rushed to the doorway, then slammed to a halt when he saw all the people. "Oh."

"Doug?" Now this was interesting. Tessa still wanted to lecture the kid, but even she could admit this was not the time.

"Tes . . ." He blushed and glanced at his feet. "Ms. Jenkins."

For a second he looked younger. Vulnerable and uncomfortable. Teen anxiety she knew all too well. "Why are you here?"

Doug looked at Ben, who nodded, before answering her. "I'm working here. You know, for credit."

Ben frowned. "You're not supposed to start this week."

"I thought you might need help." Doug looked around

as he drew out what sounded like a long *ahhhhhh.* "I could get the phones or photocopy stuff."

Exactly the topic Tessa wanted to mention. "Speaking of that, what's going on with Maddie? The phone keeps ringing."

Ben shook his head. "I have no idea. She's always been dependable but she's missing most of the calls right now."

"She usually answers on the second ring." The fact she wasn't today pricked at Tessa's curiosity. She had never seen Maddie. Several times Tessa had arrived somewhere—the lodge or the market—and been told she'd just missed meeting the other woman.

"Not today." Ben nodded in Doug's direction. "Since you're here, can you pick up and take messages? Check the messages already left as well."

"Sure." Doug looked around the crowded office. "I'll handle that out in reception."

Tessa waited until he disappeared and then she whispered, "You forgot to tell me you were making him work here."

"Seemed like a good solution." Ben shot her an I-told-you-so look. "I'm not totally useless as the law enforcement on the island."

Yeah, she'd figured that out. "We'll see."

Kerrie shifted until she stood in front of Hansen, half shielding him from the rest of the room, as if they were having a private conversation. "I was hoping we could have coffee and discuss how I can help undo some of Judson's damage."

Okay, no. That struck Tessa as a bad idea. It was just common sense for Hansen not to be alone with the woman who had a protective order against him. And then there was the other problem. Tessa couldn't kick the sensation that something was off with Kerrie. She chalked the uneasy feeling up to the role Kerrie played in making Hansen's life difficult in the past. Fair or not, the whole situation had Tessa on edge.

"You need to talk with me about your husband," Ben said, not even trying to lower his voice.

By the time Kerrie turned around again she wore a sweet smile. "Hansen and I share a bond on this issue. I'd feel more comfortable with him."

"You should rest. You've only been out of the clinic for a few hours." Hansen answered her but shot Tessa a help-me, wide-eyed stare.

The poor guy held his body stiff, not touching the woman who had jammed her body next to his. Tessa felt a spark of compassion for all of it—for Hansen for being stuck and for Kerrie for all she'd been through and her misfire in attaching herself to Hansen. "He's right. This is the time for napping."

"I'm going stir-crazy." Kerrie's voice sounded strained as her hands dropped to her sides. "Does the sun ever shine here? Not just for five seconds at a time like today, but all day?"

Hansen shook his head. "No."

"Two or three times per year," Ben said at the same time.

Tessa took pity on Kerrie and walked over to her.

"They're not exaggerating as much as you want them to be. Where are you staying?"

"I . . . uh." It was as if the thought had only just occurred to her. Kerrie glanced around, looking as lost as she had back at the hospital. "Have no idea. I thought the boat, but . . ."

"No."

Tessa didn't find Ben's curt response all that helpful, so she took over. "Let me take you to Berman's Lodge and we'll get you a room."

"It's getting crowded there," Hansen mumbled under his voice.

Yeah, she got it. He wanted them to go back to his place. So did she, but she had to get Kerrie settled first.

"I can go back home when my brother comes." Kerrie didn't ask. It was clear she had a plan.

Tessa appreciated the way the other woman fought to take back some control, but she wanted Kerrie to be realistic. "He's not here yet. The storms might delay him another day."

Kerrie just nodded. Tessa took that as a sign it was time to go. She guided Kerrie into the reception area but not before shooting Hansen an eye roll. "I'll text you."

THE WOMEN WERE barely out of the main door and on the street before Doug shot back up from his seat at the reception desk. He hovered right in the doorway as he looked at Ben. "Should I go with them?"

Hansen had planned on ignoring the kid, but not now. "Excuse me?"

"Ms. Jenkins shouldn't be alone."

The waver in his voice. The way he kept turning around and watching Tessa leave. Hansen was starting to get Doug's issue now. "You mean both women."

He made a not-really face. "Sure."

"They're fine." Hansen knew his tone came out sharper than intended when Ben frowned at him.

"You're watching over the one who just showed up." Doug shook his head. "I'm not talking about her."

He sounded . . . judging. Yeah, because that wasn't annoying. "Kerrie? Her husband died."

"I know, but I mean, maybe someone should watch Ms. Jenkins. Since you're busy and all."

Before Hansen could respond, Ben jumped in. "For now, I need you to answer the phones and keep an eye out. I don't want you investigating, but if you see anything out of place, let me know so I can check it out." Ben nodded toward the reception area. "Not right now though. I need you on phones. Use the conference room."

Doug's shoulders fell and Hansen had his answer. The kid had a crush. For the first time Hansen felt bad for him. They'd all been there. Teen love came with a knock-you-on-your-ass feel. Everything seemed larger than life and impossible.

Still, Hansen wanted to be clear on one point. He didn't play with Tessa's safety. "And I'll take care of watching over Tessa. To the extent she'll let me."

"I thought . . ." Doug started and stopped the sentence twice before abandoning it. "Never mind."

Hansen watched Doug go. Made sure he walked

into the conference room before moving across the desk from Ben and lowering his voice. "Is it just me or does the kid have a crush on Tessa?"

Ben smiled. "Yeah, I think we know why he made the stupid move in the parking lot. His friends likely found out and he was trying to impress them and touch her."

"Still not okay."

"Nope and I'll talk with him about that." Ben inhaled a long, dramatic breath. "Then there's the other crush."

Hansen didn't even pretend not to understand. "*Boyfriend* is just a word."

Ben chuckled. "Oh, we'll get back to that interesting bit. I meant Kerrie."

Damn it. "What are you talking about?"

"You really don't see it?" Ben leaned against the side of his chair, looking far too comfortable with the subject matter. "She hangs on you. Drops hints. Wants to meet for coffee."

Hansen knew because it freaked him the fuck out. She'd cried about him in front of a judge. Now this.

He taped the notecard he still held in his hand to the board. "Her husband is dead and she needs support."

"She might be looking for someone to rescue her, and you did try that once, so her perception could be off about what role you're playing for her now. Be careful."

Hansen did not want any part of this. He'd tried to save her from Judson for her own sake, not because he wanted her. "She's in mourning."

"She was married to an abusive jackass who probably killed your sister."

Wrong word. "Did kill."

"The point being her main emotion right now might be relief, not sadness." Ben pulled out his chair and sat down. "Now, about Tessa and the boyfriend thing."

"You should go check on Maddie."

Ben rolled his eyes. "Subtle."

"I never claimed to be." But Hansen wasn't wrong about Maddie. She didn't fall down on the job. The fact she was now meant something was wrong.

"The only thing that's saving you from a conversation that would make me laugh and you squirm is that I actually do need to see Maddie. I texted and said I'd be there in . . ." Ben glanced at his watch. "Oh, shit. Five minutes from now. Damn it. Where did the morning go?"

"Want me to tag along?"

Ben shot him a quick look as he grabbed for his keys. "I can't have you playing amateur detective on this case. Not until you're officially cleared."

Hansen knew Ben had been working every second since they'd found Judson's body. Checking the island and interviewing witnesses and anyone with potential information. But the whiteboard was right there. Hell, Hansen had helped to fill it. "Aren't we too late for that?"

"Yes, but I can pretend to follow the rules." Ben slipped his wallet into his back pocket and slammed and locked his top desk drawer.

"Interesting."

"And the answer is no."

Hansen must have missed the question. "What?"

"No talking to Arianna and Ellis. Stay away from Cliff. Don't even look at Ruthie."

Oh, that question. Hansen absolutely intended to ask around. There were things people might say to him that they'd hold back from Ben because he was an official. Residents took the we're-private-here unofficial motto of Whitaker seriously. "Sure."

"Why don't I think you're listening to me?"

Hansen winked. "I'll let you know what Cliff says."

CHAPTER 20

When Hansen called to see if she wanted to come with him to "visit" Cliff, Tessa jumped at the chance. She'd been hoping to talk to Cliff. She also needed some space from Kerrie.

That part made her feel like a shitty person. The other woman had been through so much and deserved patience and understanding. Tessa could handle all of that. The problem came from Kerrie talking nonstop about how decent Hansen was and how he deserved better. Tessa wanted to keep her feelings for Hansen, which were still in the blurry stage, separate from Kerrie's newfound adoration of him.

Tessa understood Kerrie's obsession, mostly because Sylvia explained it to her. Kerrie needed a lifeline and she'd grabbed on to Hansen. That all made sense and Tessa would make room and keep her mouth shut if Hansen wanted to be a support for Kerrie, but Tessa was pretty sure he didn't. He looked ready to jump out of his skin whenever Kerrie showed up. Tessa couldn't blame him since one of the court orders that had sent him traveling across the country away from his family stemmed from a run-in with her.

Fake or not, imposed by Judson or not, Hansen needed to exercise a bit of self-protection in case someone other than Kerrie wanted to enforce the order. Or if he continued to be the number one suspect in Judson's murder. Ben might not think Hansen did the deed, but sooner or later, and likely sooner now that the storm had moved out, investigators would work through any jurisdictional wrangling and arrive on Whitaker, ready to solve the case.

"Ben thinks Kerrie has—"

"A crush on you." So much for not thinking about Kerrie for a few minutes. Tessa held in the eye roll but just barely. "Definitely."

Hansen stopped on the uneven pebbles leading in a path along the side of the house to Cliff's front door. "She's grieving."

She was. All true. That wasn't really Tessa's point. "She praised you during the entire ride to the lodge. We're sleeping together, and I don't say such nice things about you."

"Dating."

Oops. "Hmm?"

This time he sighed at her. Didn't even pretend not to be annoyed. "We're dating."

Tessa bit back a wince. "I'm not really used to the word yet."

"Join the club. But I would point out Kerrie also told a judge I scared the shit out of her because I went up to her and . . ." His words trailed off as he slicked his hand through his hair. "Forget it. I screwed up. It doesn't matter that I was trying to help. I should have left her alone and didn't."

"You thought you were protecting her." Tessa didn't doubt that at all. Now, neither did Kerrie. Ruthie seemed to be the only one in town holding on to the idea of Hansen's guilt.

"And I was wrong. Going to her might have made things worse for her with Judson."

All the grumbling in Tessa's head had blocked out the problem right in front of her. If she thought Hansen were violent or dangerous or engaged in harassing behavior, she would have been the first one protesting outside of his cabin. But Judson set Hansen up. Killed his sister, and when Hansen got too close or made things too uncomfortable, Judson unleashed, using his wife as a weapon. He'd put her in a terrible position. Abused her. Used her.

Judson was a terrible man and Tessa just couldn't figure out a way to mourn him, but she understood why Kerrie would. They built a life together. Judson, not Kerrie, had ripped it down. Hansen hadn't done anything other than get lost in his grief.

"Judson insisted she get the order to get back at you. She's said that more than once." Outside of the abuse and the orders, there was one other thing Tessa tried to make sense of in her head and couldn't. Maybe Hansen had an explanation. "Speaking of Kerrie."

Hansen's head dropped back and he looked up at the

clouds racing by on the wind. "I'd be fine if we talked about something else."

"I helped check her in and went to have a cup of coffee and a bit of girl chat with Sylvia."

He lowered his head again and looked at her with a guarded expression. "Not sure if that should scare me or not."

"You were discussed. Get over it." Only men thought women didn't talk about sex when they got together. "But when I passed through the lobby on my way back out to meet you, I saw Kerrie in the dining room."

"Okay."

"Sitting with Ruthie."

For a few seconds Hansen stared at her with his mouth open. She took pity on him and hooked a hand under his elbow and guided him on toward Cliff's front porch.

Finally, Hansen shook his head. "That's the kind of news that makes a grown man shiver. And not in the sexy, very welcome way."

"How would they even know each other?"

"Ruthie probably sat down, introduced herself, and is right now trying to convince Kerrie I killed her husband."

That was the conclusion Tessa had reached as well. She had to give Ruthie points for consistency. "That does sound like her."

They came around the end of the porch and froze. Ellis and Arianna stood there on either side of Cliff's empty porch swing.

Ellis was the first to move. He came down the steps with his hand out, greeting them. "Hello."

"The weather is finally clearing." Arianna's smile didn't reach her eyes.

Tessa dropped her fingers from Hansen's arm. She didn't know what to do except stand there and soak in the surprise visitors. "And you thought this was the perfect time to say hello to Cliff?"

Arianna folded her arms across her chest. "We wanted to check on him."

Hansen's eyebrow lifted. "Do you even know him?"

"I thought I heard voices." The screen door smacked against the jamb as Cliff stepped onto the porch. He wore a heavy flannel shirt and brown pants. Still had his bedroom slippers on as he sipped on a steaming cup of what Tessa assumed was coffee. Although, with Ellis and Arianna hanging around, they might all need something stronger.

"Hey, Cliff." Hansen touched his hand against Tessa's lower back. "Do you know—"

"Tessa." Cliff nodded before taking a long sip. "The one you're sleeping with."

"The gossip on this island can outrun a violent storm," Hansen said.

"Nah, no big deal. People talk." Cliff shooed Arianna out of his way, then sat down on his porch swing. "Besides, we've been making bets on whether Hansen would stick around on the island if he found some young thing."

"Young thing?" Tessa decided to be flattered.

Cliff glared at Ellis and Arianna over the rim of his mug. "Are you two done here?"

"It was nice to see you." Ellis gestured for Arianna to come off the porch and turned back to Hansen and Tessa. "And you two as well."

Arianna flashed them a smile. "We should have dinner one night."

"Nope." Hansen added a what-the-fuck expression to make his position on that idea clear.

Even though neither Ellis nor Arianna looked offended, Tessa rushed to clean up Hansen's response a little bit. "Once things calm down."

She could feel Hansen glaring at her as she watched the couple leave. When she turned back around, his expression hadn't changed.

"Are you serious?" he asked.

Now was not the right time for this but easing up on the grumpy attitude would not kill him. "I was trying not to be rude," she insisted.

"Hansen's right. They deserve to be run off. Nosy jackals." Cliff practically shouted the last part.

Tessa ignored the male-bonding moment. "That's some impressive name-calling."

Not waiting for an invitation that Tessa assumed would never come, she and Hansen walked up the steps and joined Cliff on the porch. He sat in the middle of the swing, which struck Tessa as one of the most impressive turf-defending, don't-even-think-about-sitting-here gestures she'd ever seen.

Hansen leaned against the railing and she stood

next to him. If Cliff started yelling about that choice, they'd move somewhere else. He ran this show.

"They've been around twice. Yesterday, in the middle of all that rain, and I pretended not to be home." Cliff used his foot to keep the swing moving. "Even saw the lady peek in my front window."

Now that was interesting. A little bold even for them and not very covert. Tessa immediately wondered if they had a secret relationship with Judson and why they'd be so obvious about it. "What did they want?"

Cliff shrugged his thin shoulders. "Same thing you do, I'd guess. Information on the fight I overheard."

"They specifically asked about that?" Hansen asked.

"Who knows? I wasn't listening because they talk over each other." Cliff swore under his breath. "The man never shuts up."

That sounded pretty accurate to Tessa. "Ellis."

"What?"

Hansen shifted his weight around. Scanned the area but hid it pretty well. "That's his name."

"I don't care." Cliff used his mug to point at the railing behind them. "Stand there and ask your questions. I've already talked but I can do it some more."

His head bobbed as he blew on his coffee. She could smell the delicious aroma. Not that he offered them any, but if he had she would have been stunned.

"Could you identify the voices?" Hansen asked.

"Nah. They were over by the treeline." Cliff pointed to the far right of the house. "It started as mumbling. I could only make out a man's voice. Little else."

Tessa looked over the property. Cliff had an amazing hundred-eighty-degree view of the water about fifty feet below. His two-story farmhouse sat up high enough to clear the trees on the incline in front of the house that would otherwise block his view.

She couldn't see Throwaway Beach or the marina from here. But she'd been cursed with a challenged sense of direction and a total inability to read maps. Directions made her brain go blank. But the area did look familiar, as if she'd been on the beach around here.

"I'm trying to get my bearings. What's over there?" She pointed to the treeline he referenced, wondering if the marina and downtown lay that way.

"The hill down to the lot people park in to walk that trail to the beach."

That was not exactly helpful. "Wait, which trail?"

"Not Throwaway Beach." Hansen shook his head. "Pioneer. Where kids fish."

"Stupid kids."

Sounded like Cliff was two seconds away from saying *get off my lawn*. His mop of white hair and the way he had his shirt buttoned all the way up to his neck, almost choking him, fit with his grumbling attitude.

Reminded her of another guy she knew.

"The Ridgewells and the Taylors live just up the hill from the lot. They're my closest neighbors on that side, but a shock of trees separates us." Cliff returned to sipping on his coffee.

Tessa's brain started spinning with possibilities. "The Taylors?"

He scowled at her. "That's what I said."

"Could you make out any words?" Hansen asked.

"When?"

She assumed he was being purposely ornery now. Hansen must have thought so, too, because he shot Cliff a look that said *come on*. "In the argument you overheard."

"He sounded pissed . . ." Cliff pressed the back of his hand to his mouth and peeked over at her. "Oh, sorry."

"I've heard worse." She'd thought worse when they turned the corner to find Ellis and Arianna on the porch.

"Dating Hansen, I'd guess you would." Cliff saluted her with his mug.

She had to admit that was cute. "Who told you about that?"

"The dating? Saw it in the paper."

Hansen's eyes bulged. "What?"

The laughing started a second later. Cliff had managed to crack himself up and send Hansen into an emotional spiral with just a few words. "Calm down. That was a joke. The kid that delivers my groceries said it. That weird couple that just left mentioned it. And I have friends."

That was a lot of people. Tessa almost broke into a coughing fit. She struggled to come up with a question instead. "Was anyone with you the night of the argument?"

"Some things are private, young lady."

Hansen rolled his eyes. "So, that's a yes?"

"No, but I'm tired of all these new people moving in and being nosy." His stare moved from Hansen to Tessa. "Walking across my land like they think I don't see them."

She was about to point out how Whitaker needed a bit of new blood when Cliff dropped that bombshell. She glanced at Hansen and he glanced back.

He took the lead on the question. "You mean Arianna and Ellis?"

"What?"

This conversation made her smile. Cliff not wanting to answer. Hansen being annoyed at having to ask the questions more than once. She stayed in the middle, keeping them from trying to out-grumpy each other. She got a flash of an older Hansen, sitting on his porch, watching every move, and being annoyed twenty-four hours a day. She should have hated it, but no.

Instead of dwelling on that, she flipped back to questioning mode. "Who was walking across your land? Maybe Ellis and Arianna?"

Cliff snorted. "I would have heard their voices since they never shut up."

She couldn't argue with that.

"When?" Hansen asked.

"A few nights ago. Saw a shadow and heard a crash when they ran into the trash cans."

Hansen stood up and went over to look around the side of the house. "The cans by the back door?"

Cliff's scowl deepened. "Where else would I keep the cans?"

Hansen looked ready to snap, so she took over. "I think he was pointing out that the person, whoever it was, got close to your back door."

"I'm neighborly." Cliff muttered something into his mug that she couldn't hear. "They just needed to ask first."

Sure, *neighborly*. That was the word she'd use to describe Cliff.

"Did you tell Ben?" Hansen asked.

"He knows he's welcome here."

Hansen made a strangled noise. "No, I mean—"

The chuckling cut off the question. Cliff laughed for a good minute before responding this time. "You're easy to rile. And I know what you meant. No, there was no need for the police. We handle our own."

She really needed him to explain that. "Meaning?"

"If someone around here did some killing, there was a reason."

Hansen shook his head. "That's not—"

"I understand." Cliff winked but had to use both eyes to do it. "Whatever you did to the unwanted stranger with the boat is fine with me, just be less sloppy next time."

WHEN HANSEN OPENED the front door to his cabin a few hours later, a familiar scent hit Tessa. The mix of shampoo and soap. Clean and inviting, it drew her in. She'd missed it on her one night away in the lodge, though she did have the live version with her.

After all the chaos of the day, she wanted to fall

into bed and sleep for a week. She blamed everyone on Whitaker for that. Talking to Cliff exhausted her. He switched directions every few seconds and delivered half answers. Kerrie, whom Tessa didn't quite understand, was only a bit better. Then there were Ellis and Arianna, who were mysterious in the most irritating way.

At least she'd realized one interesting bit of geographical information. Tessa decided to highlight it even though she knew Hansen had picked up on it. "The short distance between Cliff's house and the Taylors might mean something."

She walked the whole way to the kitchen area before she realized she didn't hear footsteps thumping behind her. When she turned around, she saw Hansen standing by the ladder to the loft, his expression unreadable.

"Could we, maybe, for the next hour not talk about murder or Judson or try to dissect anything Cliff said?"

His tone gave him away. Not tired or angry but definitely on edge. All rough and grumbly. Ready for something other than investigating.

She drank him in, letting her gaze travel over him. Took in those broad shoulders and the formfitting zip-up pullover that hid a flat stomach outlined with the sexiest muscles she'd ever seen. It was like he lifted houses for exercise rather than worked in them.

Her breathing grew uneven just from watching him. She inhaled, forcing her body to stay calm. Asked a question she hoped she already knew the answer to. "Tell me what you'd rather do."

He didn't even move. His hands stayed balled into fists at his sides. "Get both of us naked and into bed."

"That's a pretty clear response." She moved out of the kitchen and toward him. "I have one teeny adjustment to your plan."

"Whatever it is, the answer is yes."

"This wall." She leaned back against it. Ran her open hand over it in a slow motion that had his gaze snapping from her fingers, then back to her face. "We'll get to the bed later, but I was thinking we should see how sturdy your wall is first."

"Yes."

So eager to please. "Try it fast, hot, dirty, and . . ."

He visibly swallowed. "And?"

"Now."

He slipped his fingers into his back pocket and lifted out a condom. "I'm prepared."

She loved that he'd carried it around all day. She was half surprised he wasn't already wearing it. "That's why we're dating."

The corner of his mouth kicked up in a smile. "You said the word easier this time."

"You should stop talking and get over here."

He moved in a blur. One minute he stood by the loft, looking all hot and ready. The next he had his palms slammed against the wall on either side of her head and his body pressing against hers.

"Take off your shirt." He stared at her as he delivered the order.

His voice scraped across her senses. She felt the thin

vibration unspool all the way through her. Her need for him spurred her on as she fumbled with the buttons. She looked down, but she could feel the heat of his stare on her hands. With each one she unfastened, his breathing kicked up. His chest moved up and down on rough intakes. She heard the soft gasps as they escaped his throat.

So very eager. She slowed down, wanting to draw this out. Ratchet up the tension a bit more before diving in.

He did not let her win this round.

He wrapped his arm around her waist until she went up on tiptoes, then he pulled her off the ground. She grabbed on to his shoulders for balance, letting her shirt gape open. One lift and her body balanced between the wall and his hips. Her legs curled around him, one near his waist and the other slid down the back of his muscled thigh.

She'd dreamed about this. Being covered by him. Letting loose and letting go. Seeing the swirl of emotions he kept banked behind that sturdy wall of control.

Heat pounded between them. She heard a buzzing in her head and chalked it up to need. His lips caressing hers. His tongue tickling the roof of her mouth. A kiss that sent her stomach tumbling.

She couldn't move her hands fast enough. She ran her palms over his chest, grabbing handfuls of fabric and tugging until he gave in and helped her pull the top over his head. Next, his jeans. He'd skipped the belt and she almost missed it. Something about yanking it open and hearing the buckle clank as her fingers worked on him turned her on. She settled for the button. Flicked it open and pushed her hand inside. He was already hard and waiting.

His breath blew across her ear and echoed through her. His lips trailed to her neck while his hand yanked at her pants. He had them open and shoved down before she could catch her breath.

She gave as much as she received. No way would he be the only one granting pleasure tonight. Her hand slipped up and down his length. His traveled between her thighs. The touching took off in a frenzy of need and motion. Neither of them careful. There was nothing slow and sweet about this. Need burned through them. It wound around them.

His finger plunged inside her and both of them moaned. She had no idea where he put the condom or how she folded his briefs down. He was in her hand, pulsing and warm. So hard as he bucked his hips against hers.

"Hansen. Now." She spit out the words, begging him to go even faster. To get inside her and cool the frenzy he had touched off.

Her back knocked against the wall and she heard something fall. A crash off to the left that she ignored as he pressed a second finger inside her, readying her. She grew wet and impatient. Snaked her free hand between them to hold his hand tight against her. Pushed him tighter in the space she'd made for him between her legs.

Mini waves of pleasure crashed through her. A somersaulting in her stomach that made her light-headed. She heard crinkling. He shifted his weight, balancing her legs higher on his waist. His hand left her, leaving her achy and wanting more. She groaned to get him to come back. Then she felt his tip. He ran it over her, back and forth, teasing her.

"Now, Hansen." She shouted this time. Her mind fuzzy and her control gone.

He pressed inside her, slow and without stopping. Filled her. Her body betrayed her then, turning itself over to him as her head fell back. It thudded against the wall. With each thrust, she slid against the surface. He set the pace. Her body moved with his. Up and down, riding him and depending on the combination of his weight and the wall to keep her upright.

She turned boneless as she clenched her tiny muscles against him. The move made him freeze, just for a second.

"Fuck, yes." He brushed his mouth over her cheek. "Do it again."

When she didn't move, because she couldn't, he slipped a hand between them. Touched that spot that made her breath leave her lungs. She came as she whispered his name. The pulses continued as he pumped inside her, not granting her any respite. The tightness inside her let go and the spinning in her head started. She felt relaxed and free. Her body, so sensitive, still jerked at his touch. The way he pumped into her milked the last of her need.

One of her legs slid down the outside of his. She reached around and grabbed on to his ass. Pushed him tighter against her as his body began to buck. She rode the wave with him. Enjoyed every push and pull as his orgasm hit.

After a few minutes their bodies stopped moving. The sound of their heavy breathing still floated in the air. She would have slid to the floor, but he held her up, stayed inside her.

He rested his forehead on her bare shoulder. Kissed the spot where his mouth could reach. It took another few minutes for him to relax against her. The steady crush of his weight anchored her.

"You get to decide where we do this from now on."

"Smart." She smiled as she kissed the spot above his ear. His damp hair tickled her nose. "It's about time you ceded control of your body to me."

He lifted his head then. "You can have any part of me you want."

She searched for amusement in his voice but didn't hear any. "I like being your girlfriend."

"Good." He managed a half smile but looked exhausted doing it.

"And now I want to be your girlfriend upstairs."

CHAPTER 21

The banging on the door started around one in the morning. Hansen turned over in bed, bringing Tessa with him. They'd just fallen asleep after a quick shower. She'd wrung every ounce of energy out of him and all he wanted was quiet and a few hours for his muscles to recharge.

Thump. Thump.

"What is that noise?" She shot up and the blanket fell down to her waist, revealing those amazing breasts he'd spent a good half hour worshipping with his tongue earlier. She pushed the hair out of her eyes and flicked on a light.

"It's the sound of someone who wants me to punch them."

She sat in the middle of the bed, naked with her legs curled under her. "The last time there was knocking, it was at my house and . . ."

That woke him up. "Get some clothes on."

Adrenaline flowed through him as he threw the covers off and bounced out of bed. He jumped up and down on one foot as he struggled to pull on a pair of sweatpants in his exhausted state. Looked around for shoes and socks but gave up, opting for his worn Princeton T-shirt instead.

When he started down the ladder, she scrambled to the side of the bed closest to him. "Please be careful."

He wanted to kiss her again, but they were too far apart. "Find something to wear just in case it's Ben."

"Ben would have called."

Hansen ignored that truth as he climbed down. Being as quiet as possible, he walked across the floor. The only light downstairs came from a soft one over the stove and the reflection from the one on the front porch.

He didn't have a peephole. The guy who lived here before him believed even less in guests than Hansen did. But he looked out the narrow strip of glass next to the door, not sure what to expect.

Not her.

"Kerrie?" He reached for the lock.

"Are you serious?" Tessa's voice sounded right behind him.

He did a quick check. She wore one of his shirts and a pair of boxers. He had no idea where she found them, but he gave her a nod before opening the door.

Kerrie stood under the light wearing what looked like lounge clothes of some sort. They hung on her and she kept picking at the sleeve where it fell down her shoulder and tugging at the waistband of her pants. The clear dark night enveloped everything around her. "Hi."

Not the greeting he expected either. "Are you okay?"

"I thought you'd be alone."

Tessa made a strange noise as she grabbed on to the back of his shirt and leaned over his shoulder. "Why would you think that?"

Kerrie blinked a few times before focusing on Tessa. "You have a room at the lodge."

"So do you." Not to state the obvious, but Hansen thought it sounded like the right call here. Especially since Tessa wound his shirt tighter in her fists. Seemed like she hated company even more than he did tonight.

"I just couldn't . . ." Kerrie rubbed her hands up and down her arms. She carried a small plastic bag with the hospital's logo printed on it, but hadn't worn a coat and he could see the goose bumps on her skin.

He had no idea what was going on. "What?"

"Be alone." She glanced behind her before looking at Hansen again. "Until we figure out who hurt Judson, I don't feel safe."

Letting her in struck him as a bad idea. Her being there could lead to trouble or confusion . . . or Tessa strangling him with his own shirt. "Other people live at the lodge."

Suddenly the pulling and tugging stopped, and Tessa stepped up beside him. She edged him back and made room for Kerrie. "Come in."

"Thanks." Kerrie walked over to the couch but didn't sit down. She brushed her fingertips over the top of the cushions and bent down to fluff up a pillow.

"So that I understand this. You came here thinking Hansen would be alone?"

Kerrie exhaled as she lifted her head and met Tessa's gaze. "He's proven he's very protective. That means more to me than anything else right now."

Hansen stood there, not sure what to say. The right answer was to put her in the car, call Ben, and figure out how to get her protection that was not him. The tension between Tessa and Kerrie didn't help to resolve the situation. Tessa continued to be friendly and concerned but she studied Kerrie when she wasn't looking, and Hansen understood. Kerrie had been forced to get the court order by Judson but that didn't make him any less wary of what being near her could mean for his future.

After a few seconds Tessa seemed to snap out of it. She pointed toward the kitchen. "Do you want some water?"

"I could curl up on your couch." Kerrie wrapped her arms tighter around her middle. "Sleep here, but I don't want to bother you."

Jesus, no. This was his nightmare. Hers, too. He got that, but he'd watched all those months ago as she'd begged the judge to keep him away from her. She'd been through hell, but she'd also helped to unleash a hurricane through the center of his life. Every time compassion and sympathy hit him, a wave of wariness crashed over him right after. He feared getting too close or trusting too much.

But Tessa nodded. "Take the bed upstairs."

He rested a hand against her lower back and leaned in. Didn't exactly whisper but tried not to be too obvious about the shock running through him. "What are you saying?"

Tessa touched a hand to his cheek, then dropped it again. "We can sleep down here."

"Forget I bothered you." Kerrie knocked into the table as she rounded the couch in a rush to leave. A table wobbled and the lamp moved back and forth but didn't fall. "I can head back to the lodge."

Tessa glared at him before smiling at Kerrie again. "Absolutely not."

Now he felt like shit. "How did you get to my cabin in the first place?"

Kerrie reached out to steady the lamp. "A man named Paul gave me a ride."

"He still drives?" Tessa sounded horrified at the thought. "Isn't he ninety?"

"Eighty." And last Hansen checked, Paul drove a golf cart.

"Oh, that's better." She snorted. "And what is he doing out this late?"

Kerrie sat on the armrest of the couch. "He was in the dining room at the lodge. Said he couldn't sleep with all the excitement and Ruthie calling him every few seconds about things the board needed to handle."

He thought back to Tessa's news from the lodge earlier. "Do you know Ruthie?"

"No."

He was about to ask a follow-up when Tessa jumped in to help. "You should change the sheets upstairs and bring some fresh ones down for us."

He wasn't even sure where he kept the sofa bed sheets. "Uh . . ."

"This is so nice of you." Kerrie slid from the armrest onto the sofa cushion. "I am sorry about the trouble. Any other time I would be fine, but . . ."

And he'd lost the argument. He felt it, saw it, and heard it. "I'll go find those sheets."

He glared at Tessa as he started up the ladder. She glared back. All that did was make him move faster. Something about leaving Tessa and Kerrie alone together for too long made anxiety pump through him.

TESSA WAITED UNTIL Hansen disappeared to turn back to face Kerrie. She was fiddling with the tassel on one of the pillows and tugging at the drawstring holding up her pants. Then there was the lie about Ruthie. Tessa didn't know what to do with that piece, so she filed it away for later.

Kerrie looked lost and uncomfortable and Tessa felt a punch of guilt. "Did you really feel unsafe at the lodge?"

Kerrie's chest lifted on a deep breath as she looked up. "I didn't want to be alone."

"That makes sense." Not sure what else to do, Tessa went to the kitchen and got Kerrie that bottle of water. "The bathroom is through there and—"

"Did you know Judson?"

Tessa froze in the act of handing the water bottle over. "How would I have known your husband?"

"You're with Hansen . . ." Kerrie took the bottle.

She turned it around in her hands and picked at the label. "I thought maybe you came from D.C. You look familiar."

That was not a topic Tessa wanted to explore. "No."

Hansen appeared a second later. He had a blanket and a few pillows in his arms. "All done."

"You're quick." Which was a good thing because Tessa guessed things were about to get awkward with Kerrie. The sooner they all went to sleep, the better.

Hansen winked at her as if to apologize for the night's really sucky turn. Then he looked at Kerrie. "Head up and we'll talk in the morning."

"Thank you both." Kerrie screwed the bottle cap on and off. Back and forth. "You've made a terrible situation tolerable."

Going up the ladder, Kerrie looked small and vulnerable. A new wave of guilt smacked into Tessa. The other woman really had experienced the worst. Having some company wasn't too much to ask.

Ready to be done with this day, Tessa went over to the couch. She threw the pillows on the floor, then started on the cushions before glancing at Hansen. "Since you're so quick at making beds, want to do this one?"

"I want to find another island." His low voice bordered on a whisper.

The light clicked off upstairs, so Tessa matched her volume to his. "Next time, get a house with a wall around it."

"You read my mind." He unfolded the bed. "I think the sheets are on here."

The idea made Tessa cringe. "Have they been washed this century?"

"They were clean last time I made up the bed."

It was late and she was done, so she accepted that answer and crawled beneath the covers.

After relocking the front door and switching off the night-light over the stove, Hansen slipped in next to her. The mattress was smaller than the one upstairs. Also, less comfortable. Tessa guessed she'd regret offering the good bed after a night of sleeping with a bar sticking into the middle of her back.

Hansen wrapped an arm around her and tucked her body close to his. "This isn't how I intended to spend the rest of tonight."

"Me either." But resting her head on his shoulder wasn't a hardship.

"I meant sex. What are you talking about?"

She smiled against his shirt. "Something sex-ish."

"That's an intriguing answer."

"Hmm."

Hansen pulled back and looked down at her. "What's that sound about?"

"She was with Ruthie in the dining room. Funny she didn't mention that."

"Yeah, I know."

Even in the darkness, Tessa could feel him staring. She debated pretending to be asleep but knew he'd never buy it. "Sylvia gave me this lecture about how some survivors make this connection with their rescuers and the lines can blur."

"Ben said the same thing." Hansen rubbed a soothing hand up and down her back. "You were talking to Sylvia about this situation?"

"About a woman who can't see you without touching you? Yeah."

Hansen made a hissing sound. "Please tell me you're not jealous."

"No, that's not it." It was all mixed up in her head. Kerrie needed security, and Tessa understood that. But Kerrie had skipped from fearing Hansen to emotionally grabbing on to him, and every now and then she'd make a stray comment that didn't fit with anything else. And where did that leave him? "Some guys like to save. They want a woman who needs them."

He didn't say anything for a few seconds. "You think you're describing me?"

"I have no idea."

"What?" His voice rose on that question.

"No." She balanced on her elbow and loomed over him. Skimmed her hand over his chest with the need to comfort both of them. "Look, I'm not good at this sort of thing."

"What exactly?"

"Dating. Opening up."

His body seemed to relax again. "I'm rusty, too."

She hated this part. Sharing was one thing. Cutting her heart open and peeling back the layers was something completely different. All these insecurities kept bubbling to the surface, and instead of shoving them back down like she usually did, she wanted to confide in Hansen. To make him understand.

"She makes me feel . . ." Her mind sputtered. She mentally reached for the right word and couldn't find it. She wasn't even sure what she was trying to say.

He rolled over to face her. The light sneaking in from the porch gave the area by the door an eerie glow. It also let her see his expression when they were this close. "Tell me."

"Unsettled." That fit. Not jealous. Not uncomfortable. But not right either. "I feel sorry for her but confused about her. I'm on edge. It's like an explosion is coming and I don't know if I should duck or run or what."

"You're not alone."

"Really?" For some reason having a partner in all this wallowing was a relief.

"My life imploded and now Judson is dead. In any given minute I waffle between relief, which makes me feel like a crappy human being, and worry for what's to come." He traced a finger over her nose and down to her mouth. "So, yeah. Unsettled. Except with you. Do you know how you make me feel?"

"Annoyed?"

He laughed. "Sometimes."

"The feeling is mutual."

"Lighter."

Not the word she expected at all. "Lighter?"

"With you, all the heavy baggage and problems battering me fade into the distance. You are hot, smart, nosy, and strong. I don't really know a sexier combination."

She slipped a hand over his chest. Let it travel down to his flat stomach. "You're pretty irresistible yourself."

He grew more so every single day. She'd gone from having a little crush to hating the idea of going a half day without seeing him. The cracks had started to form. Little breaks in her defenses that allowed him to move in.

She refused to think about love or a relationship that stretched past the unreal situation they were in now thanks to Judson. Hansen had a life in a city she despised. Power and money—two things that scared the crap out of her. But those feelings hovered there, in the background. She could feel them sneaking up on her no matter how much she pretended not to.

Not something she could handle. Not fair to suck him into her family drama. There were so many reasons and excuses floating through her head to justify them being apart that she started to sound like her mom. But she could enjoy some parts of this dating thing while she figured out the others.

He ran his fingers through her hair, bending her head closer until he placed a light kiss on her forehead. "We need to sleep."

She leaned into the touch, loving the dance of his fingers against her skin. "We could cuddle."

"I used that word one time and now you're throwing it back at me."

She smiled because the man made her smile. "You're good at it. One might even say an expert."

"Appealing to my ego works every time." He rolled onto his side, tucking her back against his front. "I like your style."

She liked everything about him. It was starting to be a problem. "Remember that when I whine about this mattress tomorrow."

"Something to look forward to."

Quiet settled around them. His arm fell heavy across her waist, holding her against him. And she loved it. "Thank you."

He answered after a few beats of hesitation. "For?"

"Listening."

"That's what boyfriends do." He dropped a kiss on her shoulder. "Go to sleep. Tomorrow is going to be a long day."

CHAPTER 22

Hansen stumbled over a piece of driftwood as he got out of Ben's car the next day. Tripped over the damn thing in Cliff's driveway.

"Is your head in the game?" Ben asked as he closed his door.

"What?"

"You're mumbling under your breath. Looks like you haven't slept, though that could be a good thing."

"Kerrie showed up on our doorstep last night." Hansen still didn't believe it. He hated guests and surprises; literally everyone on the island knew that and gave him space. Not Kerrie. Not the one woman legally guaranteed space from him.

"Why was she there?"

Ben didn't seem nearly as shocked as Hansen had been when he opened the door well after midnight to find Kerrie standing there. "She said she was scared to be alone."

"You don't believe her?"

They walked side by side, marching on the trail

Cliff or someone who once lived in this house had laid out. The warm sun beamed down and the wind had all but vanished. The weather still was seasonably cool, maybe in the low sixties, but a stunning day broke through on the other side of the storm. Except for swampy grass and a few downed trees, no one would have known they'd had four solid days of rain and whipping winds.

"No, I do. She was nervous and . . . off. Like she didn't know what to say, which makes sense under the circumstances." He didn't like being around her. He'd trained himself not to be, to lock away his concerns for her safety because of what happened to Alexis. He'd abandoned his life and family, at least for a short time, in order to move a country away from her and stay out of trouble. Despite all that, she kept popping up. "I just get twitchy when I'm around her."

"Understandable." Ben skidded to a stop. "Wait, you don't mean you're attracted to her, right?"

They were not on the same wavelength at all. "I mean she could sue me. Have me arrested."

Ben shook his head. "Not sexy."

"There's only one woman I find sexy right now." Not a subject he should broach but he found that he wanted to say it out loud. He thought about calling Connor this morning and telling him about Tessa.

Ben made a humming sound. "Because you love her."

"It's been awhile since you dropped that. You used to say it every day whether it made sense in context or not."

Ben laughed as he started them walking again. "I stopped because I think you actually do love her now. Before it was a joke."

"Why are we friends?"

"I ask myself that all the time." Ben waved his hand as if dismissing that topic. "So, Kerrie. What did you do?"

"She slept in the bed. Tessa and I took the sofa."

Ben threw Hansen a what's-the-matter-with-you look. "Your personal life is odd."

"Tell me about it."

"But with the sunshine here and the storm gone, the weekly ferry runs should resume tomorrow. I've asked for forensic and investigative help. All that might give Kerrie some comfort. It also means, at some point, we can officially clear her and she could go home."

"It doesn't bug you that police might come here and take over, or at least share the workload?"

"We need the help. That's why I called in the first place. But I'd like to be able to hand them something other than you, which is why we're talking to Cliff."

"Again." Cliff had been ornery last time. Hansen couldn't imagine him taking the double team any better today. "Did you find Maddie?"

Their shoes crunched on the gravel walk. "She called and apologized. Said something about a family crisis."

"Families can be messy."

Ben glanced at him. "But I haven't seen her. Did she somehow get off the island to see them?"

"Good point." She rarely interacted with the other people on Whitaker, worked out of her home, and always showed up alone in town, if she showed up at all. She made Hansen look friendly and easy to pin down.

Ben shook his head. "Something isn't right."

"When was the last time you saw her?" Hansen watched as Ben rubbed the back of his neck and stared at the lawn around him instead of giving eye contact. "And why are you blushing?"

"I asked her out for coffee. She, uh . . ." Ben shook his head.

"What?"

"She walked to the coffee place with me, ordered hers, and left."

That didn't . . . Oh, damn. She *went out* for coffee with him. Hansen tried hard not to laugh but it took a lot of effort and more energy than he had after his night with Tessa. Even silently making out with her drained him.

Hansen whistled. "Wow, I thought I sucked at dating."

"You probably do."

"Tough talk. You might want to remember one of us has a girlfriend."

"At least you finally admit it . . ." Ben's smile faded as they turned the corner of the house. "Oh, shit."

He took off on a run. His shoes slipped on the wet grass as he pivoted around the porch and bolted up the steps. He thudded up to the porch without looking back.

"What are you . . . ?" Then Hansen's gaze fell on the swing. On Cliff's body slumped there. "Damn."

He followed Ben, taking the steps two at a time. His

heartbeat thundered as he took in the mug on the floor and the coffee spill.

Ben was already moving. He had his cell out and continued scanning the area. "Stay here."

Too stunned to answer, Hansen did just that. He reached out to check for a pulse and felt nothing. Cliff's body was ice-cold. He wore a jacket and thick socks with his slippers. It looked like his stiff body had been there for a while.

His hands shaking and mind racing with a thousand questions, Hansen crouched down and touched a fingertip to the coffee stain. Also stone-cold. From this position, below Cliff, Hansen could see the blood. It stained Cliff's side near his armpit. Another slice low on his neck had blood pooling by his shoulder.

The last of Hansen's energy drained from his body as he squatted there. "Son of a bitch."

Footsteps thumped off to the right of the house, then Ben appeared. He had gone in through the front door. Hansen figured he'd checked the area for any signs of who might have done this and come out the back.

"Well?" Ben asked with a nod in Cliff's direction.

"He's dead. Stabbed in the stomach and chest multiple times. Just like Judson." Hansen was no expert, but the blood had congealed and nothing about this looked fresh. "I think he's been here awhile."

Ben bent over the body. Looked around, even sniffed. "No defensive marks on his hands." He glanced down. "Dropped his mug."

"He might have been asleep on the swing or sitting

there." Hansen knew Cliff liked to sit out here. He was aware. A smart-ass. Not an easy person to fool.

"When did you see him last?"

Hansen knew Ben had to ask the question, but it still punched through him. "He was alive when we left yesterday afternoon."

"And you, Kerrie, and Tessa were all at your cabin last night until early this morning." Ben made the comment as he walked around the swing. Seemed lost in whatever he was calculating in his head.

"We drove Kerrie to the lodge around nine, then I swung over to see you." But when Hansen listened to Ben discuss the sleeping arrangements, Hansen had to admit it sounded weird.

"The three of you together all night, no one left the place. That's actually good news because, depending on the timing, it sounds like an alibi for all of you."

"Maybe I should thank Kerrie for showing up." As odd as the situation was, she may have cleared his name in a second murder. Since this one had to be tied to the first, that should take the target off his back. At least for now.

"Everything looks fine inside. Something could be missing, but I'm not sure how to tell."

Hansen hated that the most. A man's life came down to trying to find one or two people who had been in his house recently. The loss carried a lonely, haunting quality that made him want to kick something. "I guess he really did hear an argument. Looks like someone got scared about what he might know."

Ben unlocked his cell phone. "State police are going to move in. I say we have a day before they figure out the jurisdictional details and a swarm starts."

"Then we have a day to solve this." As soon as he finished the sentence, Hansen heard the roar of an engine overhead. "Or maybe I overestimated. A private plane?"

"Police would come by boat."

"Then we have company." His least favorite thing.

IT TOOK ANOTHER hour for Hansen to leave Cliff's house. Lela arrived and the ambulance crew unloaded equipment. Everyone moved in stunned silence. Professionals cordoned off another crime scene on an island that had remained mostly crime free, except for something getting stolen here and there, for decades. Ben took photos and Lela went to work. It was a scene Hansen had hoped he'd only ever see once on Whitaker; now it had been twice in a week.

Cliff had been a staple on the island. He'd sat on that porch and relayed gossip like a pro. Hansen had watched the older man back down Ellis and Arianna, which was not an easy task since they never stopped talking. He'd made jokes and held his ground. Refused to let anyone suggest that he hadn't heard a fight that night. It was clear now he had.

An unsettled feeling rolled over Hansen. So much loss and no real explanation. A horror of sorts unfolded on the island and it connected, at least tangentially, to him. The idea that he brought the danger, that without him Cliff would be alive, ate at him. All he wanted was to see Tessa, take her back home, and shut his eyes for a few hours.

A wall of noise hit him the second he opened the main door to the lodge. Voices, some loud, and Ruthie's overriding all of them.

Fuck. This was not what he needed right now.

He looked into the dining room. The board members were there spread out among the other tables. Sylvia and a few of her staff served drinks and food. Kerrie and Tessa sat at a table by the window, out of the fray in the center of the room but not saved from the chaos. Even Ellis and Arianna sat at the bar. Those two. Hansen had to clamp down on the urge to go over and question them.

Tessa treated him to a big smile when she saw him. She got up and met him in the doorway. "Where have you been?"

The words stuck in his throat. He was about to wipe all of that light out of her eyes. The kicking in his gut told him not to do it, but he had no choice. People were watching them. The news would be out soon. She deserved to hear it from him.

"Cliff." That's all he got out.

She ran a hand up and down his arm as if she knew he needed some encouragement to get the next part out. "What did he say?"

He leaned in. Tried to whisper the horrible news. "He's dead."

"What?" Paul whipped around in his chair. Forget being eighty. The man moved and heard just fine. "Who is?"

Tessa's fingers dug in to Hansen's arm as the color left her face. "How?"

"Stabbed."

"Someone killed poor Cliff?" Paul yelled the news now.

All talk in the dining room stopped. A glass shattered as it fell to the hardwood floor. Everyone turned, as if waiting for an explanation. Even Sylvia froze in the middle of pouring coffee at one of the tables.

Hansen glanced at Paul. "Your voice carries."

The talking ramped up again. People started moving. Chairs scraped against the floor. Some took out their cells and started making calls. Sylvia's voice carried above it all. "Did you say—?"

"Everyone calm down." Hansen knew it was a stupid comment. He felt anything but calm. If the pounding in his head got any louder, he'd need to sit down. "Ben is there now. So is Lela. They are securing the scene and trying to figure out what happened."

Ruthie slowly rose. "How is that supposed to be a comfort?"

At the sound of her voice, the talking died down again. Her voice shook with anger. This time Hansen couldn't blame her.

"You hate Lela, too?" Tessa asked.

"I believe Lela and Ben and everyone handling this case are ill-equipped for this sort of violent emergency." Ruthie looked around at the board members in the room, which was all of them. "It's time for professionals to step in and we need to make that happen."

Tessa seemed to shake out of her shock. She aimed all of her focus at Ruthie. "You could be supportive."

"I need to keep this community safe."

Ruthie wasn't wrong. But she wasn't the only one watching out for Whitaker, and Hansen wanted to make that clear before she started an incident. "Ben already called for reinforcements."

"A plane landed," someone called out from the back of the dining room. "They must be here already."

Hansen couldn't identify the voice through all the people and movement, but that didn't matter. "No, that one is private."

"Anyone know who's visiting?" Paul asked.

Someone else jumped in to explain as the conversation pinged around the room. "A few wealthy families with summer rentals fly in."

Sylvia frowned. "That's rare. Most people come by boat."

"It's happened."

Sylvia cleared her throat, which seemed to quiet things down again. She looked at Hansen. "Is what happened to Cliff related to Judson's murder?"

All the attention switched right back to Hansen. He could feel the weight of their judgment pressing on him. "We don't know."

Tessa stood next to him the entire time. Halfway through the bouncing topics, she slipped her hand into his. Now she gave his fingers a reassuring squeeze.

He was about to talk when Arianna spoke up. "How was Cliff killed? He's an older man. Maybe he had a heart attack—"

"No. This was intentional." Hansen did not need her spreading false information. She and Ellis had done enough of that in the days after Judson was found. All that talk of blood and fighting. "And, please. Let's be respectful."

"This is a nightmare." Tessa whispered the comment under her breath.

"You visited him yesterday. Right, Hansen?" Ruthie threw down that comment. If her intention was to drive the focus back to him, it worked. Everyone watched him now.

Interesting how she forgot to mention he was just one of the people at the house. Hansen figured if she knew about his visit, she knew about the others. "How did you—?"

"Excuse me." A deep male voice filled the room.

Hansen glanced over his shoulder and saw a pilot. He wore a uniform, which was a bit unusual for the private planes that flew out this way. He also held his body stiff as he entered the room.

Sylvia fumbled the coffeepot in her hands before setting it down on a nearby table. "May we help you?"

"You there." Paul looked past the pilot, into the hallway. "You look familiar."

A man in a navy suit stepped forward. Tall and distinguished. Hair graying at the temples and trim. Only a bit of a double chin hinted that he might not be as fit as he once was.

Tessa groaned. Her fingers clenched around Hansen's in a death grip. Nothing about her expression looked welcoming or happy.

Hansen cut through the bullshit. "Senator."

"Wait . . ." Ruthie's eyes bulged. "Senator?"

"I'm here for . . ." The man took one more step as he glanced around the room. He didn't even smile when his gaze fell on Tessa. "There you are."

"What are you doing here?" Tessa blinked as if she could blink him away.

His expression said he wanted to scold her. "I think you know."

Sylvia's eyes narrowed. "How do you two know each other?"

"I'm her—"

"Okay." He looked like he was actually going to say it. To pin down Tessa without her consent, so Hansen stopped the talk cold. "That's not important."

"I think it is," the senator said.

Tessa rolled her eyes. "Of course you do."

CHAPTER 23

Sylvia showed the small group to her office and shut the door, closing them inside. Tessa flattened her back against the door and stared at the man who ignored her until it was convenient for him to stage a meeting without his handlers present. She wanted to yell the walls down.

Of course he sat in the big, comfortable desk chair.

Of course he looked at her like *she* was the problem.

The only thing that calmed the restlessness churning inside her was Hansen. He stood on the side of Sylvia's big desk, between Tessa and her father. He hadn't said anything but the twitch in his cheek suggested he had a few things he wouldn't mind unloading on her father.

Fury seethed inside her. Today, of all days, when poor Cliff was killed, he showed up wanting to play Daddy.

She forced her voice to remain even. She refused to give him the satisfaction of knowing his presence mattered to her in any way. "Why did you think you could just drop in like that and tell everyone we're related?"

"It's true. I'm your father."

The words pummeled her, but she managed to stay on her feet. For so many years she'd ached to hear him say that. Her mother told her the truth when she turned eight. Before that, she'd lie in bed with the lights off and spin wild tales of why her father didn't live with them but would one day. Despite the pile of disappointments and no-shows, she'd wait at every birthday and holiday, even though her mother insisted he'd never be back.

All those years she'd wanted him to pop back into her life, take her to a park, say he loved her—anything that acknowledged she mattered to him. And nothing. He only traveled to find her now to save himself from additional embarrassment, not caring if he upended her life in the process. "Interesting that you remember our family relationship now."

Her father flicked a gaze in Hansen's direction. "This talk is private."

As if he got to pick who stayed in the room for this unwanted talk. "And this is Hansen."

Her father let out a dramatic sigh. "Now isn't the time—"

"My boyfriend." Now that she'd gotten used to the word, she really liked it. Especially in cases like these when she could use the backup.

Her father looked Hansen up and down. His eyes narrowed but he didn't roll them. Instead he nodded. "Charles Michaelson."

Hansen shifted, inching his feet apart and linking his hands together behind his back. "Hansen Rye."

Her father continued to stare. "The name is familiar."

She could almost see the wheels turning in his head. Running through his donor list, trying to figure out if Hansen owed him or he owed Hansen.

This topic made her uneasy, so she rushed to quash it. "Back to your visit. How did you know to find me here?"

"I pay people to tell me the things I need to know."

"Give her a real answer." The edge to Hansen's voice suggested her father get to it.

Something about the man-to-man thing or the lack of wiggle room in Hansen's tone worked because her father nodded. "I've been looking for you, as you know. Someone here on Whitaker reached out to my people. Suggested the woman in the middle of this ridiculous scandal was here. Tracking you down from there proved easy. Although why you would come to somewhere so remote is unclear."

"Who? And why would someone contact you?" Because that meant someone knew who she really was and worked to undermine her. Tessa didn't know how to process that information.

"When did this happen?" Hansen asked, not even attempting to soften his tone.

"I don't appreciate the interrogation." Her father brushed a nonexistent piece of lint off his dress pants.

"Two people have been murdered." She pointed that out since, in her mind, the deaths took precedence over one senator's quest to clear the name he deserved to have muddied.

"What?" He sat forward in the chair. "On the island?"

That answered the question of whether the news of Judson's death had gotten out despite the weather—no. "Yes. Over the last week."

He made an annoying tsk-tsk sound as he got up from the chair and pushed it in. He put his hands on the back of it and stood there. "That's unacceptable."

"Thanks for clearing that up. We'll let them know." Hansen leaned against the wall, seemingly unimpressed with her father's outburst.

Her father inhaled as if he were about to deliver an important lecture. "I mean I can't have us implicated in another scandal."

And there it was. Being here could further tarnish his name. Drag him into another mess that people could use against him. It was the playbook he used, so he expected others to follow it as well.

"Aren't you responsible for the first scandal?" Hansen asked.

"I'm going to have to ask for privacy."

Too late. As far as she was concerned, this was the one reason to come out as his daughter. To let people know what a hypocrite he was. "Hansen knows about you pretending I didn't exist. About you tracking me and Mom. About the threats and people following me."

Her father held out his hands and pressed them down, likely a way to tell her to calm down. "Let's not get dramatic. I asked you for a simple favor."

"You blackmailed me by using my mother."

"You left me with no other choice." He sighed at her. "I need you to step up and tell the truth."

"You're talking to me about the truth?" He either had zero self-awareness or his narcissism had exploded. Maybe both.

He dropped his hands again. "There's an easy way to do this. We control the damage and the story. Your mother will be fine. So will you." He shook his head. "But if you force my hand, then I'll need to tell my PR team to switch to protection mode."

Hansen stiffened. "You're threatening her."

"I'm reasoning with her."

The longer she stood there, facing the man she thought of as *the senator* and not her father, something she'd waffled between wanting and dreading for years, the more a sense of peace washed over her. She was not the same shy, hidden little girl he'd left.

She'd told Hansen about her past and he put the blame fully on her father. None of this was her fault. In a tiny darkened part of her soul, a piece of her had always believed she caused the rift. Her mother was beautiful and determined. Nothing about her could have driven him away. No, Tessa had convinced herself the fault rested with her. If she had been more lovable, more talented, smarter, cuter, quieter, louder. Someone other than who she was.

But the picture had cleared. This was on him. Her mother had made mistakes and she never should have let him plow her under or change who she was, but Tessa understood how easy it was to get overpowered by a man like him. She would not let that happen no matter what leverage he dangled.

"Oh, you've been clear." His people had contacted her mother and threatened to expose her, completely upend her life and threaten her job and privacy, if she couldn't get Tessa to play along. She'd gotten the visit when she stopped in her work office for a weekly in-person meeting. Then there was that guy in the car parked across the street from her window. Her father had tracked her down and used intimidation to scare her into agreeing. "My job is to come out as your daughter and pretend we've always been a big happy family despite how my terrible mother ruined your life."

"I have a job. An important one. Constituents depend on me. The people who work for me. The committee. Frankly, the American people." His voice grew deeper, more solemn as he talked, which suggested he might buy the garbage he spewed. "This is bigger than our petty differences."

Hansen let his head fall back against the wall with a thud. "You've got to be kidding."

Her father ignored the comment. "Coming here borders on a waste of my time. I did it for you. You want my attention, you have it. There is no need to prolong this. It's a distraction."

She was pretty sure she was the *it* in her father's sentence. "You can leave."

Hansen lifted his head again. "Please do that."

"I am your father."

He said the words as if they meant something. They didn't. Not to her. "You donated sperm."

"Theresa, that's enough." For the first time her father's voice rose.

If he wanted to snap, she would snap right back. "I haven't gone by that name since I was eight. I dumped it when I dumped all hope of a relationship with you."

Getting the words out hurt. Pain sliced through her and she had to fight to keep the tears from forming in her eyes. She would never cry another tear for him. She made that vow then and planned to honor it now.

Hansen snapped his fingers, drawing her father's attention. "Who was it?"

"Excuse me?"

"Who contacted your office?"

Her father snorted in derision. "I don't see how that's your business."

But Hansen didn't back down. "You know the name. You probably have a file on this person."

"I would think you'd want to know who wasted your time because I am not leaving with you or being a part in your lie." Every time she said the words they reinforced the wall of defiance inside her, strengthened her resistance. "I told you this already."

The senator managed to cool down. When he spoke again, his voice had returned to his usual lilting tone. "There is a lot at stake here."

"For you." The list of all the ways this impacted *him* ticked off in her head. "Your reputation."

"Your career," Hansen added.

"Your family, which has never included me."

Her father shook his head. "You have your mother's temper."

"Thank you."

His hold tightened on the back of the chair until his knuckles turned white. "And her refusal to see reason."

"Stop blaming everyone else for your mess," Hansen said. "Tessa's mom didn't get pregnant on her own, Mr. Married Man."

That's when it happened. In the short time she'd known him, she'd morphed from crush to interested to girlfriend, and now, to love. Right there in Sylvia's light blue office. The possibility had been looming out there, maybe since the day they'd met. The thick layer of grumpiness Hansen used to hide his charm won her over. He'd grouse and whine, but he never said no to her and he said no to everyone else.

That should have been a sign.

Hansen, the man whose real life made her want to run screaming in panic, a guy who in so many ways stood for all the things she'd fought against her entire life, now filled up that empty space in her heart. She didn't believe a woman needed a formal partner to feel whole. She'd seen her mother thrive and love without ever walking down the aisle. But the idea of sharing the burden, having someone to help her fight in situations like this . . . The way he kissed her, touched her. The smile he saved only for her. Yeah, love.

Talk about terrible timing. Their lives didn't make

any sense right now. His was on hold and hers . . . Well, she didn't know what she wanted or if she'd ever leave Whitaker. But love. It knocked her down and wrestled her into admitting that it pulsed awake and alive inside of her. Silently, and only to herself, but happiness flooded her.

At some point they'd talk and she hoped she wouldn't leave brokenhearted, but for now the knowledge soothed her. Made her feel invincible. And when he winked at her across the room, her insides melted.

"I would like to talk with Theresa alone."

"It's Tessa." Hansen didn't even look at him. "And no."

"I'm not leaving until I do."

Hansen finally turned his head. Hit her father with that step-the-hell-down expression he did so well. "The police are going to come. The press. Murder means publicity. You really think they won't notice a senator walking around on a small island?"

Bull's-eye. Such an impressive hit. "I'd say you have a day before Whitaker becomes a lot more popular."

A sly smile formed on her father's mouth as he spoke. "Then that gives me twenty-four hours to convince you."

Crap. She looked at Hansen. "We tried."

He winced. "Didn't think he'd do the ticking-clock thing."

"I'll stay with you." Her father came around the chair to stand in front of the desk, in front of her, after he dropped that command.

She pointed at Hansen. "I'm living with him."

It was true, mostly true. Didn't matter because she knew Hansen would back her up. That's what he did. Supported her.

Her father shook his head. "For heaven's sake, Theresa."

The name grated across her nerves. "It's still Tessa."

Her father clasped his hands together in front of him. "Dinner this evening then."

Hansen shook his head as she answered. "No."

"We'll have a nice family visit—"

This was her nightmare. "No such thing with you."

"—then I'll fly back."

Silence skidded through the room as he ended the comment. Any other man, and she might have bought the act. From this guy? No. "I don't trust you to go."

"You don't have a choice."

Hansen pushed off from the wall. "On two conditions. First, you don't announce to anyone that she's your daughter."

Her father opened his mouth once and closed it. After a few seconds he nodded. "Fine. Not right now I won't."

Typical of him to fudge the answer. She didn't even bother pointing it out.

"Second," Hansen continued, "you tell us who tipped you off that Tessa was here."

"Some woman named Ruth. She thought I'd be concerned about a scandal. I thought she meant the false stories about me, but now in light of the murder I'm not so sure."

A million questions spun around in Tessa's head. She couldn't grab on to any of them long enough to ask. Ruthie?

"How did she contact you?" Hansen asked.

"You can ask me any questions you want." Her father buttoned his suit jacket and tugged on the bottom to straighten out the material. "At dinner."

She wondered if he did that out of habit. "You should change."

Her father looked down at his jacket. "Why?"

"You don't want to stand out during a murder investigation." Hansen sounded amused as he laid it out.

She filled in the rest. "Then a new scandal is inevitable because no matter what, people around here will talk about a senator being on the island."

THEY WAITED UNTIL her father checked in. Hansen planned to take her home and tell her how proud he was of her. That talk was brutal. Whatever feelings lingered inside the man, he held them back. Tessa could have been his employee with all the care and compassion he showed her. More than once Hansen wanted to throw him through a wall, but that would guarantee Hansen could never return to D.C. and his regular life.

The thought popped into his head for the fifth time today. He lived in the city Tessa avoided. She didn't trust wealthy men and Hansen had money. She feared power. Some would say his family, because of the business, wielded a lot of it.

They were mismatched and didn't make sense. And he didn't give a shit. They'd find common ground. Her father wasn't the only one with power in that town.

But Hansen's attention needed to stay on the here and now. Another murder, one clearly tied to Judson, which meant it was tied to him. He feared Tessa's proximity to him made her a target as well. He dreaded having that conversation and explaining why he wanted her to be even more careful and limit where she went. That last part was sure to invite some yelling.

They walked out of Sylvia's office and made it part-way to the main lodge doors when a couple stepped in front of them. It took a few seconds for his vision to clear and who they were to make sense in his head.

Then he got pissed off. "What are you doing here?"

Tessa elbowed him after he delivered that non-welcome.

Kerrie flashed a wide smile as she made the introductions. "You remember Allen."

"Her brother." The last meeting between them hadn't gone well and Hansen was not ready for a repeat.

"Hansen?" Allen held out his hand. "I just wanted to say thank you for helping Kerrie with everything since . . . well, you know."

Hansen stared at his hand. Debated whether to shake it. Throwing off the image of this guy in the courtroom, the things he'd said, struck him as impossible. It took Tessa shaking his hand first to get Hansen moving and doing the same.

"When did you get here?" Hansen asked because he had no idea what else to ask.

"I flew in with the senator. We were both waiting out the storm in Seattle. Sitting in a private terminal until we got the go-ahead."

"I didn't realize you were this close by." Because he would have warned Tessa. Maybe given Ben a heads-up.

Kerrie frowned at Hansen. "I told you in Ben's office."

Seeing her with Allen brought it all back. He'd felt so helpless back then. Wallowing in his grief over Alexis and desperate not to let Kerrie get hurt.

Tessa's comments about his rescuing nature had validity. This family had burned it out of him, but it once existed. That was the role he took on back then, but he'd underestimated his opponent. Judson rallied the troops, including the two in front of him.

"The senator was so busy with calls I doubt he even saw me at the back of the plane." Allen smiled at Tessa as if he were confiding some great secret with her.

Kerrie moved in closer to her brother. "He's here to help me settle everything."

Allen nodded. "Then I'll take her home."

They talked in sync. Even looked alike. Both with light blond hair and bright blue eyes. They were the type to turn heads. Stunning and stylish. More than one D.C. businessman commented on how Judson liked to show off Kerrie, like she was his possession and not his wife.

None of that was his business now but Hansen would feel better when they left the island. "You might be delayed. Now we have a second killing."

Allen's smile fell. "Is this tied to Judson?"

"Cliff had—"

"We're not sure." Hansen hated cutting Tessa off, but he didn't know what specifics Ben wanted out there. It could impact his ability to test witnesses later. "You might want to speak with Ben, but I suspect he'll be at Cliff's house for another hour or so."

Allen nodded. "I'll get checked in."

"Sylvia must be running out of rooms," Kerrie said.

Tessa smiled. "She can use mine since I don't need it."

"Look, about Judson and the court order." Allen looked at his feet. Ran a hand over his mouth. Generally looked out of place and ready to run, before looking up at Hansen again. "I had no idea what kind of pressure my sister was under. I was trying to . . ."

"Protect her. I get it." Part of Hansen really did. He'd spent so long being angry. All that pent-up frustration from not being able to get anyone to listen to him about Judson. But he'd been in Allen's position. As much as he hated to admit it, he understood how a person could block everything else out and become obsessed with the rescue.

"I figured you would, but I'm still sorry for the way I acted. You deserved better. Kerrie has been clear that you made the past few days bearable." Allen turned to Tessa. "And you, of course."

Tessa smiled back. "She's been through a lot. We were happy to help."

"We'll let you go." Allen shook her hand again. Held on a bit too long, but finally dropped her hand. "Nice to meet you."

Hansen watched the two of them head for the check-in desk, then talk with Sylvia. He looked back at Tessa, not sure what her impression would be. Many people got blinded by the siblings' ability to work a crowd.

"Did we even tell him my name?" Tessa asked.

A shot of relief surged through him. Hansen didn't know he needed her to say something like that until she did. "Last time I met him he punched me, so this was better."

She looked ready to forge into battle. "What?"

Hansen slipped his fingers through hers. "He went from wanting information from me when Kerrie and Judson started dating to believing I was harassing his sister."

"Why didn't you get a protective order against him?"

He lifted their hands and kissed hers. "Because I would have done the same thing if I were him and someone were bugging Alexis. Hell, I should have stopped her wedding."

"You've had a shitty time of it."

Funny how since meeting her the sharp edges had dulled. Things that once made him furious now bounced off him. He shrugged. "I have a pretty cool girlfriend now."

"You do." Then she sighed. "With an idiot father. What are we going to do about him?"

"Tolerate him, I suppose."

"And Ruthie?"

Hansen's anger level kicked right back up again. "That's a different story."

CHAPTER 24

Ruthie didn't appreciate being called in to Ben's office and made that clear by complaining for a solid ten minutes when she got there. She talked about board votes and hiring someone new. Threw in a bunch of threats. Ben waited until she ran out of gas, then guided her into the conference room. Hansen and Ben stood on one side of the table with Ruthie on the other.

He and Ben had talked about the contact with the senator before Ruthie arrived. Ben knew what Hansen knew. Neither had seen the evidence, but they couldn't think of a reason for the senator to lie. And how would he have guessed at Ruth? That would require some luck. No, it made more sense Ruthie had been pulling strings behind the scenes all along.

They all took a seat. Ben had a notepad in front of him and a recorder between them on the table. "Something you'd like to say to start?"

Ruthie folded her arms in front of her. "We are all relieved the real police are coming."

Ben didn't even flinch.

"We talked to the senator." Hansen figured he'd dive right in. He'd dropped Tessa off at the lodge with Sylvia after a few hours of relaxing at home together. The days of awful things happening, one after the other, needed to end.

Ruthie rolled her eyes. "Who knew you had such impressive connections?"

Her. She'd investigated Hansen and his background. Knew about the protective orders. It wasn't much of a leap to think she'd checked out Tessa as well. The tattling to the senator didn't make much sense. That would be a pretty deep dive for Ruthie, and how that fit in with anything else was a mystery. But that's why they were here.

Ben tapped his pen against the desk, not having said anything since they sat down. Then he started. "Honestly, Ruthie. What's wrong with you?"

Hansen hadn't expected the burst of anger or the frustration threading Ben's voice. From the way her eyes widened, he guessed Ruthie hadn't either.

"Excuse me?" She sounded appalled at being dragged into the office and accused of anything. She clearly viewed her standing as above reproach.

"You're going after Tessa," Ben said.

"Oh, please." She rolled her eyes a second time.

Hansen guessed that would be her reaction to every question—denial and deflection. "Honest, decent, charming. People love her."

"What's your point?" Ruthie emphasized each word.

Despite the tension choking the room, Ben didn't

ruffle. He rode out the tension and kept his focus. "Why did you tell Senator Michaelson that Tessa was on Whitaker?"

From the narrowing of her eyes to her screwed-up lips, she looked confused. "What are you talking about?"

"He implicated you." Ben tapped his pen against the notepad, end over end.

The surprise looked genuine. Ruthie wasn't exactly the type to hide her schemes. She tended to celebrate them. Show them off so everyone could appreciate her power.

"In what?" She shook her head. "I don't understand."

"Letting him know that she's here," Ben said.

"That's ridiculous." Her gaze zipped between the men. "I had no idea Tessa being on Whitaker was a huge secret. And why would the senator care about Tessa?"

No way was Hansen offering up that information. It was bad enough he had to fill in Ben. Even then he'd gotten Tessa's okay and kept the details to a minimum. "Try again."

"I don't have to. I know I'm telling you both the truth, though we all know I don't owe you any explanation for anything I do."

"You contacted him." Hansen guessed by email because a letter would take too long, and a call could raise too many questions.

"That never happened." She didn't waver, and the questioning edge never left her tone.

"Ruthie, come on. You led the senator directly to Tessa." Ben set the pen down. "What was the end goal? Did you recognize her from the paper and want to make money or cause trouble? Explain it to me."

"Was she in the newspaper?" Ruthie took a deep breath before talking again. "Look, your information is wrong. I didn't know about Tessa's background. Honestly, I didn't think she was interesting enough to investigate. I guess the joke is on me."

The subtle delivery of that last line. The rest amounted to pure bullshit, but that one . . . Hansen wondered if she meant to spill it. "Who did you investigate?"

Her face went blank and her mouth flattened. It was as if a shield clunked down. Her entire affect changed.

The woman should never play poker. Hansen started to question the senator's intel but now he had a new concern—who else was in Ruthie's crosshairs? Ben, likely, but this felt bigger, as if Ruthie had accidentally let a point slip.

She glared at Ben. "I'm leaving, and if you try to stop me, I'll call an emergency board meeting and have you fired."

She just didn't know when to pull back or stop. She had one speed and didn't seem to care if it slammed her into a wall or not.

"Sounds like an abuse of power to me." Hansen could think of other words for it but went with that.

"You will stop talking unless you want *another* protective order brought against you."

Now she was threatening him. That seemed to be her go-to move. "That's not how it works, but go ahead and leave."

She didn't say another word. Just left and slammed the door behind her.

"That went well." But Hansen had to admit the meeting ended about how he thought it would. Except for the peek into Ruthie's investigative habits. That bit of news was problematic.

"I don't know, Hansen." Ben shook his head. "She looked stunned when we said she contacted the senator."

Hansen couldn't disagree. "But she's hiding something."

Ben smiled. "True."

"What are you thinking right now?"

"This might be a good time to follow her. If I'm going to get fired, I might as well go out big, right?"

"That's the spirit."

"You in?"

A quick glance at the wall and Hansen knew he was in trouble. He'd lost track of the afternoon and now they'd entered the countdown to dinner. "Shit."

"What?"

"I'm supposed to meet Tessa at the lodge in a half hour."

Ben stood up and took his blank notepad with him. "Can it wait?"

"She's going to kill me." But then, she'd hate it if Ruthie knew something big and Hansen didn't follow up. It was a battle between dealing with her father and satisfying her nosiness. "We have fifteen minutes."

TEN AFTER SEVEN. Not that Tessa kept looking at the wall clock or anything. She sat at a table in the corner of the dining-room close, tucked behind the door. A few other residents were there, some who lived there, but not all. Most people chose to stay in now that the news of Cliff's murder had seeped out.

She'd granted Hansen a brief reprieve, but he'd better not push it. There was only so much small talk and water she could drink before she dumped something over the senator's head. And that would be a headline.

Her father unfolded his napkin and placed it on his lap. "Where's your young man?"

He had ten minutes to show up. When he texted earlier about Ruthie lying, it had taken all of her control not to insist he take her along for the questioning. Ben said no. He even threatened to text her his stupid rules and protocol speech.

"I don't think of him as young." She smiled when she thought about Hansen and those dark glasses. "He's very hot though."

"That's enough."

"If you say so."

Her father frowned at her. "Theresa, really."

She wasn't even sure what she had done to disappoint him this time. Breathed wrong? Wore the wrong shirt? He did shake his head when he saw her show up in dark jeans. He must not know that qualified as fancy clothes on Whitaker.

"Call me Tessa or I'm getting up." She planned to draw many lines with him and that was the first and the brightest.

He sighed as he opened the menu and studied the pages. "You really are difficult."

She wore that as a badge of honor. "You have no idea."

After a few seconds he closed the menu again and rested his elbows on the edge of the table. He did a quick glance around the room, but Sylvia had put them at a table away from the other diners. She'd also turned up the music that played in the reception hall. It was usually faint, almost imperceptible. Tessa could make out the words now.

"I've never asked anything of you."

The comment stunned Tessa for a second. She bit back a string of profanity. "You have to be kidding. My silence. My loyalty. My patience."

He leaned in and dropped his voice to a whisper. "Me being your father is the truth. We can hold a press conference and set boundaries. Say the rest is private. My wife will support us."

It was as if she were talking to herself. He didn't hear a thing she said. Didn't care that she didn't want to be put in this position or that she refused to lie about her mother or their past.

"How do you get people to do that? You say one thing and do another, preach about family values and holding off on sex until marriage, and you don't follow any of those rules." She assumed that because there had been one *other woman* that there were more. Whatever the rules in his marriage were didn't concern her, but the public lying did. He laid out a set of rules for how people should behave but they didn't apply to him. Only him.

He glanced at the couple nearest to him. They sat a good six tables away and weren't paying attention to anything other than the steaks in front of them. "Politics requires sound bites these days. Easily digestible pieces of information that people can believe in. Thoughts delivered in a few words that play well on social media and the news."

"Lies. That's the word you're searching for."

"The people who vote for me believe in me."

Because they weren't biologically related to him. "Then they should do the press conference with you. Let them be your cheerleaders."

He sat back in his chair and crossed one leg over the other. Took on an informal, carefree affect. "I could just tell everyone who you are, name you and your mother without your permission, and ask my constituents for forgiveness. Explain that your mother wouldn't marry me and talk about how embarrassed I was for having a human failing."

He would do it, too. Throw her mother under the bus, then back over her. Ruin their privacy and drag them into the public eye with him in the worst possible way.

"You never asked her, but I'm sure you remember

that. Though I doubt she would have said yes. You inadvertently convinced her marriage was not a great thing." Her mother confirmed that once, not long ago, when Tessa had talked to her about marrying Ray. Her mom had been asked by exactly one man to marry her, never by the man in front of Tessa right now.

"She's not currently married to . . ."

"Ray." That was as much as Tessa wanted him digging around in the part of the family that made her whole. The one that didn't hide her. "Did you think about us at all over the years?"

His shoulders fell as the breath ran out of him. "Now is not the time. After we have this issue settled, then yes."

"It's the only time I've had the chance to ask." And that reality still had the power to drop her to her knees. She felt the pain run straight through her.

"You're old enough to understand it—the thing with your mother. It was a youthful mistake. She was a hostess at this restaurant. So beautiful." He shrugged. "I was tempted and she liked the idea of being with a man who could pay for dinner."

He wore a smile as if he were lost in a memory. Tessa had no idea what to do with that information. She'd always assumed he viewed her and her mother as horrors better left buried. But the look on his face, the rush of nostalgia that seemed to come over him while talking about the old days, threw Tessa off.

For a second, and not much more than that, she felt a whiff of a connection to him. "That's all very human."

Her voice snapped him out of his memory. He cleared his throat before talking again. "Well, yes."

"You made a mistake and I'm the result."

For the first time a flash of guilt moved over his face. "That's not what I meant."

"But it's true. People fail. Birth control fails." She wasn't blaming. She was trying to make a point for the other women out there who paid for the way he voted and the laws he supported.

"I can't change who I am, Tessa." His voice was softer now. Less "on" and more genuine.

"But you don't believe in the crap you spew." Part of her wanted that to be true.

"It's a persona, and I need to protect it if I want to be reelected." He sighed at her. "You may not believe this, but I'm able to create change. Bring good things to people."

"But reelection is what matters to you."

He hesitated, as if trying to figure out how much to say. In the end he went with the simplest response. "Yes. Everything else flows from that."

She didn't agree with him and sure didn't respect him, but this one time, he didn't try to dress up his deeds, package his ideas, and sell them to her. He admitted what she'd known all along—it was an act. His whole life was.

She wished she could go back and tell her younger self how lucky she was not to be wrapped up in that. "At least you're being honest."

"Neither one of us wants family holidays." He stared

at his water glass. "That sounded harsher than I meant it to."

But he wasn't wrong, and for whatever reason, that harsh slap of truth didn't sting. "I don't want to get together for family time, but the problem for you is I'm not going to *pretend* that I do."

Quiet descended between them. She wasn't sure what to say. She just wanted to leave, go find Hansen. For the first time ever, she was happy to see Kerrie when she stepped into the dining room with her brother.

Tessa waved to them. Called them over when they didn't see her.

"Hello again." Tessa pointed from her father to Allen. "You remember Allen."

"Hello." Allen gave them a little wave as he shifted his weight. "Don't want to interrupt."

Then they shuffled off without saying anything else. Tessa assumed her father intimidated some. Not her. Not anymore. Kerrie's interest waned when Hansen wasn't with her. They actually walked right back out of the dining room.

Her father gave them a quick look, then went back to the menu. "I guess they're not staying."

"He's here for tonight, like you. I'm not sure if he'll fly back with you tomorrow." She drank her water. It took her a second to notice her father was staring at her. "What?"

"What are you talking about?"

"You and Allen."

"Who is Allen?"

"The man we just . . ." The entire conversation flipped, and she didn't know what was happening. Probably said something about how much she sucked at small talk. "He was on the plane with you from Seattle."

Her father slowly lowered his menu. "No, he wasn't."

What was happening right now? "Allen Bernard."

"I'm not sure why you keep saying his name, but you're wrong. The weather is still rough in Seattle. We didn't have permission to take off, but I called in a few favors."

"Despite the danger?"

"I didn't have a choice. The press refuses to let the scandal go. Some members of my party, in particular a certain senator from Texas who is looking to climb up the ladder, are on television, questioning my integrity. And the opposition? They would love to see me fall."

"Is this the part where I'm supposed to feel bad for you?" The question slipped out before she could stop it.

"The owner of a biotech company let me borrow his plane and I was the only one on it other than the pilot and copilot." Her father made a noise that sounded like *humph*. "I'll likely need to pay a fine when I get back, or he will, but that's the point. That's how important it was to see you. I risked upsetting the ground crew and the FAA to get to you and get the truth out."

When he started to pick up the menu again, she pushed it back down to the table with her hand. "He wasn't on the plane."

"We've been over this. Only one plane came in. I was on it. That man was not." He finally leaned in as if he realized something had happened. "What is wrong with you?"

Allen hadn't been on the plane—the only plane to land since the storm. The same plane he'd insisted he arrived on. She tried to remember what he said . . . something about her father working during the flight.

The liar.

She didn't know what this meant but it meant something.

She took her hand off his menu and stood up. "For the first time since you stepped into the lodge I'm happy to see you."

He did a quick look around before staring at her again. "Where do you think you're going?"

"I need to find Hansen."

"No." When she didn't sit down he took the napkin off his lap and put it on the table. "Fine. Then I'm coming with you."

Lord, no. "That's not necessary."

He pushed his chair back and stood up. "I still have about fifteen hours left to change your mind and I'm not wasting them."

"Lucky me."

CHAPTER 25

Hansen wanted to be anywhere but here. He thought the conference room with Ruthie was bad. Being in a car, conducting surveillance with Ben was worse. Ten times worse. They sat in relative silence, watching Ruthie's car on the other side of the marina parking lot.

"She's been sitting in the front seat for twenty minutes." Hansen glanced at his watch. Debated texting Tessa with a renewed apology and a promise he'd be there very soon.

Ben's attention didn't waver from the window in front of him. He stared at Ruthie's car. She'd turned it off a few minutes ago and now just sat there with the windows fogging up.

"You're late for your date." Those were the first words Ben had said between all his off-key humming.

Understatement. "I promised her."

"You don't want to disappoint her dad."

Hansen could see why this sort of thing ticked Tessa off. It was annoying. "She doesn't consider him that, and I don't care what the guy thinks. He's a jackass."

"Her jackass."

Hansen knew Ben was trying to make a point, but he had no idea what it was. "Explain."

Ben shifted in his seat, not far but enough to sneak peeks at Hansen in between watching over Ruthie. "Be careful. She may hate him, but there could be a time, far in the future, where they reconcile. What you say about him now will matter then."

That sounded . . . personal. Hansen understood the no-background-questions here and Ben's reluctance to share anything about his romantic life before or during his military years, but he asked anyway. "Are you talking from experience?"

"Comments can have more than one meaning." Ben tapped his fingers against the wheel, then stopped. "She's moving."

They watched as she shut the door, then stood at the side of her car. The brake lights flashed, then flashed again as she aimed her key fob at it, as if she were trying to decide whether to lock it or get back in. After a few minutes, she pulled up the collar of her jacket and did a quick scan of the lot. It was dark and Ben had parked away from a light, so Hansen assumed they were safe.

Ruthie didn't do a thorough look. She started walking toward the slips. She walked past the docks with the sailboats and the smaller motorboats. She kept going until she reached the gated area on the far left side.

She stopped under the light because she didn't have a choice. It hung over the locked entrance. A few seconds there, then the gate opened, and she stepped through.

"Does she have a boat?" Hansen asked.

"She sold it a few months ago, but that's not the pleasure boat area. That's the houseboat section." Ben tapped his fingers on the wheel again. The thuds matched the song he hummed. "That's why it's locked. Gives those who live there an extra bit of protection."

The answer hit Hansen then—Ellis and Arianna. "This is interesting."

They lived in that section. Ruthie's presence could mean a friendly visit, but he didn't have the impression they all got along. Ellis and Arianna weren't the easiest people to like.

Ben's fingers froze in mid-tap. "Let's go."

They eased their car doors open, then shut them and started walking. The sounds of the marina covered their footsteps: the boats bobbing in the water; the creaks of the dock and the slips as the water rushed in and out.

It didn't take them long to find the houseboat. There weren't any lights on, only the quick beam of a flashlight zipping past a window now and then. Ruthie was inside and searching for something. The darkness inside gave it away. Whatever she was doing, Ellis and Arianna didn't know about the visit.

Ben ducked as they got closer, and Hansen followed his lead. The faint sound of movements and a soft bang inside the house welcomed them as they sneaked onto the boat's small front porch. If Ruthie heard or saw them, she didn't come out. The scratches and thuds continued.

A few more steps and Ben opened the door, not bothering to keep their final entrance quiet. They got halfway through the main area, past the couch and the kitchen, before Hansen saw her. Her back end stuck out of the closet as she pulled on something inside. Something heavy by the sound of her grunting.

Ben leaned over the sink and flicked on the light. "We have a problem."

The scream came before the fall. Ruthie fell back on her ass and stared up at them with a face gone pure white. "What are you two doing here?"

Wrong question.

She dropped the flashlight and it rolled next to her. That's when Hansen saw her hands . . . and the safe. A break-in didn't fit with what he knew about her, but then nothing on Whitaker matched up cleanly at this point. "Watching you break in to someone else's house."

"Care to explain that?" Ben asked.

She sputtered for a few seconds. "You followed me."

That seemed obvious, so Hansen responded. "We did."

"I don't have to—"

"You actually do, Ruthie." Ben gestured for her to get up and come out of the closet. "Let's sit out here."

He guided her out of the bedroom and into the living area. She sat on the love seat and they stood over her. All of her usual bravado failed her. Her shoulders slumped and her hands fell on her lap. Hansen didn't know what was going on, but seeing her fold in on herself like that made him think tonight and this errand were bigger than simply Ruthie thinking she had the right to know everyone's business.

"Something is going on with you, Ellis, and Arianna?" Ben held out his hand as he looked around. "Obviously."

But that was only part of it. Hansen had so many more questions. "Your conversation with Kerrie."

Ben looked at him. "What?"

It wasn't until right then that Hansen realized he hadn't told Ben that part. About how Tessa had told him that Kerrie had met Ruthie at the lodge yesterday.

"Those are two different things." Ruthie blew out a heavy breath. "You don't understand."

Ben shrugged. "Fill us in."

"This is a misunderstanding. I was looking for—"

"Don't." Ben stopped her with one curt word. "We can call Ellis and Arianna. Get them to come back here and help clear this up."

She shifted to the front of the small sofa. "You can't trust them."

Ben grabbed the only other chair in the room and dragged it over to sit in front of her. "Tell me why."

"They know things." She looked like she was going to give him a list but then she shut down. Folded her arms across her chest and slipped back into the cushions.

Ben balanced his elbows on his knees as he leaned forward, got closer to her. "Where is Daniel?"

"His ass should be in jail." The words burst out of Ruthie. Not in her usual lecturing way. This was an emotional explosion. Her hands shook at the mention of her husband and she practically spit the comment out. "This is all about him, covering for him." She rubbed her hands together. Kept rubbing them. "I don't know what their real names are, but that money Ellis and Arianna live off of? It's mine."

The story started to make sense. Ellis and Arianna not being what they seemed was no big surprise. How this all fit together and pointed back to Judson . . . Hansen had no idea.

Ben being Ben, he stayed calm. Pitched his voice low and soothing. "What did Daniel do?"

"Stole money. Original, right?" She swiped at her eyes as soon as the tears formed. "Apparently it costs a lot to have a family here and then go spend days with your girlfriend in Seattle."

That was the piece Hansen saw coming. Daniel the asshole, leaving his wife and son. Screwing up in a way that emotionally sliced her in two. "Oh, Ruthie. I'm sorry."

"He stole from the ground rents. He was Board treasurer and siphoned off the money. I figured it out and we fought . . ." She swallowed a few times before continuing. "I have no idea how Arianna and Ellis learned about it."

The mechanics of home ownership on the island were so odd to Hansen. He'd forgotten about the ground rents, the quarterly amount each house renter paid above the actual rent to cover the fact that none of the land belonged to anyone living on the island. The ground rents literally covered the use of ground. In legal terms it was called a leasehold and it had been the practice on Whitaker forever. The owner—one very private and mysterious person—leased the land, people built houses, they paid to use the land, and then renters paid the usual rent to live in them.

It all worked, until the treasurer ran off with the funds. As the board president, everyone would look to Ruthie for answers. As the wife of the man who stole the money for personal use, she could be hit hard with the blame.

"They're blackmailing you." That was the only answer that made sense, so Hansen threw it out there.

She nodded. "It's what they do. They're grifters. They bragged about how they collect information, and information is valuable."

"What happened?" Ben asked.

"Apparently Daniel's girlfriend is part of their setup. She met him, showed him attention. They had sex and he thought he was in love, so he started taking the money for her. Then Arianna and Ellis moved here to finish the deal."

"They threatened to let everyone know what Daniel did and you paid them to not say anything," Ben said, filling in the blanks.

She leaned back and let her head rest against the window. The words flowed easily now. All her usual defiance and anger faded into monotone answers. "We hold the ground rents and pay them quarterly into an account held by the island's owner."

Ben didn't move from his position in front of her. "The corporation."

"Right." She shut her eyes for a few seconds before opening them again and answering. "They're due in six weeks. I don't have the money. What I did have in savings, I paid to Ellis and Arianna to keep them from saying what Daniel did."

Hansen felt sorry for her. "It's his crime, Ruthie. Let him fix this."

"I'm in charge. I run the board. I oversee the accounts." She exhaled. "I failed to see what Daniel was doing and it was my responsibility to watch."

"How are you going to pay the ground rents now?" Hansen couldn't imagine the pressure she was under. Losing her husband, her financial security, and potentially her reputation all in the same moment. Devastating emotional blows, especially for someone like Ruthie, whose self-worth was wrapped up in her board position.

"I've been selling things. Trying to track Daniel, but it appears he and the girlfriend are vacationing with a portion of the stolen funds. I'm sure Ellis and Arianna have the balance of the money, along with what I've paid for their secrecy."

Ben stood up and put the chair back where he found it. He gave the house a quick scan before facing her again. "Where are they now?"

"I heard them say they were going to dinner at the lodge, so I thought—"

"You'd come here and find some dirt on them." Hansen admired the quick thinking. That survival instinct was no joke.

In her position he would have done the same thing. He'd also have safeguards in place for the checks and would have run to Ben at the first note of blackmail, but he understood the choices she'd made.

"I was desperate."

"While you're being honest, tell us about the contact with the senator." Hansen took a shot.

"That wasn't me. I promise." She couldn't quite meet his gaze when she looked up. "But . . ."

This had to be bad. "Just say it."

"I investigated you."

Not a surprise. She'd already made that clear. "Why?"

"You were with Ben all the time. He confided in you and not the board about what was happening on the island. You were a wild card and I thought I should check you out, especially since I knew what could happen when a con artist moved to town."

"Anything else?" Ben asked without a note of emotion in his voice.

"Once I knew about your past, I told Judson you were here." Her gaze continued to bounce around the room before it finally landed on Hansen. "Not on purpose. I asked questions and Kerrie emailed me back. Told me how dangerous you were."

Everything inside Hansen froze. "Kerrie?"

Ben pushed ahead. "When?"

"Maybe three weeks ago."

Ben whistled. "That's interesting."

Not the word Hansen would use. He thought of all those times Kerrie had grabbed on to him. The way she thanked him. Then Allen. It all felt off to Hansen. The tears seemed real and the shaking a symptom of genuine fear. The talk of Judson being dangerous rang true.

The pieces spun in his head until he questioned every interaction with Kerrie on Whitaker. Now he knew she played him, and he'd been so desperate to believe Judson was a violent piece of garbage that he didn't question the sincerity of her grief or her forgiveness.

Ruthie looked from Ben to Hansen. "Judson came here because of me, didn't he?"

The anger and confusion pummeling Hansen eased long enough for him to hear the pain in her voice. She had enough guilt without him piling onto it. "He came because of me. You just made it easier for him."

She shook her head. "I didn't mean to put you or anyone else in danger."

"We know." Ben touched her shoulder. "Okay, you're going to go home and gather any evidence you have on the blackmailing scheme."

Ruthie blinked. "Wait—"

But Ben was off and issuing orders. He turned to Hansen next. "You find Tessa. I'll pick up Ellis and Arianna because I'm betting after I dig a bit, we'll find a trail of victims." He glanced at Ruthie again. "Clearly you were not their first target."

"And Kerrie?" Because Hansen wanted a crack at asking her a few things.

"I'll take care of her." Ben continued to stare. "I'm serious. You're too close to this."

"Are you going to arrest me?" Ruthie's voice sounded small from her seat on the sofa. "For hiding the information about Daniel."

"You're going to have to tell the board. Probably step down. There will be an investigation," Ben explained. "Sylvia will help you maneuver through it."

"She hates me."

"You know, if you trust people just a little, you might be surprised how much they'll help you." Hansen knew that from experience.

THE WIND HIT Tessa the minute she stepped out of the lodge. She missed her jacket and regretted not bringing a purse with her. She had a wallet and her cell stuffed in her back pocket. And her father. He would slow her down.

He stepped in front of her, blocking the light and casting his face in shadow. "What's the plan?"

She grabbed her phone. "I need to find Hansen."

"How is your boyfriend going to help us here?"

This would go faster if she didn't have to stop every two seconds to answer her father's questions. She should appreciate the attention, but she knew this was really about his fear of letting her out of his sight before he got his way about the press conference.

"He has connections. Here and back in D.C." She lowered the phone before she hit the button to call Hansen. "He's not as powerful as you, at least not in politics, but he knows people. He might be able to get a lead on Allen and—"

"This isn't your job, Tessa."

More lectures. *Great.* "I've been wrapped up in this since the first murder."

He shook his head. "You can't get involved in this sort of thing."

"I actually can."

"Hansen should know better than to play with your safety."

"You care?"

"When have I put you in harm's way? If anything, not being connected to me let you have a normal and safer upbringing."

Maybe part of that was true, but the response seemed rehearsed. A total rationalization for his failure to be there.

She glanced at her phone again. "Hansen trusts me."

"He needs to rein you in."

Her hands dropped to her sides. If he was going to say that garbage, then she wasn't going to ignore him. He deserved the lecture this time. "He's not you. He actually loves me."

She didn't know if that last part was true, but it

didn't matter. She knew what she felt for him and he was not the type to tell her to stay home and out of the way. Sure, he protected her, but he was never a condescending dick about it.

She went back to her phone. Had to turn up the backlight when the night grew darker around her.

The *whack!* caught her off guard. She looked up just as her father's eyes rolled back and he crumpled to the ground in a heap. Before she could go to him, the figure behind him smiled at her.

The feral expression made bile rush up the back of her throat. "Allen?"

"It's a shame about that love thing."

"What are you—?" A hand knocked the phone out of her fist. She turned and saw the woman who'd touched off an alarm in her head since the moment they met. "Kerrie?"

"All you had to do was stop investigating long enough for us to get out of town, but no." Then she put something over Tessa's mouth and the world went blank.

CHAPTER 26

Hansen couldn't breathe. When he'd called Tessa and couldn't reach her, he swung by the lodge. More than one person talked about how she and the senator rushed out without saying anything. The easy explanation was that they'd fought over family issues and left, but then why not answer his calls? No, something felt off and the longer he went without talking to her, the harder it became to stay rational.

He paced the small open space in Ben's office in front of his desk while Ben made a series of calls. When he finally hung up the phone, Hansen turned on him. "Where's Maddie? We need her here."

"I got a call from a government official earlier today."

Hansen stopped walking. "Meaning?"

"Maddie is fine and my job is to stop asking questions about her."

That sounded more covert than Hansen expected. Maybe witness protection? At the moment, he didn't care. All he wanted was to find Tessa, and Ben had dragged him back here instead of letting him search the island.

"She's not at her house or mine. I checked with Sylvia." He ran through the list of possible whereabouts a second time, hoping whatever he missed would jump out at him. "The last anyone saw her was when she was having dinner with the senator and now both of them are missing."

Whitaker wasn't a place with lots of security cameras. There were a few around stores, but none at the lodge. None in the parking lot. Nothing pointed them in the right direction.

Ben studied the notes he wrote out as he made his calls. "Could he have convinced her, or forced her, to go back to D.C. with him?"

"The plane is still here."

The knock on the door startled Hansen. He spun around hoping to see Tessa but she wasn't there. Disappointment swamped him. Weighed him down. He fought to keep his mind working.

Doug stepped into the doorway. "Hey."

Ben held up a hand. "Now isn't a great time."

"I'm here, too." Ruthie followed her son inside the small office.

Seeing them, not having answers, ratcheted up Hansen's anxiety. It soared through him, cutting off his breath.

"Ruthie, I caught them," Ben said, referring to Ellis and Arianna. "One is in the cell. The other is locked in the conference room." He'd grabbed them at the lodge in the middle of dinner. They were so sure in their blackmailing scheme that they hadn't even tried to run. They'd thought Ben was saying hello . . . and then the yelling started.

Hansen knew because everyone was talking about it. Every place he stopped on the island in his futile search for Tessa, people were talking about "poor Ruthie" and all she'd been through. That was the right answer, of course. He just hoped she learned from it.

But that's not where his mind was right now. His thoughts jumped around. He couldn't concentrate.

Ruthie waved off Ben's concern. "We're not here about that."

Hansen's control snapped. He fought to keep his voice even but he could hear it shake. "We can't discuss this now. Tessa is missing."

Ruthie put her hand on her son's shoulder. "Doug, tell them."

"She's on the boat."

Hansen knew he meant Tessa. Doug didn't even need to say her name for Hansen to know. "What boat?"

"I was following her." The words raced out of the kid. He talked with his hands as the sentences tumbled out. "I know I wasn't supposed to, but everyone keeps dying and you weren't around, so—"

"It's okay." Ben inhaled as he watched Doug, getting the kid to mimic him. "There you go. Stay calm and tell me where you saw her."

"The man was dragging her to a boat."

Hansen's heart stopped. The beats cut off in a shrill screaming second. "The senator?"

"The man that looks like Kerrie."

TESSA TRIED TO stop the shaking moving through her body. It was a cool evening that only got cooler out on the water. And that's where they were. On a yacht in the middle of the water somewhere. Water lapped against the side and the smell of water filled her nose.

She'd been knocked out and she had no idea for how long. They could be anywhere. She looked around for lights and the shore but it was hard to see anything from where she sat on the deck. Her vision blurred and she had trouble focusing. Whatever Kerrie had hit her with, something to knock her out, left her fuzzy. But in the distance, she could see the outline of what she thought was Whitaker—but it could be any one of the islands in the area.

Bands held her wrists and ankles together in a tight grip. She moved her legs and her foot hit against something. She blinked, trying to make out the form in the darkness. Then she saw the blood dripping down the side of her father's face.

They'd hit him in the head with something. That fact registered in her muddled brain.

Before she could lean over and check on him, she heard Kerrie's voice. It hadn't lost any of its breathiness. "This is all Judson's fault."

Tessa's head shot up and a shock of pain moved through her. Crashed from one side of her brain to the other.

She heard footsteps right before men's shoes came into view. Black dress shoes. Had to be Allen. They were all out on the deck now.

"He was supposed to come here, implicate Hansen. But Judson had this elaborate plan to destroy the guy, as if killing his sister wasn't enough." Kerrie took a sip of her drink. Some sort of cocktail. "And then he got angry when I questioned him. He spent most of our time together angry."

Allen topped off her drink from the pitcher in his hand. "He was a bastard."

Leave it to these two to celebrate killing. Tessa could see it all so clearly now. The facts pushed through her clouded mind. The setup. The crying. The lies that put Allen on Whitaker long after he actually arrived. She guessed he came on the yacht with Judson and Kerrie.

She looked at Kerrie. Noticed her jewelry and the makeup. She'd bounced back from her grieving phase pretty quickly. "You killed him."

Tessa didn't ask it as a question because she didn't have any doubt.

"No, I did." Allen set the pitcher down, then rejoined them on the deck of the yacht where Hansen and Ben had found Kerrie tied up days ago. "See, Judson had a plan, but so did we."

"I learned from him. Take out an insurance policy

and kill the spouse." Kerrie shrugged. "He admitted what he did to Alexis one night. Got drunk and dropped the bombshell as if I didn't know the truth already. As if I hadn't dropped hints that we couldn't be together while he was married and how nice it would be to have a piece of her money."

"You convinced him to kill Alexis?"

"I gave him a push. Trust me, it wasn't hard to get him there." She took another long sip, as if she were at a wedding and not talking death while waves lapped at the sides of the boat. "Once he killed Alexis, I made plans to set *him* up, take the money, and get out. I wasn't about to be dead wife number two."

"Enterprising." It was the only word that popped into Tessa's head.

"I think you're kidding, but it's true. I'm a survivor and when Judson made it clear there was only one way for me to leave our relationship, I knew what I had to do."

Kill or be killed. If it weren't so sick and hadn't destroyed innocent people, Tessa might admire the ingenuity on principle. "All of this, the crying and clinging to Hansen . . ."

Kerrie smiled over the rim of her glass. "Convincing, right?"

"He was a dream. Barging in all heroic. It was a pleasure to punch him." Allen threw his head back and laughed. "We knew everyone would believe he killed Judson."

"One problem." Kerrie made a clicking sound with her tongue. "He was sleeping with you at the time."

"None of our background research pointed to that," Allen said.

"Cliff heard you two fighting." The answers clicked in Tessa's mind. She said them as soon as she thought them. Looked at Allen. "You're the one who staged the scene on the boat and Kerrie's injuries, then stole the clothes and tried to get into my house."

"Judson was long dead. I killed him in the woods and covered his body until night fell." Allen smiled. "I improvised the rest, but I could hardly walk around the island in my clothes. I needed to blend in as much as possible, so I stole some from the locals. Then I had to take the old man out because I had no idea what he heard and he kept getting all these visitors. Thought it would be more believable if Hansen went on a rampage after you turned him down."

"But you didn't." Kerrie lifted her glass in a toast. "Good for you, Tessa. Getting a piece of that. Hansen is a handsome one. And that bank account." She whistled. "Impressive. Well, knowing him isn't really that great because your connection with him is why you're not going to make it off this boat." Kerrie set her glass down and pushed her foot against the senator on the floor. "You and the senator will go missing. Allen and I will cease to exist but people who look just like us will turn up very far from here and start over."

"We'll lose the insurance money, of course. And some of Judson's assets." Allen glanced at his sister.

"It's a good thing Kerrie has been stockpiling money. Faking documents. Opening new accounts. Collecting what we'll need to disappear."

"It's amazing how easy Judson was to con when he drank." She shrugged. "A little flattery here. Some flirting and sex there. The guy was not that deep."

Her father's body moved but he didn't make a sound. Didn't lift his head. The blood pooled on the deck. Continued to pool. The dark circle seeped out from beneath him.

"He's a senator." Tessa didn't know why that mattered, but she thought, maybe, these two would care about money and power. They'd certainly done horrible things to collect both. All those lies and the bodies in a trail of destruction behind them.

Kerrie shoved at him with her foot one last time. "He'll sink just like anyone else."

The water. That's how this would end. Not with an amazing rescue or her declaring her love for Hansen. With a dark cold cloud of water sweeping over her head and choking her.

The only thing she knew to do was stall for time. Hope was all she had left. That and the vow that when she went overboard she'd grab one of these two and drag them with her. "How many people do you plan on killing?"

Allen didn't hesitate. "You two will end it. Hansen will walk into a cell, end of story."

They were quite the pair. Kerrie walked with a bounce to her step and could cry on cue. Allen answered each question with a mix of sarcasm and a slap of anger. Hansen had told her about Allen's temper. She could almost see the furious heat lurking behind his eyes.

"Thanks for offering his bed the other night." Kerrie shook her head. "You made it so easy to plant evidence in his house. The knife used to kill Judson and Cliff. A shirt with Judson's blood on it. The fibers from that one should match fibers that doctor collected on the yacht."

"But the best part is the money." Allen nodded. "Judson died with forty-two dollars on him. Additional money—with Judson's blood on it—is also in Hansen's house."

Tessa closed her eyes as a wave of desperation moved through her. Her muscles went lax as a wave of exhaustion hit her. They talked tough, but they'd been seen, and disappearing would make them the obvious suspects. Ben wouldn't buy the trumped-up evidence. No one would. She had to believe, in the end, Hansen would be fine.

But she would still be dead. "You'll never get away with this."

"All we need is to create confusion, then we'll slip away."

HANSEN OPENED THE car door and ran as soon as Ben's car stopped in the parking lot. He took off down the dock until he slammed into the locked gate at the end. His gaze went to the empty slip where Judson's boat once sat.

"The boat is gone." He repeated the phrase a few times. It ran on a loop in his head.

Ben was out of breath and disheveled by the time he slid to a stop next to Hansen. "Shit."

"It was in a locked slip." This shouldn't have happened. None of it. He came here to get away from the killing. To let Judson move into the future without any fear of being dragged to prison or run over by Hansen's car.

All those sacrifices meant nothing. His past had thrown Tessa into danger. He'd spent so much of his time with her in this stupid cycle of wanting her and fighting it. He'd worried about being in a relationship and stumbled over the word *girlfriend*. Now all he wanted to do was hold her and tell her he loved her. Because that's where he was. Panicked and afraid for her and unable to think because he'd fallen in love with her and put her right in danger's path.

"They broke the lock." Ben held the piece hanging off the gate and moved the broken one on the ground around with his foot.

"Now what?"

CHAPTER 27

Tessa stood near the side of the boat because Allen had yanked her to her feet. He kicked back the last of his drink and shelved the charm. His fingers tightened around her biceps and he held her in a punishing grip. The kind that cracked bones and left bruises.

Kerrie had the harder job. She pulled the senator to his feet. Forced him up when his legs folded underneath him again.

"What's happening?"

Tessa's father kept blinking. The blood covered his eye and when he lifted his bound hands to touch it, Kerrie smacked his hands away. Since she held a gun, she got her way.

"You're about to die." Kerrie shoved him down on the bench near Tessa.

"I'm a senator."

The words rolled out of him. Tessa almost laughed at how, right to the end, he held on to his position.

Allen did laugh. "Did you really just do a do-you-know-who-I-am thing? Come on, really?"

"Because we do know. That's why we contacted you and told you Tessa was here." Kerrie pulled bullets out of her pocket and loaded the gun. Made them watch as she did it. "We thought you'd drag her away, so we'd have a clear shot at Hansen without interference or an alibi."

"No one could have predicted the storm," Allen said.

"Anyone who lives here could." The second after Tessa made the comment, Allen dug his fingers deeper into her skin.

"Shut up."

Kerrie's voice remained light, as if she wasn't a few minutes away from adding two more murders to her list of accomplishments. "Why would anyone live here?"

What she said no longer mattered, so Tessa didn't hold back. She'd visually searched the boat, looking for a way out. Thought about how much weight she'd have to put into tripping Allen to make him fall overboard. Tried to calculate how long they could be in the water before it was too late. Even allowed herself to believe, just for a second, that the splashing she heard was about a rescue and not the sound of waves.

She could tread water. That would have to be enough. "You seemed to like Whitaker well enough when you were crying all over Hansen."

"Don't kid yourself. I thought about ending this whole thing with Hansen on my arm. Taking care of Judson, then playing the role of the grieving widow, helping Hansen clear his record, then hooking up with him." Kerrie sounded almost wistful as she laid it all out.

"Rye." Her father groaned when he tried to move. "I think I know his father."

Making connections to the end. Tessa supposed it was habit for him. To her it showed that his priorities were so skewed. No pleading for his daughter. No talk of his family.

"That's not going to help you very much now," Allen pointed out.

Tessa made one more grab for time. "But Hansen wasn't interested in you. You made him wary."

Instead of flailing or striking out, Kerrie just smiled. It was as if there was nothing inside of her. "I could have made him feel good, but we ran out of time."

Allen glanced over the side of the boat. "We're out far enough."

"What's the plan? Throw us overboard and leave?"

"Shoot you first and weigh you down, but yes."

Allen grabbed the gun before his sister finished the sentence and fired off a quick shot. The bullet slammed into the senator's arm and he yelled as he grabbed for the wound. Blood seeped through his fingers.

Allen kicked out, putting all his weight behind it as he shoved the senator into the water.

"We need the weights!"

Tessa heard Kerrie's yell and watched her father fall. He didn't put out his arms or try to brace himself. Without thinking, she jumped after him. Her body plunged into the icy water. It enveloped her, dragging her under. She tried to move her arms but the binding around her wrists held. Kicking failed until she wiggled her hips in a modified mermaid kick.

Water splashed around her and she heard yelling. Allen's voice floated above her, then a beam of light skimmed along the water. She ducked under right before it hit her. Held her eyes open against the crush of waves. Frantically searched for her father.

The harder she shifted and kicked, the deeper she plunged. She struggled to reach the surface. She could see the darkness of the water give way to the darkness of the sky. She strained, trying to break through the surface and grab a breath.

Almost there, something closed over her ankle. She screamed underwater, losing the last of her breath. The tugging and pulling had her free-falling into the freezing blackness. Then something covered her mouth and air filled her lungs. She opened her eyes again, no longer desperate to send a private thought to Hansen before she died.

There he was. His face swimming in front of her. She almost cried out. He held a mask to her face and pointed in the direction he wanted her to go. The directions refused to register in her head.

When her head broke the water and the cold smack of air hit her face, it revived her. They bobbed up and down on the waves near the back of the boat, opposite of where she'd gone in the water. She looked at Hansen and tears formed through all the wetness splashing around her.

He leaned in and kissed her on the side of her head. It was the sweetest touch, but it didn't last. He pointed to her father, who was out cold and drifting in the water with a preserver keeping him upright. Ben was there, cutting the ties binding her legs and arms. When she broke free she reached for Hansen but he put a finger over his mouth.

"Save your father." The command was little more than breath. Barely a whisper.

Then he disappeared.

IT KILLED HANSEN to swim away from her. Seeing her dive into the water. Watching her body disappear under the waves. He died a thousand times. Made promises to the universe and swore he wouldn't let anything drive them apart. He'd sacrificed so much for so many and now it was her turn. Whatever she wanted, he'd give it to her.

He had to survive the next ten minutes first.

Back on the boat Allen yelled. Their plans had unraveled when Tessa jumped over the side of the boat. He could hear the rising panic. Listened for the footsteps. Heard the crashing of a glass or bottle.

He and Ben had taken the boat out as far as they reasonably could without giving away their location, hoping the sound of the waves would cover their entry. They swam the rest of the way.

"She went under. We're fine."

Kerrie's voice. Nowhere near as calm and inviting as usual. The tension hummed in her tone. She was trying to placate Allen. Hansen wanted them to turn on each other but he didn't have the time to wait. He needed to get Tessa out of the water and the senator to a doctor. They were so far from being safe.

Terror had gripped him from the time they left the marina on the small inflatable until now. His mind kept flipping to Allen and his anger. He imagined being too late. The whole time Ben ran over a plan. Repeated it.

Hansen had left the small oxygen tank and the senator with Tessa. Now he had to move.

A few strokes and he reached the back of the boat. He could hear Kerrie and Allen talking inside the cabin. They looked at a map and in the middle of their conversation Kerrie shoved him. No question she'd married a violent man. With the murders they'd tallied, Hansen couldn't help but think she was just as violent and dangerous now.

He pushed up, balancing his stomach on the edge of the boat. Tried not to make a sound as he lifted one leg, then the other to the deck. Just as he got to his knees, Allen turned. His eyes widened and he started shouting and running toward Hansen.

"The gun!"

Hansen didn't know where it was and didn't care. He jumped to his feet and barreled toward Allen. Took them both airborne as they smashed into the hard bench lining the sundeck. Hansen fought for his footing, but his shoes slipped on the boat's surface. He came up swinging, nailed Allen right under the chin.

The skirmish had them rolling on the floor as Kerrie ran out to them. She held the gun and yelled for them to stop but the battle frenzy held them. Hansen punched and kicked, twisted around, making it hard for her to get a shot off.

The bang echoed through the quiet night. Hansen waited to feel a sharp pain through his side or back, but nothing came.

Allen went limp under him. Not sure if the move was a ploy, Hansen held on to him. He felt the slick wetness on his arm. Warm and new. He looked down and saw the blood. The instant he dropped Allen and jumped to his feet, something hard stuck against his back. He didn't have to turn around to know it was Kerrie and the gun.

"You're next."

He glanced over his shoulder and saw the panic in her eyes. "Lower the gun."

"Check on him."

Nodding, Hansen went down to his knees. The shot had clipped Allen's side but he was conscious. He gripped the wound and curled into a ball. Swore as he shifted around, likely trying to block the pain.

"You did this." Kerrie's voice was flat. Lifeless.

She held the gun out. Aimed it at Hansen's head. Opened her mouth to say something, then Ben was on her. Knocked her to the ground with a knee in her back and held her arms.

He didn't ask questions. He worked, then stood up, pulling her next to him and cuffing her to a railing. He pointed at the bench. "Sit."

Tessa.

Hansen went to the end of the deck. "Tessa!"

He called twice but didn't hear anything. Waves kicked up around them, tossing the boat, but still nothing. Ben was on the radio, notifying the coast guard of their position. Mentioning the senator's condition.

Hansen needed her. He put one foot in the water and prepared to jump in.

"Stop." Tessa threw the tank on the deck and it landed with a clank. "Help."

She sounded exhausted and her head barely stayed above the waterline. Ben joined him in dragging the senator's still form out of the water and pulling Tessa up with him.

Hansen didn't wait. As soon as her feet hit the deck, he wrapped her in a hug and kissed her hair. He mumbled words he hoped were comforting. He had no idea what he said.

A few seconds later, she dropped to the deck to check her father. Hansen stood in the middle of the chaos of bodies and blood as Ben went back to the radio. He still held Kerrie's gun and didn't look like he intended to give it up any time soon.

The quiet had settled in. Hansen closed his eyes for a second and breathed in the cool night air. Soaked in the calm in the middle of the wild frenzy. He smiled when he heard the senator cough. Any sign of life worked for him right now. He stepped over the senator's prone body and crouched down across from Tessa.

Her hair hung down and her clothes stuck to her. He

could see the blue tint to her lips and the way she kept shivering. He turned to get a blanket when suddenly an arm wrapped around his neck. Allen grabbed him and pulled him back, taking them both crashing to the deck.

Blood stained his shirt, but his eyes looked dazed. He mumbled something about Judson and tightened his hold. That was enough to get Hansen moving. He kicked out and he heard Ben shout. He waited for the gunfire, but it never came.

He heard a scream of pain and Allen's grip fell away. When Hansen looked up, Tessa stood there with the oxygen tank dangling from her fingers. She'd slammed it against Allen's elbow. Ben skidded to a stop.

"Enough!" She shouted the word and dropped the tank.

Hansen couldn't wait to get her home.

IT TOOK THREE more hours, rounds of questioning, and all sorts of coddling from the ambulance crew until they left the marina. Attacking a senator carried a high penalty. The coast guard, the navy, and a whole bunch of people who looked like they should be in uniform but were wearing street clothes showed up. There was talk of a special ferry landing and a ship sat close to shore.

Tessa had blocked out all of it. Everything except the man underneath her.

They'd gotten as far as the lodge. Their clothes came off the second they closed the door to the room Sylvia gave them. A hot shower came next and now the bed.

Tessa had demanded they skip the foreplay and move right to the main event, just for tonight. That was twenty minutes ago. Now she straddled his hips, riding up and down on his length. Loving the feel of him deep inside her.

Bruised and a little battered, he sat up in a pile of pillows with her curled around him. The thrusts moved through every inch of her. She came up off the mattress, then sank back down on him again.

She slapped a hand against the wall for better leverage. Hovered over him and lost her breath when he lifted his head to lick his tongue over her nipple.

Her body both begged for more and ached for rest. Making love with him gave her a burst of renewed energy, but her muscles started to shake. Her body, wet and sensitive and clinging to him inside and out, cried out for mercy.

Through it all he hadn't said a word. None of his usual dirty talk. No begging. He let her set the pace and arched into her with every plunge.

She tried to focus on his beautiful face. On the relief that flooded through her when he popped up in the water. But the waves of pleasure shook through her now. She tipped her head back and let her hair fall over her. Dug her fingernails into his chest.

When the orgasm hit her, it stole the last of her breath and all of her energy. Her body pulsed and she squirmed on top of him to find the position she liked best for the end.

"Damn, woman." He grabbed her hips and guided

her up and down when she lost the ability to move and the orgasm started to ease.

Boneless and satisfied, she slid down until she lay on top of him. The move earned her a gasp, then he enjoyed his turn. By the time they finished, he lay sprawled with his arms out to the side on the mattress. She covered him, unable to shift to the bed next to him.

“That was almost worth drowning.” His bare chest muffled her words, but she got them out.

“No.”

She didn’t have the strength to fight him and her eyes wanted to close. Right before she gave in to sleep, she lifted up so he could pull out of her. She thought about snuggling against his side but went right back to sleeping on top of him.

“I almost lost you.” He whispered the thought into the dark room.

She said the only thing she could. “Never.”

CHAPTER 28

Two days later the senator stood at the private airfield with a crowd of handlers and assistants hovering nearby. He'd been checked out and approved for travel by Lela and two military doctors. His arm was in a sling and he'd forsaken his usual tie in favor of an open-collared button-down dress shirt.

Tessa pretended that was progress.

Hansen had asked her this morning why she dove in after her father. He'd been watching and lost it when she went in. She understood the confusion. It wasn't as if Charles Michaelson had ever done anything for her other than donate sperm. For him, fatherhood ended there. That would never change. But neither would she. She would never be the person to watch someone disappear under the water and not make a move. That explanation Hansen understood.

He stood with her now in front of the senator. They were far enough away that the distance and the roar of the plane's engines blocked anyone but them from hearing what they said.

"I came here to insist you come back with me." But this time there was no harsh demand in the senator's voice.

She thought she'd comment anyway. "No."

"I meant originally. Not now." He ran his fingers over the edge of the sling. "An argument could be made that you don't owe me anything after saving my life."

Hansen shook his head. "Yes, that is *the* argument."

Tessa realized that was as close as she'd likely ever get to a thank-you. She'd saved his life and in return he no longer threatened her. Or he'd at least taken a short break from the practice.

"I was thinking of retiring from the pressure. Maybe leave the Senate and try lobbying."

Not what she expected him to say. She figured he'd die in his office chair, still casting a vote for something that pissed her off.

"Is that a better career?" Hansen asked.

Tessa didn't really care what he did or how he earned his money. They would never agree on politics or most other things. But she did still have one bright line he could not cross. "You either have to admit you had a mistress and kid you didn't want back then or pretend you have a mistress now. But if you use my name or my photo, I will spill the truth and you will not like the way I frame it."

She was done hiding and worrying she'd make his "people" angry. She had no desire to be part of his campaigning or tracked down by people who wanted to destroy him. Whatever game people wanted to play, they needed to do it without her. She had a life to live and it didn't include him.

"We'll see. I'll get together with my people. My wife might have an opinion. We've let the bad press go on long enough. It's time to bring it to an end, even if it's not the end I prefer." Her father turned to Hansen. "What about you?"

His eyes widened. "Excuse me?"

"You're no longer under suspicion. You can clear your name and get back to your old life."

Panic ran through her. Her stomach turned over and wave after wave of dizziness hit her. This was the moment she dreaded. Hansen had a life in D.C. without her. One with echoes of her father's. As much as she wanted to be with Hansen, she couldn't just ride along and accept his power and wealth in place of the power and wealth she never had from her father.

She didn't want any of it. She wanted the man who treated her like she mattered and loved his family to the point of being willing to give up everything for them. She wanted to be a part of that.

Hansen nodded. "True."

The word shot through her. She felt the ache straight to her heart.

"Then grab a bag and hop on." Her father gestured toward the plane.

Hansen stepped forward and she grabbed his arm. "Wait. Are you really leaving?"

He frowned at her. The same frown he'd been throwing at her since they met. "What?"

"You're looking like you want to go."

"I was trying to figure out if it was wrong to tell my girlfriend's father to go fuck himself as I shook his hand or if I should shake his hand first."

"Oh." She followed the small word with a big hug. Threw her body right at him, knowing he would catch her like always.

Her father cleared his throat. "That's inappropriate talk."

"It's totally fine," Hansen said without looking at anyone but her. Then he kissed her. Right in front of all the people gathered there, most of whom had no idea what they had to do with the senator other than that she saved him.

It felt like minutes passed before she lifted her head. Her lips hummed from the feel of his. Touching her feet to the ground again helped shift her world back into position. He would stay here for her. He didn't say it, but she heard it in his kiss.

Hansen still held her as he glanced at her father. "You have my answer."

For the first time in literally forever, her father laughed in her presence. The rich sound poured over her. She didn't understand his amusement, but she loved the deep hearty sound.

He reached out and shook Hansen's hand. Then he touched his palm against her arm. Just for a second. "That's my gift to you."

"I have no idea what you're saying right now." She

went to Hansen's side, loving the feel of his arm around her waist.

"He passed. I gave him a way out and he chose to stay with you."

He really was the most exhausting man. "I don't need to test him or trick him." No, she trusted Hansen. After everything, even through the fighting, he was hers. She was his.

"Loyalty is a rare commodity."

She thought it was so much better than that. "We are still talking past each other."

"Maybe." Her father's eyebrow lifted. "Last chance to come with me?"

She knew what he meant and nothing had changed. It never would. "You made the mess."

"Maybe your mom will help me fix it."

"Not after I call and warn her you're coming." She'd already called and let her mother talk with Hansen. They'd bonded over their joint concern for her and a laugh over a joke about letting the senator drown. Neither of them meant it, but still. "This is on you."

"Your spunk. I like it."

She wrapped her arms around Hansen and held on tight. "That's not what you said before."

"You take after me."

"Not even a little bit."

He took a step closer. Inhaled and exhaled. Made quite a scene before he spit out another sentence. "Goodbye, daughter."

It wasn't much but it was more than she ever expected.

She nodded and watched him go. He climbed the stairs, waving to the military folks who had gathered. Acting every inch the well-known senator he was.

She waited until he was inside to turn to look up at Hansen again. "Thanks for not leaving."

"You thought I would just say 'the sex was great but I got my life back' and bolt?"

She shrugged. "Something like that."

"You need to have a little faith. I mean, with that guy as your dad, I can see why your trust is shaky, but come on."

"You're nothing like him."

"Good."

THE PLANE TOOK off but the military presence remained. Law enforcement types filed onto the island. The press had started to arrive. Basically, it was Tessa's nightmare and she was ready to run. She was about to suggest they do just that when Ben stepped in front of them on their way back to the car in the private airport lot.

Hansen nodded a hello. "I didn't expect to see you today."

Ben glanced around at the people standing in the hangar, bent over a table, reading something. "Let's just say I have a lot of help."

"What are Kerrie and Allen saying?" Hansen asked.

"Nothing. Neither is talking. Their attorney is on the way. He argued that you're dangerous and mentioned the protective order." Ben shook his head. "The poor guy is a couple of steps behind."

"They tried to kill me." Tessa thought it would be years before she forgot those minutes on the yacht. She might not be able to go on any type of boat for a decade or so.

"Oh, the senator's statement is pretty clear. They might think they can weasel out of this because the senator has a secret to hide."

"It will be fine." Because she knew that her father would not let some con artist get away with shooting him. He'd maneuver and come up with a story. He'd use his power. She didn't doubt that.

People moved around them in the gravel lot. Some shouted orders back and forth. Captain Rogers was in the middle of it all. Looked to be in his glory as he talked with members of the coast guard as they stood next to his prized fire engine.

"True," Ben said. "The senator made it clear he will expose the secret if needed to make the case. He left one of his people here to coordinate communications." Ben pointed at a random guy in a navy suit without a tie. "That one."

The comment stunned her. "What?"

"He told me he can't let a criminal go free." Ben smiled. "I'm assuming he didn't tell you that."

The criminal comment sounded like him. The rest? No. "We'll see what truth he tells."

Ben frowned. "Truth is truth."

"You don't know the senator."

"It's never dull on Whitaker." Hansen laughed. "Speaking of which, what about Ellis and Arianna?"

"The Seattle police were pretty interested in those two. So were police in Phoenix, San Diego, and Denver. They left a trail. Which reminds me . . ." Ben did a quick check of his phone before slipping it back into his pants pocket. "I have a conference call in a few minutes about them. Everyone wants to pick them up. The courts are going to have to sort it all out."

"That's the one problem with being so odd. They stand out," Hansen said.

Tessa almost hated to ask, but she wanted to know. "And Ruthie?"

Ben's smile fell. "Her marriage is over and she's broke. She'll also lose her position on the board, which is likely the biggest hit for her. But Sylvia said it's inevitable."

That might be Ruthie's issue, but she had a problem that was much bigger than a board position. "But the money that was stolen?"

"Funny thing about that." Ben did a quick look around before lowering his voice a bit. "The mysterious owner of the island has a representative on the board. The owner knows the situation and, so long as Ruthie steps down, is willing to overlook this quarter's payment in light of the circumstances."

Hansen whistled. "That's generous."

Tessa's curiosity ticked up. "Who is the representative?"

"Sylvia."

"Of course she is," Hansen said.

The news managed to be both a surprise and not. "Everyone around here really does have a secret, don't they?"

Ben's smile came roaring back. "Welcome to Whitaker."

CHAPTER 29

The next morning Hansen wanted to sleep. Between the near-drowning, almost being strangled, dealing with Tessa's father, and all of Ruthie's emotional angst, he was ready for a vacation. The only caveat was that the woman next to him had to come along. The same woman who kept shifting around on the bed.

"Why are you moving? It is too-fucking-early o'clock."

She sat up in the middle of the mattress, naked and not even a little self-conscious about it. "We'll need to eat eventually. That's the one downfall of Whitaker. No takeout."

He rolled to his back, mostly because he wanted to get a good look at her. He'd made so many promises if she came off that boat safe, and he intended to honor them. "We could start a business. Of course, we'd need more restaurants."

She gave him the side-eye. "You already have one."

That tone didn't sound good. He was smart enough to know going back to sleep was off the table. He settled for moving up higher on the pillows and waiting to see what happened next. "Are we fighting?"

"No, we're being grown-ups in a grown-up discussion."

That sounded . . . really bad. "Ugh."

"Hansen."

He held up both hands in mock surrender. "Fine. What about exactly?"

"We need to go back. You can clear your name and give your family some peace. Reassure them that you're okay."

He wanted all of that, but not if it meant throwing her into the middle of the city she hated so much. He could give her time, bring his family out here first. But she'd said the magic word. "We?"

She stopped picking at the blanket and looked at him. "What?"

"You said we."

"I planned to come with you. Meet the family. Show you off to my mom and Ray."

He didn't fight the smile. He felt it down to his soul. "So, we're definitely a *we* now."

She crawled up the bed, which he thought just might be the sexiest thing he'd ever seen. He could see every inch of her as she moved, and hoped they were nearing the end of this conversation.

She threw one leg over his thighs and straddled him. "Did the sex weaken your brain?"

"Probably." Man, he loved this position. "But I just want to be clear that if we leave, it's together, or I'm not getting on a ferry or helicopter or anything else that moves."

She looped her arms around his neck. "We agree on that."

Too easy. Letting it go there and turning back to where they were before Allen and her father showed up tempted him, but he wanted more with her. For the first time in his life, informal and low commitment made his chest ache.

"Things will change." An understatement but it was a good place to start talking.

"It won't be easy, and I'll need some time. I still associate the D.C. area with my father. And that photo is floating around out there. If he doesn't come clean, being there could be rough for me." Her body stiffened as she talked.

"Then we won't go." He knew that wasn't realistic but for her he would try to make this shift to his life permanent.

She relaxed against him again. "I'm asking that we go slow, not that we don't go. My life, my work, is mobile. My mom and Ray are back there. It makes sense for us to be there, but I don't want to totally detach from here."

"Agreed." He met her here. Everything changed here. "I have a certain affinity for this island and the people on it. Most of them anyway."

"But it will be interesting to see you as something other than a handyman." She slipped her fingers through his hair. "I'll get to see you in a suit."

"And see me pissed off from bad days at work and traffic. Grumbling over how shitty D.C. is about clearing snow. Fighting with Connor about bullshit. Angry that the take-out driver is late." He wasn't an easy guy. He knew that. Hell, he thought she knew that. But island Hansen and city Hansen were not exactly the same.

"So, real life."

"Exactly."

Her head tipped to the side. "Are you afraid I'm going to run and hide the second I meet Hansen Rye, the businessman?"

She might know him too well. "I'm better here. The slower pace. Less stress."

"You were almost thrown in jail for murder."

Valid point. "You know what I mean."

She exhaled, bringing their bodies closer together. "I hate to break this to you, but you can be an ass here, too. Just saying."

"The idea of being with you and then having you bolt because you hate our life back there . . . I can't do that. I don't want to lose you." There, he said it. The point. The thing that had been on his mind since he realized he loved her. He didn't want to be without her or push her away. She'd spent so much of her life in hiding and he never wanted to be the one who dragged her back to that place.

Instead of panicking, she smiled. "It's about time you said that. Man, I thought I'd have to wait forever."

He had no idea what was happening. "Huh?"

"I have been falling for you since the day we met

and have no intention of stopping now. You're not getting away from me. And if the grumpiness gets out of control, though it can't be worse than when we first met—good lord—then I'll whisk you away. We're in this together now."

He could see from the shine in her eyes that she meant it and happiness soared through him. She might be a few steps behind him, but they were headed in the same direction. "Falling?"

"Fallen, falling. Same thing."

She wasn't behind at all. They were together in this. "It's not, but okay."

"Tell me where you are on the whole we're-stuck-with-each-other thing."

The words no longer scared him. The sensation actually grounded him. "Stupid in love with you and thinking about chucking everything to live on an island with you and become a handyman."

"Or—and don't think I don't love that fantasy, because I do—we could go back, set up a life there. Give your dad and Connor a break but set new priorities. Less work. More fun time. When you start acting like a powerful jerk, I'll tell you and you'll adjust."

Everything. She handed him everything. "Promise you'll stick by me because that last one might get bumpy."

"I have faith you can learn." She shifted on his lap until only a small strip of sheet separated them. "And we'll need a second home on Whitaker. I'll insist on vacations here and other places."

He could barely think. He wanted to kiss her. Roll around on the bed with her. "That's a good compromise."

"Until the kids come, of course."

A ringing started in his ears. "Sorry?"

She traced a finger over his lips before placing a quick kiss there. "Your family deserves some joy and you'll be great at the dad thing."

He hadn't even let his thinking get that far. She wasn't with him, she was miles ahead and he vowed to sprint to catch up. "All this for a man you're *falling* for."

"I'm in love with you, stupid. Want to have your babies. Yell at you when you work too much. Conspire with your brother to get as many vacation days with you as possible." Her fingers massaged the back of his neck. "My footprints will be all over your life."

He couldn't fight the urge one more second. He rolled until she lay under him. "So, babies."

Her smile beamed up at him. "That's all you got from what I said?"

"I knew I wanted the rest of that with you. The babies part is new."

"Interesting." She dropped her arms back on the bed. "You up to speed on the concept yet?"

Sexiest. Woman. Ever. "Getting there."

"That's what I like about you. You catch up fast."

"We should start practicing. The babies thing."

She wrapped her legs around his waist. "Hold up there, stud. I love you but we're not trying to get pregnant yet."

Sure felt like it but he could wait. She should probably meet his family first anyway. He knew they were going to love her as much as he did. "And I love you, so just tell me when you're ready."

"Love, huh?"

"Not falling. The actual kind."

"I can work with that." Her hand slipped beneath the sheet. Over his waist, then lower. "But we really should practice the sex part. You know, just in case."

"In case what?"

"I have no idea, but we start there and then we move on to building the rest of our lives."

He lowered his head but stopped just before kissing her. "Thank you for saving me."

"Thank you for saving me right back."

ACKNOWLEDGMENTS

Thank you to my amazing editor, May Chen, who didn't balk when we pitched this series as "imagine Jessica Fletcher's Cabot Cove with more sex, more killing, and a lot of dysfunction." Thank you for believing in me. And thank you to my agent, Laura Bradford, for making that bizarre book pitch. I've always wanted to write a romantic suspense series set on an island, especially a fictional one where I can do anything I want and design the island to fit my needs, and now I am. Go team!

As always, a huge thank-you to my readers and to all the librarians and booksellers who talk about my books and grab a copy when they come out. I am so grateful for all of you.

I'm also grateful to my husband, James, whose support makes all of this possible . . . and who has the job with the steady income and great benefits, which keeps us from having to live in our car. I never take that for granted.

At Avon Books, we know your passion for romance—once you finish one of our novels, you find yourself wanting more.

May we tempt you with . . .

- **Excerpts** from our upcoming releases.
- Entertaining **extras**, including authors' personal photo albums and book lists.
- Behind-the-scenes **scoop** on your favorite characters and series.
- **Sweepstakes** for the chance to win free books, romantic getaways, and other fun prizes.
- Writing **tips** from our authors and editors.
- **Blog** with our authors and find out why they love to write romance.
- **Exclusive content** that's not contained within the pages of our novels.

Join us at
www.avonbooks.com

An Imprint of Harper Collins*Publishers*
www.avonromance.com

Available wherever books are sold or please call 1-800-331-3761 to order.

FTH 1013